THE
TOWER
STRIVE

THE TOWER STRIVE

BOOK ONE

Walsh Bear

Podium

ISBN: 979-8-3470-0563-5

Published in 2026 by Podium Publishing
www.podiumentertainment.com

Podium

THE
TOWER
STRIVE

Mountains beyond mountains, towers beyond towers,
Revels at West Lake for hours beyond hours.
Travelers drunk on a flowering wind
Mistake Hangzhou for lost Bianjing.
     —*Inscription at an Inn of Lin'an*, Lin Sheng

CHAPTER ONE

Expedited Delivery

It was that damn raccoon again. Every night at half past two, like clockwork, I'd hear loud banging noises from the trash cans in my backyard. You could set an alarm to them, if you needed one for an oddly scheduled night shift, or maybe an après-smoke trip to 7-Eleven to grab Doritos.

It was enough to constantly be woken up by the revving assholes who treated the highway as their personal F1 racetrack. The four-lane interstate that was my next-door neighbor, buzzing late into the night with the sound of commerce. No wonder this apartment had been listed so cheap. Good sleep was like a distant memory.

Slowly, I crept downstairs and grabbed my newly purchased air rifle. *No more*, I thought. *This ends tonight.*

I pushed open the back door and stepped outside. The shadow of the freeway overhead bisected the yard, and it rumbled with the constant drone of vehicle traffic. That low rumble combined with the continued sounds of my garbage being ransacked, forming an irritating duet. Still, I felt a grin on my face at the silliness of the situation. As I skulked toward the trash with gun in hand, I felt like Elmer Fudd on the hunt.

Come on out, you wascally waccoon.

The plastic bin jumped up and down, lid flapping like a cartoon mouth. With every bounce, it exhaled a scent of moldy vegetable scraps. I moved to open it, and time stopped.

The world was frozen by the shriek of metal on metal from far above, as something smashed into the freeway's guardrail. I looked up and recognized the letters on its side, reading OTHERWORLD DELIVERIES. I'd seen those long-haul trucks before, barreling down lonely midnight roads to make their shipping deadlines. Their accident rates were apparently atrocious.

The truck broke through the railing, and gravity took hold. There was a yawning moment of silence as it plummeted toward me, packages tumbling off the rear. I clutched my air rifle, the one I'd been so pleased to get with free next-day shipping, and the second-to-last thing that went through my head was a terrible sense of irony. The last was the front grill of the semi-truck as it smashed me into the pavement.

(Interstices 1)

I sat in a classroom staring blankly at a test handout. It was a thin packet, stapled at the upper-left corner. The upper right had space for a name, and my hand filled it in automatically. Xavier S.

Where am I? I haven't been in school for almost a decade. The thought surfaced briefly in my mind before suppressing itself.

The first question on the exam read:

1) An elderly neighbor asks you for a ride to the train station, but you're already late for work. How do you respond?
   a) Call the office and give her a lift
   b) Don't call the office and give her a lift
   c) Ignore her

It's C. "What is this?" I demanded, standing up.

"Sit down," said the teacher. He sat at a large metal desk—the kind they used to call a *tanker*—at the front of the room, grading papers with a studied nonchalance. The desktop was strewn with a chaotic assortment of doodads and gizmos—whirling, gleaming things in glass spheres that I couldn't make heads or tails of. There was also an apple.

The other student desks were empty, except for one that held a raccoon, who seemed just as bewildered as I was.

The teacher slammed a desk drawer shut, and I jumped. That desk felt like pain somehow, the hard angles of weighty steel—

"I died. Holy shit, I died." Memory came flooding back, and I pushed my chair aside and ran over to the window.

The sun was low and reluctant. It cast long shadows over a world I didn't recognize, a graveyard world with obelisks and towers reaching up like spindly fingers. High-flying bridges of impossible geometry criss-crossed an orange sky. Everything swam and shifted in non-Euclidean ways that made my brain hurt.

"What is this?" I said again. The raccoon hissed. *That's right, the raccoon in my garbage. He died, too?*

"If you sit down, I'll tell you."

My pulse pounded in my ears as I returned to my desk. Someone had drawn a skull and crossbones on it, I noticed, as well as a few "Cool S" shapes. These were mostly backward.

"Well?"

The teacher sighed, took his glasses off his face. "It's a placement exam."

"A placement exam . . ." Suddenly, my mouth was dry.

He smiled at me then. A welcoming smile, a leering grin? I couldn't tell. There was a flickering suggestion of some shape above his head, a halo or horns. "Just answer to the best of your ability."

My vision swam as I considered the next question.

2) Your best friend in college likes a girl, but she seems to like you instead. What do you do?
   a) Talk to her
   b) Check with your friend if it's okay before making your move
   c) Do nothing

Another missed opportunity, I reflected. *One in a long series of roads not taken, one after another, until now. And now it was too late to go back.*

"You're taking this better than I expected," mused the teacher. "Are you sure you don't want to panic a bit first? I find it often helps people to get it out of their systems."

I ignored the offer. "All these questions are about things that happened during my life. Or didn't happen, I guess."

"So you already know the answers." His head was back down in his papers. "It should be an easy test then, shouldn't it? It's open book, even." He indicated that I should reach underneath my desk, then took an absent-minded bite of his apple.

His teeth might've been straight and white; they might've been filed to points.

Below my chair, I found a hefty volume that barely fit on my student-sized desk. I flipped to a page at random, and it was me, sitting in front of my computer, watching some YouTube explainer video about the lore for a film I'd long since forgotten about. Another page had me lying in bed on my phone, swiping on something. A catalog of my full life, from the very beginning.

My days of school and the hundred extracurriculars. College days at Cal, dropping out. Gig work here and there. Oddjob, my friends had called me. We didn't play much *Goldeneye* anymore, but I was always bouncing around between different employers, side hustles, or whatever. It was an apt nickname, except I wasn't short. A solid 5 foot 11 inches, thank you very much, and 6 foot on the apps.

A depressing number of the pages looked almost identical. Pictures of myself screen bound—at the TV, at my desk, in bed. It was all laid out here, plain as day, and I felt a terrifying sense of déjà vu as the age of the thirty-minute show gave way to the rise of the ten-minute video essay, then to the ten-second reel. I watched as Vanna White spun the *Wheel of Fortune* night after night, as Charlie bit my finger, as ice buckets were dumped and Tide pods consumed. Over-stimulated yet under-invested, until the pages and the days finally ran out, and the back cover closed with a thud of finality.

What did I have to show for it all? A second-hand life, a head stuffed full of a thousand useless memes and factoids. That was what I had amounted to. Tears welled up in my eyes. Over at the other desk, the raccoon was eating its test papers.

"It isn't fair," I whispered. "I didn't do enough. I'm not ready."

As if in response, light flared from a far-off tower outside the window, blinding us. The teacher raised his head to look, and the raccoon took advantage of his momentary distraction to leap forward and seize the red apple with greedy paws, then took a chomping bite out of it. The teacher backhanded the raccoon, sending it flying.

But it never hit the ground. The beam of light fixed itself onto us, and we were levitating in the middle of the classroom. I yelled and scrabbled at a desk for purchase. The teacher was shouting with a look of anger on his face, but I couldn't hear him. Everything outside the cone of light felt muffled somehow.

The light pulled at us, and we were yanked out the window like a bad vaudeville act. Glass shattered at the impact, but I felt no pain.

"Am I dying again?" I wondered aloud as the ground zoomed past upside-down.

"Your guess is as good as mine, friendo," said the floating raccoon.

CHAPTER TWO

The Tower Strive

(Interstices 2)

We slammed our way through the branches of lush fruit trees, then barreled onward in the column of light. Outside, the deep-orange sky swirled with dark and undefined shapes, and other structures flew past. I saw a field of roses surrounding a squat, round turret of brownish stone, then a tall spire, slim and white, with currents of air and water circulating around it.

There was a sharp *crack* as something slapped against the outside of the beam, then a sound like hail raining down. Shadowy arms tried to beat their way to us, like a car wash from hell, and I shivered as they passed by.

When I twisted my body to look forward, all I could see was a blinding brightness. It figured. Our destination was the most important thing, and I couldn't see shit. Still, the ride had become oddly smooth once we'd stopped accelerating, and my brain finally had time to review the events of the last few seconds.

I turned to look at the raccoon. Somehow, I thought it had spoken to me, but it was just an ordinary raccoon, gray-furred with a black and white mask. It had a scar above one eye that made it look like it was perpetually raising one eyebrow, and I started to laugh.

"What's so funny?" said the raccoon.

"Oh shit." I tried to stop laughing, but failed. "You actually *can* talk."

"Damn straight." The raccoon pulled out the apple he'd stolen from the teacher. "Turns out this ain't no ordinary apple. It's the fruit of the Tree of Knowledge or some shit."

"How could you possibly know that?"

The raccoon flipped over in midair and shrugged, a bizarrely human movement. I chuckled again, but just then a tower that seemed entirely made of human organs blurred past, sobering me up. "Alright," I said, regaining my composure. "That makes about as much sense as anything else that's happening." I paused and thought for a moment. "But why the Brooklyn accent?"

The raccoon took another bite of the apple. "Did I say 'fruit of the Tree of Knowledge?' Slip of the tongue. I meant 'fruit of the Tree of *Street Smarts.*'"

Absurd. The word lodged itself in my brain and refused to leave. An absurd death, an absurd afterlife, and now this. I was still contemplating the absurdity of it all when the column of light brought us to our destination and we crashed through the wall of the tower.

(Strive 1:1)

The floor was cold and hard, not the brutal coldness of metal, but the slick marble of an upscale hotel lobby. It was carpeted with plush Persian rugs—though not where I lay, unfortunately—and handsomely bound books lined the walls. The arched ceiling had a fresco of a sky in sunset, deep blue and pink, and a multitude of lit chandeliers dangled. Next to me, the raccoon was out cold, and I felt a twinge of pity for it.

I rolled over to find a moist towelette hovering inches from my face. It was in the hand of a gentleman wearing an old-fashioned concierge uniform. I looked down at my T-shirt, sweatpants, and Crocs, suddenly self-conscious.

"Sir, if you please," the man said. "We also have complimentary robes available for guests."

My head spun, from the fall and the illogic of this statement. Guests? Robes? Something in me gave out, and I decided to roll with things for now. Processing could happen later, after whatever the hell this was.

The man was still holding the towelette, and I took it, wiping my face and hands. "Not to be rude, but who're you again? I've had a hell of a day so far."

The hotelier nodded and gave me a sympathetic look. "Most people tell me the same. You can call me Hilbert. I'll be your—"

"What the fuck!" The raccoon lifted itself off the tile floor. "What's this now?"

"Ah, welcome, welcome!" Hilbert clapped his hands briskly. "Now that we're all here, we're ready for the first order of business." He turned and bent to reach behind the front desk, rummaging for something in a drawer. "You, my dear friend, need to select a legal name to be entered into our system."

"My parents already did that for me," I said wryly.

"He's talking to me, you lunk," said the raccoon. "Don't be so self-centered."

"Ah." I thought about the ruckus of those sleepless nights. "How about Dumpster Boy?"

"Not a boy." The raccoon sauntered behind a bar counter and somehow located a bowl of peanuts.

"Well, now I feel like an asshole."

"You should." She started to crack one open. "What, you think all dogs are boys and all cats are girls, too?"

"Your name, madam?" Hilbert prompted again.

"I got it, I got it." The raccoon stood on her hind legs. "Let's go with . . . El Bandito."

The hotelier put up a finger. "I feel the need to point out that, if madam is going for Spanish, the correct pronunciation would be El Bandi*do*." He emphasized the last consonant. "Also, that would be the masculine form of the title. *La Bandida* might be more apropos for a lady such as yourself."

The raccoon looked at him for a long moment. "Get a load of this guy," she said. "Thinks he knows everything."

She reached for the hotelier's pen, took it with a paw, then promptly dropped it. She tried again, this time with both paws, but once again it slipped out of her grasp. "Fucking A," she said.

I bent to pick up the pen and paper with a sigh. "How about just Bandit?"

She twitched her whiskers in frustrated thought. "Doesn't have the same ring to it. Nah. First name El, last name Bandito."

I glanced up at Hilbert, who shrugged.

"See if I care," I muttered, scribbling it down. "Current age?"

"Two and a half."

"Place of birth."

"Dumpster behind BJ's Brewhouse."

"M—" I looked at the hotelier, who watched impassively, then back at El. "Myers-Briggs?"

"Chaotic neutral."

I waved the paper to dry the ink. "ID number not applicable, taxable income—I'm going to assume that's zero—former address the same as mine, since you seemed to mostly live in my backyard, and . . . that should be it. Congratulations, El Bandito. The first raccoon with a legal name."

"Oh, that's not true," interjected Hilbert. "We had another one a few years ago."

"Really?" I was curious. "What did they pick for their name?"

The hotelier allowed himself the smallest sigh. "They also picked El Bandito."

"Good taste," said the raccoon through a mouthful of peanuts.

"What about me?" I asked. "Don't I get a form?"

Hilbert smiled. "Not necessary. We already have you in our system."

"Okie-doke," I said, feeling like pressing him wouldn't get me any more of a satisfactory explanation.

"Now onto the fun part." Hilbert brought out a smooth wooden box and handed it to me. "A welcome present for our honored guests."

The box was inset with a hieroglyph of a hand and eye. I undid the clasp, and inside was a round bracelet made of smooth gray stone, next to a clear contact lens.

"The bangle's called a *kada*," said Hilbert, placing a matching box in front of the newly christened El Bandito. "The lens is an *udjat*-eye. They'll enable you to connect to the system here and become a full resident."

"Is that a good thing?" I asked. "What if I don't want to stay here?"

"You could leave, but I wouldn't recommend it," Hilbert said quietly. "There's nothing but chaos in the land between the towers. Or perhaps you'd like to return to your test?"

My mind shied away from remembering the monstrous tendrils that'd tried to beat their way to us through the light as we moved through the air, and the half-smile of the teacher who seemed to know everything about me. That placement test that had the ring of finality about it . . .

"Fair enough." I slid the bracelet onto my right wrist. Nothing happened.

Next, I turned my attention to the contact lens. It was slightly soft and squishy, and popped easily into place over my right eye. I waited for another moment, but everything remained the same as it was, aside from a minor twinge of discomfort.

"What do I do now?" I asked Hilbert, covering my left eye with my hand. "Nothing's happen—"

Text appeared right in front of me, and I blinked in surprise.

Registering new output peripheral . . .

Sync with Udjat-001 OK . . .

There was a pause while the text scrolled away, and then ornate lettering swelled to fill my vision.

Welcome, Xavier Shaw, to the Tower Strive.

CHAPTER THREE

Dookie

It has often been said that the journey is of greater importance than the destination. From this, we may deduce the following corollary: Progression is, in and of itself, a virtue.

—First Sender, *Records of the Tower Strive*

(Strive 1:2)

Hilbert held his arm up, and I noticed for the first time that he was wearing a bracelet like the ones he'd given us, only transparent. "Since you're both from the modern era, this will be simpler to explain. Think of this kada bracelet as a wearable computer and input device. It detects gestures via nerve impulses and translates them into actions. Your udjat"—here he pulled down his lower eyelid, and I saw that he had a lens in, as well—"functions as the output."

El Bandito, whose name I'd begun shortening to El in my head, stared at Hilbert, her eyes beginning to glaze over.

Hilbert sighed. "Maybe an example would be more helpful." His fingers moved, and the bracelet on his wrist glowed white. His right eye flared briefly as well, and suddenly he was holding a fluffy bathrobe. He tried to hand it to me, but I was staring dumbfounded.

"How'd you do that?"

Hilbert smiled benignly. "Let's teach you two your first few commands, shall we? Hold this bathrobe for a moment, and ball your right hand into a fist."

I clenched my fingers tightly. Almost immediately, a serpentine curve wrote itself in light on my stone bracelet. The cursive letter *S*. It pulsed gently as if waiting for something.

"Now, place your thumb between your index and middle fingers."

As I followed his instruction, a glowing *T* joined the *S*. Both letters flashed, then replaced themselves with the full phrase "Stow Item," wrapped around the bracelet in a hovering circlet of script.

A moment later, the bathrobe vanished from my hand. I gaped at the bracelet, which had reverted to dull gray stone and felt slightly warm. It seemed almost like it could've been a hallucination, if it weren't for the lingering bright spots in my eyes.

"Well done. Your bracelets are both configured to read the American Sign Language finger-spelling alphabet. That command you just used allows you to store items in your inventories." Hilbert raised his hand. "Now copy me."

Hilbert moved his fingers into various shapes, and I copied him. Each time I did so, the corresponding letter illuminated on my bracelet. I saw the characters *I* and *N* appear, then pulse and replace themselves with the full word *Inventory*.

Immediately, a transparent window labeled **Inventory** appeared in my contact lens, overlaid on my field of vision. It was filled with empty squares, except for two—the bathrobe and a familiar pellet gun.

"Huh." I waved my hand through the hologram. "The air rifle carried over?"

"Indeed," said Hilbert.

I chewed on it for a minute. "I had a smartphone charging on the nightstand, an old Camry in the garage, a few tins of CBD gummies . . ."

"I'm sorry," Hilbert said. "The only thing that came with you is the rifle, since you had it with you when you . . . you know. Anyway, you can sign *X* to close the window, like so."

The rest of the interface was empty anyway, so I curled my finger to dismiss the overlay. El was still struggling to form a fist with her non-opposable thumbs, and I felt a slight tickle of human superiority.

"Maybe try both hands," I suggested. "Wrap one around the other."

"Maybe try fucking off," she grumbled. "Smug asshole."

"I do apologize," said Hilbert. "This system is more analog than some others. The physicality of it provides a more grounded experience."

"Fuck your grounded experience," said El, but she used her left paw to guide her right. A rough *S* flickered into place, and with some struggle, she managed to form a *T* as well. Her right eye and bracelet flashed white. "Whoopee. It works."

My mind had been racing for a while. "Correct me if I'm wrong, Hilbert, but this is some kind of D&D-type RPG system. Will we be taking on quests to save the world and fighting kobolds and liches?"

"Well," Hilbert said, "there are a few steps to get to before that."

"Character archetypes," I said. "Class selection."

"Ah!" Hilbert smiled broadly. "Genre-savvy, are we? You're thinking of becoming a [Demolitionist] or perhaps an [Innkeeper]?"

"I was actually thinking something more basic, like a warrior or mage." I furrowed my brow. "How are you talking with square brackets?"

"What?"

"Demolitionist. *Demolitionist.* Innkeeper." I tried different inflections.

"InNkEePer," said El.

"Yes," said Hilbert. "[Innkeeper]."

"Weird," I said.

"I want to be a thief," announced El.

"Aren't thieves supposed to be stealthy?" I asked dubiously. "Your loud ass woke me up every single night."

"That's ridiculous." She cracked open another peanut. "I'm as quiet as the night. I garb myself in the embrace of shadows."

"How about you garb yourself in some actual clothes, now that you're sentient and all?"

Hilbert cleared his throat. "To answer your original question, you do actually get to select something akin to a class today." He stepped toward the side of the room, fine boots clacking on the tile. "If you'll both proceed this way."

We followed him down a corridor decorated with gilded sconces and mahogany trim. He stopped beneath a crystal chandelier, indicating a handsome wooden door, and we entered.

At first, the room reminded me of a wine cellar with its subdued lighting and the dozens of recesses in the wall. Each was about the size of my hand, and they were all empty, as if waiting for something.

"Try placing your kada hand into a slot," suggested Hilbert. "Any will do."

With some trepidation, I submerged my right hand wrist-deep in the nearest one, and my udjat display came alive.

Aspect of Plantera

This aspect is the basis of botanical spells, spells of vegetation, and spells of life. It provides a passive bonus to nearby plant growth.

You currently have 0/2 basic slots filled.

Accept this aspect (Y/N)?

"Underrated," commented Hilbert. "People never seem to realize how terrifying a ten-foot-tall Venus flytrap can be."

I took a deep breath of ancient-smelling air. "This whole room is magic? We get to learn magic?"

Hilbert grinned. "Eases the sting a bit, does it not?"

"I'll say." I ran a hand across the wall in awe. So many options.

Hilbert spread his arms wide. "It's my pleasure to welcome you to the Room of First Principles. You may select one aspect here, which will grant you passive effects, as well as continuous unlocking of spells via your kada bracelet."

A million questions bubbling inside me finally breached the surface. "What is this all for? Why all of this in the first place? And you mentioned a name, the Tower Strive?"

"Yes," Hilbert said. "Great questions all. But we should sit down for this discussion. It might take a while."

My stomach rumbled. "Actually, before we do that . . . you guys got a restroom nearby?"

Hilbert graciously pointed me to a door down the hall. It was single occupancy, but just as opulent as the rest of the place, all dark jewel tones and brass finishes. There was a toilet, spotless of course, as well as a litter box set unobtrusively in one corner. *Considerate of them to provide that,* I thought, although I wasn't sure El would know how to (or decide to) use it. As I sat, I found my emotions to be surprisingly calm, with a growing undercurrent of fear or excitement. I wasn't sure which one.

I was deep in thought when I felt a splash of cool water, and then the horrible feeling of something wet against me. Something slimy. A burning sensation.

I swore and jumped upright. From the depths of the toilet on which I'd been sitting, a mass of green goop was sending up an inquisitive arm. I felt my rear with my hand, and it was tender. There was a patch of skin burned away where I'd felt the slime touch me. I thought about going out to fetch Hilbert, but something told me that I should deal with the situation myself. It might've been simple pride, but it seemed improper to involve another man in my bathroom affairs.

There was a fancy-looking plunger underneath the sink, and I grabbed it. Better not to touch the acidic toilet slime with my bare hands if I could help it.

The slime was still emerging from the toilet bowl, so I mashed the plunger into it and pressed down. Every thrust brought a disturbing sucking noise from the slime. It compressed, stretched, and executed all kinds of topologically unlikely transformations. But it refused to reenter the bowels of the toilet. In fact, my assault only seemed to make it more determined. The goop began to work its way up the plunger handle.

I looked around. There was a closet I hadn't noticed earlier, right by the litter box. *Do I dare to relinquish my grip on the toilet slime for a second?*

I had no choice. I waddled over with my boxers still around my ankles and flung it open.

It was just what I was looking for. A chemical closet, with all the usual suspects—toilet bowl cleaner, Windex, bleach, ammonia. I grabbed the last two. Unscrewing the cap on the bleach, I lobbed the whole jug at the slime. The container spun through the air, spraying liquid, and landed a direct hit. I held my breath for a long moment as it was slowly absorbed, hoping it was enough.

The slime stiffened into a hard lacquer-like substance and sent out spikes. It seemed to be trying to build a protective shell around itself. But it was too late. The bleach had already begun to damage whatever innards it had.

It collapsed back into the toilet with a splash, and I sighed in relief. Ammonia would've gotten it for sure, but the off-gassing might've done me in, too. I'd seen that combo send people to the emergency room.

Picking up the plunger, I forced the limp slime down the drain. It waggled at me weakly, sank below the waterline, and then, finally, disappeared. I gave the toilet a triumphant flush.

When I had concluded my business, I staggered back into the wine cellar room. El and the bartender turned to look at me, and I realized I was still holding the fancy plunger.

"Trying out a new career path?" asked El.

I spun it in my hand and forced a smile. "That's-a me."

CHAPTER FOUR

This Hole Was Made For Me!

(Strive 1:3)

Oh dear," Hilbert said. "Oh dear, oh dear. This isn't supposed to happen at all." He was looking down at the slime residue coating the inside of the men's room toilet. It had started to eat away at the formerly pristine porcelain, dotting it with ugly pockmarks.

"Those blasted slimes." Hilbert shook his head. "Stay on your own floor, I told them. Keep away from the sewers, I said. I should've known, they've always been terrible at taking instructions. Cute as a button, though."

"Um," I said, wondering if we were thinking of the same snot-colored acid blob.

"I really do apologize," said Hilbert. He adjusted his bowtie nervously, his face red. "Monsters aren't supposed to be encountered until the next floor of the tower. Our friend here got a little overexcited and decided to do some exploring. He didn't get you anywhere, did he?"

"Not at all," I lied, acutely aware of the skin missing from my right butt cheek.

"Splendid, splendid." He clapped me on the shoulder. "Wait for me a minute where we were before, and then we'll continue."

I returned to the Room of First Principles, where El was still perusing the magic slots.

"So," she said, "did you solve your issues with dropping the kids off at the pool?"

"Don't be gross. I was fighting for my life in there."

"I've got a gastroenterologist I can refer you to." The raccoon made a chittering sound, which I took to be laughter. "Oh, check this one out. It lets you smell really well. Probably the opposite of what you want after what just happened, though." She indicated a slot, and I inserted my right wrist.

Aspect of Nostrum

This aspect is the basis of potion-crafting and alchemy. This aspect grants passive poison resistance.

You currently have 0/2—

"*Nostrum*," I said, retrieving my hand. "Not *nostril*."

"Is that right?" said El, already moving onto the next slot.

There were so many that it was impossible to choose, especially when I didn't know what waited for us on the upper floors of the tower. The Aspect of Tempest allowed the user to create raging storms. That sounded badass, but was it better than the more practical Aspect of Gastronomy? For all I knew, this place could be a fantasy version of *Iron Chef*. Or it could be full of brainteasers. But overwhelmingly, it seemed that the various aspects tended toward combat utility. Which was all well and good for games, but . . . I looked down at my not-particularly-muscled limbs. That could be a problem.

Before long, Hilbert returned, smelling slightly of toilet bowl cleaner.

"Right," he said, gesturing to a group of plush chairs. "Thank you for your patience. Let me attempt to explain." He waited until we all took our seats, cleared his throat, and began to speak.

"On your journey here, you may have noticed a whole plethora of towers out there in the world. A tower isn't just a physical entity. It's a bastion of order within chaos, of reality within non-reality, held together by sheer strength of will. Without the towers, all would be shadows and anarchy. You are currently on the first floor of the tower named Strive, and the figure at its helm is known as the First Sender."

The first floor, I noted. *Not the ground floor. Even though his voice oozes posh Britishness.* Aloud, I said, "Why's it called Strive?"

Hilbert waved a hand at the walls around us. "As the name suggests, the conviction that holds this tower together is the principle of Progress; that is to say, the climb to the next floor. Because of this, our time together is regrettably limited. Shortly after you select your first spell, we will say our adieus, and you will be sent up to begin your trial."

"The first nine floors, including this one, are instanced—it will be you two and nobody else. In addition, there will be no way to return to a previous floor. You may think of these as the tutorial levels. There's also a rest area midway through."

"Whoopee," El yawned.

"At floor ten, everything changes. Return to previous floors becomes possible starting at that level, although you will never be able to return to floors nine and below. It's also at this point you will meet your fellow climbers for the first time—"

I couldn't hold myself back anymore. "The trials you mentioned earlier, what are they? Seems like it'd be prudent to know before picking an aspect here."

Something odd came over Hilbert. He opened his mouth as if to respond, then it snapped shut like a technical glitch. "I'm sorry, as the doorman of the Tower Strive, I'm unable to answer that question," he said simply.

"Who's the First Sender?"

In the same flat tone, he replied, "I don't have access to secret or confidential information. My purpose is to be helpful and informative based on the knowledge I've been trained with."

I felt a twinge of horror settle into my stomach. Terra incognita, no map to guide us forward, and we had to commit to a decision now. It was against all my instincts. Sometimes I'd do days of research before buying a pair of jeans or a T-shirt.

El twitched her whiskers. "This man's not human. I could bite him as hard as I could, and I bet he wouldn't bleed a drop."

"Don't be rude, El."

Hilbert shook his head. "El's correct in her suspicions. I'm more like what you would call an advanced, adaptive NPC, although this is not a game world. In the interest of fairness, there are limits to what I'm allowed to share."

If Hilbert was an NPC, he was a more realistic one than I'd ever seen. He looked fully human and seemed more intelligent than half the people I'd ever met.

"Okay . . ." I said. "So what *can* you tell us about the trials?"

"Essentially nothing more than what I've said. I'm sorry."

"Fuck me." I scratched my head. "What if I refuse to leave the first floor?"

"Look at the corner of your display," said Hilbert.

Oh, shit. A timer rolled down in transparent numerals. There was just under an hour remaining on it.

"If that hits zero, you'll be booted out of the tower entirely. You know what that means." Hilbert gestured at a window to the orange sky outside, where hungry black waves roiled in the air.

I did. It meant certain doom at the hands of some nightmare creature.

"Best get to picking a spell then," I muttered, casting an eye around the room. Another thought crossed my mind. "The slime came from the second floor, you said. So there are creatures like that in the tower that we'd need to fight. Combat encounters. And presumably the environment differs greatly between the floors."

Hilbert's face froze. "I'm unable to confirm or deny that information."

"Got 'em," said El.

Five minutes remained on the timer as I stared at another hand-sized slot in front of me.

Aspect of Corpus

This aspect is the basis of spells that empower the body beyond its natural limits. This aspect grants a small passive bonus to physicality and athleticism.

You currently have 0/2 basic slots filled.

Accept this aspect (Y/N)?

"Flexible," Hilbert said from next to me. He'd been a bit distant since I called him out about the combat encounters. "If rather basic."

"This is the one," I said firmly, and extended my thumb and pinky into the letter *Y.*

"I should warn you—" Hilbert started.

My kada bracelet burned fiery red on my wrist, and half my field of view reddened as well. I gasped and tried to jerk my hand out of the slot, but it was fixed there by an invisible force.

Downloading . . .

Do not remove the kada from the slot . . .

Downloading . . .

I swore and levered myself against the wall, but my wrist stuck fast. I put both feet up against the wall and pushed, as hard as I could.

Download complete.

The suction disappeared, and my whole body launched back from the slot, slamming into the opposing wall and rebounding onto the floor in a crumpled heap. "Ergh," I said, rubbing my head.

My wrist still burned, but when I looked, there was no sign of damage, only the gray stone bracelet with a slight residual heat remaining. "I don't feel any different."

"It might be some time before it takes," Hilbert said. "And my apologies; it's not the most comfortable experience. I meant to warn you."

"Don't be sorry," El replied. "That was great."

I gave the raccoon a sidelong glance. "I'll be sure to enjoy your turn, too. Have you even picked one yet? Four minutes left."

"This one." El pointed at a slot, and I stuck my ringed hand in to read the description.

Aspect of Prestidigitation

This aspect is the basis of spells of trickery and sleight of hand (or paw). It provides a boost to manual dexterity.

You currently have 1/2 basic slots filled.

Accept this aspect (Y/N)?

"Only one per user, please, Mr. Shaw." said Hilbert. "It's part of the rules. You'll be able to find a second one later."

In all honesty, it would be nice to have more information before locking in a second permanent aspect, so I extracted my hand. "I kind of see it," I said. "Might help with handling the interface."

"And it matches my aura of sneakiness." The raccoon's eyes practically shone. "It's perfect for me. Even if I can't pronounce 'press-titty-fication.'"

"Prestidigitation."

"Whatever."

Two minutes remained on our timers as we stood by the elevator in the hotel lobby.

"I'm giving you both these sign language cheat sheets, in case you forget." Hilbert handed each of us a scroll of paper. "There are more sequences listed there that you may find useful. Remember, the kada reads *all* your hand movements as potential inputs. So use your other hand if you're planning to play rock paper scissors or something." He mimed finger guns. "Accidents happen."

I glanced over the page, which had a short list of commands as well as hand positions for each ASL letter. There was way too much to learn at a glance, so I put it away for later with the Stow Item command. El did the same, using her mouth to hold the scroll of paper while she signed with both hands. I had to hold back a laugh. She looked like a ninja from *Naruto*.

"One more thing, Xavier," Hilbert said, turning to me. "I owe you for that bathroom snafu. Trespass by a monster into this safe zone is highly inappropriate. So I'd like to bestow upon you a small gift, which I believe you've very much earned the right to have."

His fingers danced, and suddenly he was holding the plunger I'd used against the slime. It was encrusted with gems, sparkling and reflective and utterly ridiculous. But it was a gift, so I received it with both hands.

"Thanks, Hilbert," I said. "See you when I see you."

"Don't mention it." Hilbert smiled. He poured three shots of Fernet, paused for a second, and then poured one mostly back into the bottle. "Here's to you, El Bandito. And to you, Xavier Shaw, slayer of slimes." He raised a glass to each of us.

"Unclogger of drains," El said, snickering, and lapped up her half shot of herbal liqueur.

I clinked my glass with Hilbert, and at that moment, there was a matching *ding* as the elevator arrived.

CHAPTER FIVE

Slimed

(Strive 2:1)

Ding!

The second floor of the Tower Strive was not what I had expected. In my head, I'd had images of something more grandiose, more exotic, and more . . . pleasant smelling.

El and I stepped out of the elevator into a narrow alley, the floors covered with trash and the walls with graffiti. Rickety steel scaffolding blocked out the sky, dripping slightly as if from a recent rainstorm. That liquid mingled with piles of garbage to create suspicious brown puddles on the ground. Puddles of a suspiciously slime-like consistency.

El lurched over to the wall and began to make retching noises.

"Damn," I said. "I would've thought this was a raccoon's bread and butter."

"No," El panted. "That fucking Fernet. Everything . . . spinning."

I leaned down to pat her on the back. "Why don't you stay here for a bit while I look ahead?"

El weakly nodded and then retched again. It sounded less dry this time, and I backed away to avoid the splash zone.

There was a fluorescent glow and a harsh electric buzz from the end of the alley. It came from one of those Japanese-style vending machines, with the products displayed in neat brightly lit rows. There were only five items for sale, arranged in a cross formation. All of them were more or less bizarre to me.

The top one looked like a protein bar, with a green and white wrapper that had a mint leaf on it. The leaf had a cute anime face, with a dialog bubble coming out of its mouth that proclaimed, "Oh! So Fresh!"

The middle row held three individually wrapped hard candies, the kind they'd give to kids at a doctor's office. Each was a different color—red, green, and blue.

At the bottom, there was a cyan-colored soda labeled SUPER BUBBLES! with a cartoon image of a surfing shark on it.

Next to the snacks were an unmarked slot and a cross-shaped keypad.

It was all very kawaii and aesthetically pleasing but completely useless since I didn't have any coins on me. Although, looking closer at the coin slot, I wasn't sure if the machine took Japanese yen or some other fantasy currency. Maybe there was some way to acquire tokens around here.

Besides the vending machine, the path was a dead end, so I walked past where El was busy emptying her stomach, back to the elevator we'd arrived from.

As Hilbert had promised, there was no down button.

My throat tightened. It was one thing to be reincarnated and learn that the afterlife existed and you had to take a placement test and then climb a magical tower. That was all cerebral, big-picture shit. It hardly seemed real. But starving to death trapped in a filthy back alley was something very concrete. My lizard brain grokked that and wasn't happy about it.

To keep myself from dwelling, I examined the graffiti on the walls. Mostly, it looked like spray-painted tags in made-up languages, or pictures of monsters. Completely indecipherable. Finally, though, after minutes of searching, I found something clear. An up arrow.

I tilted my head back and spied a gap in the scaffolding, big enough for me to wiggle through. I jumped and caught the edge with my hands, but it was slick with an unknown substance and I lost my grip. *Gross.* One more try in a different position, a brief struggle, and I was up, standing inside the scaffolding.

A few electric lanterns in the corner lit the ramshackle space. There was a ramp to a higher level in one corner and not much else, other than the smell, which was somehow even worse here. Against my instincts, I followed my nose to what looked like an overstuffed garbage bin with something leaking out of it. Nasty but harmless.

Then the leak raised itself off the ground and lurched toward me. *Here it is*, I thought, *in its natural habitat. What is it with me and garbage cans lately?*

The slime was a congealed brownish mass, with random trash floating within its body. It moved slowly, its own stickiness seeming to hamper its movements.

With my right hand, I signed *R-T* for *Retrieve Item*, and the interface flickered up before me. I had no time to choose an item, just flailing my hand wildly, and my plunger appeared in a flash. I had been hoping for the pellet gun, but this at least extended my reach. I'd have to figure out how to select a specific item quickly later.

With a swing, I stuck the slime with the business end, then slammed it against a flat piece of plywood that comprised the wall. The goopy part deflated and stopped moving.

Well, that was easy, I thought, oddly disappointed. *I guess it's only the first enemy.*

There was no notification that I'd gained experience points or items or anything, which was a bit of a bummer. In fact, my display didn't acknowledge the kill at all.

I inspected the dead slime's contents and spied a dull glint within the ooze. I almost reached in to grab it before I remembered the burnt-off patch of skin on my ass and grimaced.

Using my trusty plunger, I fished around inside the goop until the round token came free. It bounced on the scaffolding once with a bright metallic *clink* before falling between the floorboards down to the ground below.

"Ow!" El Bandito's voice floated up. "Who's throwing coins?"

"Sorry. You feeling any better?"

"A bit."

"In that case, could you do something for me?" I called down from atop the scaffolding. "Put that in the vending machine? Any item, just see if it fits."

There was the sound of grumbling and then a long pause. I thought I heard a far-off *ch-chunk* of an item being dispensed. After another pause, El appeared below the gap of the scaffolding, using both paws to hold an opened soda can.

"Pretty good," she said, and burped.

"You drank it already?"

El chugged the rest of the can and tossed it on top of an existing pile of litter. "That'll teach you to drop loose change on me."

I put a palm against my face. "Well, did anything unusual happen? Do you feel anything?"

"Hmm." The raccoon thought for a minute. "Feel hydrated."

"Great," I said. "Thanks for the helpful report."

There was nothing else of note on that floor of the scaffolding, so I shimmied up the makeshift ramp.

On the next level, I found a slime gorging itself on a takeout container. It didn't notice me, and this time I signed *R-T* slowly, swiping in the inventory's user interface (UI) one position to the right to select the pellet gun. I quickly signed *Y* to confirm, drew the gun, and shot the creep. That worked even better than the plunger, but it felt like a bit of a waste of my limited ammo.

This slime held a coin as well, and I brought it down myself, jumping down from the scaffolding onto the ground.

"What's the matter?" El trundled alongside me. "Don't trust me to grab it for you this time?"

"Frankly, no," I said, approaching the vending machine. "I'd like to actually see what the items do."

The soda had been the bottom item, and there were four other items. I slid the coin in the slot with a satisfying clink. The five buttons all lit up, and I hit the center one at random. El tried to swipe the small wrapped candy as it clattered down, but I snatched it before she could.

"Looks suspicious," she said. "You should give it to me for taste testing."

"I'll risk it." I popped the candy into my mouth. It was intensely sour, and I almost spit it out. But I held it in, gritting my teeth, and was rewarded with a surge of energy that jolted my body like electricity as my optical display came alive.

CHAPTER SIX

Sign of the Cross

(Strive 2:2)

You feel agile! Your dexterity has increased from Unacceptable to Pathetic!

I blinked at the message that flashed across my vision for a brief moment before it disappeared. I raised my hand to my face, and as I did, my arm seemed to react a fraction quicker, my eyes tracking the motion a fraction sharper than before. At least I thought so.

You feel agile! It felt patronizing for the contact lens, the udjat, to tell me how I should be feeling. I could decide that myself, thanks. As for the second part of the message, dexterity was obviously a stat, what they used to call "ability scores" in the old pen-and-paper days. I had no idea what to make of *Unacceptable* and *Pathetic*. I supposed they might be substitutes for numerical ratings.

"So?" said El impatiently.

"Hold on." I eyed the scaffolding that had been such a struggle to climb before. "Let me try something."

Running back over to the hole in the bottom of the scaffolding, I leaped upward. This time, my hands cleared the edge easily, and I clambered up. *Not bad. Not bad at all.* The effect of consuming the item was clearly noticeable.

But the question remained: How the hell were we going to get out of this filthy alleyway? Did the scaffolding lead up to the next floor? If not, all the agility in the world would only let me bash my head against the wall more efficiently. I pictured spending months subsisting on candy and soda, finally starving when the machine ran empty. *Yikes.* I shook my head to dislodge the image.

"Mr. Parkour over here," said El, looking up at me from underneath the hole. "Now come back and give me a boost?"

I grinned. Even the squelch of my shoes landing in a puddle of garbage juice couldn't fully dampen my spirits. I bent over to pick up the raccoon, lifting her to the hole like Simba from the *Lion King.*

"Someday all this scaffolding will be yours, El Bandito," I said. "Everything the smell of garbage touches is your kingdom."

"Thanks," said El, "but I'm more of a problem-free philosophy type of raccoon. Next coin's mine, by the way." With that, she hopped into the structure, her tail disappearing over the edge.

I sighed and boosted myself up. Two floors up, I found El rooting around in the stain of the slime I'd shot with my pellet gun.

"Already looted that one. And be careful with the goop; it burns." I whipped out my plunger again from my inventory, as a squelching sound came from the far corner, behind a mesh of orange netting. "Looks like another one's on its way, though."

The raccoon was already dashing forward, digging into the slime with both paws.

"What did I just say—"

El snarled as the acid bit at her, but there was a sucking sound, and she extracted the glittering coin out of the still-moving slime. "Easy-peasy," said the raccoon, squeezing through a crack in the scaffolding to drop out of sight.

"Hey!" I said. "You didn't kill it! Goddammit, El!" The raccoon was gone without a backward glance, off to redeem her earnings. I guarded myself with my plunger as the now-coinless slime continued to advance on me. "Lazy fucking trash panda," I muttered, jabbing at the sentient ooze. It didn't give me much trouble, and I didn't know how much the raccoon could actually help in a fight, but it was the principle of it that annoyed me.

When I had finished and descended, El was nowhere to be seen. Then I heard a banging from inside the vending machine. She'd gotten herself stuck in the dispenser.

"Are you alright?" I pushed the flap in so she could scramble out. "Your paws—"

"Fucking blob of acid," El spat. As she lifted her front paws, they left damp, rust-colored imprints in the dirt, and I sucked in through my teeth, deciding against the I-told-you-so I'd been about to deliver.

"We have to wrap that up," I said instead. "It's liable to get infected around here."

I was still wearing the plush robe from the hotel lobby. Pulling hard at the belt, I managed to tear it from the body of the robe. Kneeling down to wrap the makeshift bandage around El's left paw, I saw the prize she'd been trying to reach inside the vending machine through the transparent flap. An oblong rectangular wrapper like a protein bar.

"This sucks," said El, looking down at her bloodied paws. "Can't even grab my reward with my hands like this."

I felt a twinge as I looked at her pitiful form. "I got it," I said, reaching into the slot to grab the bar. I held it out in front of her, but she just looked at it and then at me. I was getting better at interpreting the raccoon's expressions. That one meant, *Are you serious right now*?

"Damn," I said. "I guess you can't really open it."

"No," she said. "I can't."

Feeling a bit foolish, I unwrapped the bar and held it in front of El's face while she bit into it.

"It's pretty good," said El, flicking crumbs from her whiskers.

"Alright, now let me wrap up your—"

I stopped. El's paw that had been burned by acid was healing right before my eyes. With each bite of the protein bar, the bloodied skin knitted itself whole again. I rubbed my eyes to confirm I wasn't seeing things, then double-checked the wrapper.

"Health bar," I read aloud. "A bar that restores health."

"Neat," said El as a few more pieces fell out of her mouth.

Impossible, I thought as I stared at the freshly healed paw. Not a scratch or blemish remained, and El didn't seem to be in pain anymore, either. She licked the paw absently. *There should be scarring or something.*

"Now what?" said El.

I glanced at the brick walls that surrounded us. "Still no exit," I muttered. "Maybe it's at the top?"

El grumbled, but we didn't have much of a choice, so it was back up the scaffolding with us, fighting off more brown slimes. Thankfully, they were slow, easily obstructed by small barriers we could step or jump over, so we often didn't have to fight them at all. Still, with the plunger, I could fish out the loot from within their gelatinous bodies with little effort, and so we slowly built up a small cache of coins during our climb.

Finally, we made it to the top of the construction site, where the walls of the alley shot up to a sliver of night sky like a cosmic coin slot. None of the stars looked familiar to me, but I'd never been a constellations guy—I didn't know Orion from an onion ring. More importantly, it was far too high for us to climb.

"Nuts," El said. "Dead end."

I was enveloped by a sense of despair. Something about it was familiar, but I felt it deeper than ever before. *No way forward.*

"It's fine," El said. "We'll try another way."

"What other way?" I tightened my grip around the plunger. "We've explored every inch of this dump from bottom to top. There's nothing here."

El pointed ahead. "Well, not quite nothing . . ."

A drainage pipe protruded horizontally from the wall, leaking a yellow fluid. Underneath the spill, a golden slime had formed. It leaped about erratically, facing us.

"There's nothing inside it," I said. "No coins, no trash even. Just a blob of piss."

"It's not attacking, either."

I watched the movements of the slime. El was right. It never got closer, just kept hopping around in a rhythmic little dance. When this started to bore me, I grabbed it with the plunger and flung it off the scaffolding. A few seconds later, it splatted on the ground with a sickening sound.

El and I exchanged glances, then made our way down. She reached it before I did, even with my newly improved dexterity. Well, it wasn't like I'd been especially athletic before.

"It's not dead," El said in a fascinated tone. "It's still doing its thing."

The golden slime bounced cheerfully in its new spot in front of the vending machine, repeating the same movement pattern. It always made two jumps forward, two backward, then two sets of side-to-side motions before stopping and restarting the sequence.

"Maybe we're supposed to copy it," I said, imitating the movements. "Like that rhythm game, *Dance Dance Revolution.*" After a few tries, I noticed El snickering at me and stopped. We both sat there for a while, watching the shimmying creature.

Realization jolted me, stronger than the magic candy had. This wasn't the *boss* of this floor. This was the *key*. That pattern . . .

I strode up to the vending machine, punching in a code on the cross-shaped keypad. *Down, down, up, up, right, left, right, left . . .*

Nothing happened. Upside down, then.

Up, up, down, down, left, right, left, right . . .

A fanfare sounded from the vending machine, and its lights danced in a kaleidoscope of colors, before it slid aside on invisible tracks to reveal a hidden entrance in the wall behind.

I knew being a gamer would come in handy one day.

I turned to see El trying to cram a coin into the machine, but it seemed to feel its purpose had been served. Her inserted coins were promptly spat out into the return tray.

"Ah," I said as El shot me a baleful glare, "my bad."

"Whatever." The raccoon pushed in the secret door, and we entered, leaving the golden slime to its gyrations. "I didn't want them anyways."

The new room had the atmosphere of a speakeasy cocktail bar, all warm woods and luxurious carpeting. A glass dish with a few hard candies lay on the bartop, along with two pink cans adorned with flowers. Strains of light jazz piped in from an unseen source, and a spiral staircase with a gilded number three seemed to lead up to the next floor.

A large podium that I initially took to be an ice sculpture stood in the center of the room, but on closer examination, I realized it was made of a material more like a magnifying lens, flipping and warping everything on the other side. The top had a deep hand-sized slot, much like in Hilbert's wine cellar.

El sniffed at the base. "What do you think it does?"

"Only one way to find out," I said, sinking my kada hand into it. My bracelet and contact lens both burned bright with script.

Downloading . . .

Download complete.

You've unlocked a new utility technique: *Examine*.

CHAPTER SEVEN

Take a Look, It's in a Book

(Strive 2:3)

The podium sank into the ground after El downloaded the same skill, but the pale white text remained hovering in my udjat-eye.

You've unlocked a new utility technique: _Examine_.

Energy consumption: None.

I pulled my sign language cheat sheet from my inventory and looked up the letters. *E* consisted of curled fingers with the thumb held below; *X* was a crooked pointer finger. Those two letters comprised the activation command. My bracelet glowed white in confirmation as I formed the shapes, and my contact lit up with a simple statement.

A bar countertop.

I realized my finger had landed on the bar at random, and I retried the sign, pointing at El instead.

El Bandito, a raccoon who has partaken of the fruit of the Tree of Street Smarts.

So she was telling the truth, I mused, before Examining myself. This time, I got more information.

Xavier Shaw, a human. Your strength is Nada, your magic is Zilch, and your dexterity is Pathetic.

I winced. It felt a bit personal, the way it was phrased. *What good was the Aspect of Corpus if my strength still sat at Nada?* I wondered whether Zilch was better or worse than Pathetic.

The only other things in the room with interesting descriptions were the sweets and sodas on the bartop. Apparently, the red candy was a **Steel Tendon Pill**, the green was a **Quickening Breath Pill**, and blue was the mysteriously named **Dendritic Lightning Pill**. They were the same kind of hard candies that had been in the vending machine outside, and they each seemed to increase different attributes permanently. The soda cans with flowers on them were **Minor Elixirs of Replenishment**.

Since there were two of each item, I pocketed a red, green, and blue pill, as well as a soda. For starters, I popped the Steel Tendon Pill in my mouth.

At first, it tasted like a regular cinnamon-flavored hard candy, but like the green candy from the vending machine, the feeling soon spread through my whole body, only this one was supernaturally hot. Fire burned everything from my tongue to my toes until my organs seemed to be roasting in an oven. Sweat began to pour out of me. *Am I dying? Food poisoning? God, that would be a dumb way to go.*

You feel strong!

As suddenly as it'd begun, it was over, and my muscles felt intensely sore, like after a hard workout. I turned my arm over. Was its shape more defined than it'd been a second ago, or was that just my imagination?

There had been no message to indicate that my overall strength had increased, just that I "felt strong." In addition, my strength was still Nada afterward. Perhaps it took multiple candies to increase power, like an experience curve? That thought made me feel a bit better. Maybe because my strength was already higher due to the Corpus aspect, it simply took more resources to further raise it.

All the same, if this was the way we were meant to become permanently stronger, it was like a sick joke. I stared at the bright green Quickening Breath Pill and couldn't make myself put it in my mouth. I'd need a breather before the next one.

"El, you gotta try these . . ." I looked over at the raccoon, and she had shoved all three pills into her mouth and was washing them down with the soda. ". . . although I'm not sure all at once is a good idea . . ."

El sprayed liquid and all three pills bounced out of her mouth, rolling and leaving three different colored streaks on the fine Persian rug. She coughed and sputtered. "What the fuck," she said. "You trying to kill me?"

"It's not so bad if you take them one at a time," I said unconvincingly, staring at the green pill in my hand, "and with breaks in between."

I glanced at the inscribed number three on the wall by the stairway that seemed to indicate the way to the next floor. My stomach growled. "I guess we should be moving on soon anyhow. We can't live off candies and soda, even if they're magic. One of these floors has got to have real food."

A small chest with a slot hung from the banister, and I Examined it with my new ability.

Deposit box for floor two tokens. Floor two tokens may not be used after this point.

I dropped one of my remaining golden tokens into the box. When it didn't reward me for doing so, I decided to keep the rest. It wasn't like I was short on space or anything, with my dimensional inventory system. All I was carrying so far was those few tokens, a pellet gun, and an ornamental plunger that was now slightly slimy.

My calves burned as we climbed the stairs until they opened up onto a dimness that I initially thought was a cave. But the smell that hit me a second later was unmistakable—the homely scent of old paper and binding glue.

(Strive 3:1)

It was a library.

Shelves of books towered over us in hexagonal formation, stretching up into the darkness. Intermittent reading lamps perched high above, casting long shadows all around. It looked like the place kept going in every direction, and I caught glimpses of maze-like passages through gaps in the stacks.

The place was labyrinthine and otherworldly, but I still felt a pang of nostalgia. I could almost imagine being back in a school library or a deep corner in a Barnes & Noble, nose buried in some doorstopper or another.

I brushed off a dusty book and opened it. The contents seemed to be complete gibberish, random words strung together for hundreds of pages. The second book was the same, and the third as well. My Examine command unhelpfully told me all three were strange books. Worse than useless.

El wasn't interested in reading, so we moved on, passing through a space between the shelves to emerge in another hexagonal chamber. The books here were nonsense, as well, and we kept walking.

After about ten minutes of strolling and perusing, I found a book that seemed like it'd been disturbed recently. It was slightly pulled out of its row, like someone hadn't put it back properly. I retrieved it and read the first few words, but it was the same gibberish as all the others.

"Goddammit." I threw it on the ground. Closing my eyes, I tilted my head toward the ceiling. "I'm stuck."

A feeling of foolishness immediately came over me. This wasn't an escape room with some employee watching the camera feed to make sure we had a good time. Our destiny was in our own hands.

"El," I said, "stop eating that book."

"Fine." She spat out a wad of paper. "It wasn't any good anyway. Too gluey."

As we entered the next chamber, a bitten and torn volume lay discarded on the ground, and it finally clicked.

"Lost Woods," I murmured.

"What's that?" El was rooting around in the shelves, not looking at me.

"It's not that every direction *looks* the same," I said excitedly. "They *are* the same, because no matter where we go, we end up in this room. At least, I think that's what's happening. Stay here."

I walked in one direction through the stacks as straight as I could, and soon enough, I entered an identical room with a raccoon lounging on a shelf.

"Who the hell are you?" asked the raccoon.

"Not funny, El."

She sighed and flopped onto her stomach. "Killjoy. So what do we do now?"

I rubbed my chin. "With this kind of puzzle, there should be a specific sequence of directions that gets us out of here. Maybe it's in one of these books? A code?" I paled as I realized how daunting that would be. There were hundreds, if not thousands, of books surrounding us, and the directions could be ciphered in a million different ways.

"Why not try the vending machine directions from the previous floor?" El asked lazily.

"Maybe. But there are six exits here, and that code had only four orthogonal directions."

"Ortho-who?"

"Compass points. Plus . . ." I turned in a circle. "I'm not sure how we would decide which exit corresponds with which direction. We could add up and down? But there's not a clear mapping."

"Hey," said El.

"What?"

"Stop mumbling to yourself and listen. Something's there."

El was right. There were fluttering sounds coming from somewhere high up, and occasionally I'd spot flickers of shadow, if only for a second.

I cursed and readied my pellet gun. Whatever they were, they were quick, and I was no Hawkeye. Furthermore, El had no offensive abilities to speak of. She couldn't prestidigitate an enemy to death.

Too late. In a flurry of wings, they were on us, big bat-like creatures buffeting us with their weight.

"It's a flying book!" cried El with a hint of panic. "Do something!"

I peeled one off my face to see that El was right. We were being mobbed by a bunch of floating grimoires, flapping their covers like wings, with their pages hanging underneath. One dive-bombed my arm, giving me the mother of all paper cuts. It really fucking stung. Another was latched onto my leg, opening and closing like a crocodile's mouth. That one didn't hurt. It was just kind of annoying.

I managed to remember how to perform the Examine command and signed at the one on my leg.

Bookbat, an annoying but unthreatening enemy. Knowledge wants to be free!

It was followed by another line that made my heart leap.

Its knowledge could be your ticket out of here.

The thing was too close for me to shoot with my pellet gun, so I dropped it and pulled out my plunger. I stuck it on the bookbat fastened to my leg and pulled, popping it off of myself. It chomped at me impotently from arm's length while the others continued to buffet me with their pages.

Lifting the book-on-a-stick, I bashed it again and again on the nearest shelf. Scraps of torn paper flew into the air, but I didn't stop until it went limp. Breathing heavily, I looked up.

El had torn the bookbats a new page or two, and one was flapping heavily away from her. The others hovered a safe distance overhead. Then, the thickest of them made a clapping sound with its covers, and the whole flock turned and flapped away, searching for easier prey.

"That's funny," said El, sniffing my bashed-up bookbat corpse. "I never took you for an anti-intellectual."

CHAPTER EIGHT

The Variation of the Twenty-Six Letters

(Strive 3:2)

All the pages in the dead bookbat were blank, except one that had an *L* printed on it in an absurdly large font. I flipped back and forth, but the other pages remained empty. Just one massive *L*. El found that hilarious, and I was glad at least one of us was having a good time.

"Maybe we need to catch more of the flappy bastards," she said.

It was easier said than done. The bookbats were wary of us now, after I'd taken one down. I heard flapping on occasion from far overhead, but they must've had some way to tell each other to stay away from the asshole with the plunger. I switched to my pellet gun and took a few potshots that ricocheted off the ceiling, then stopped. *How much ammo did I have left, anyway?*

I checked through the window on the air rifle's magazine and blinked. It was fully topped up with pellets. But that was impossible, given that I'd already used some on the bookbats and slimes. Had the gun been augmented with infinite ammunition, another magic trick of the tower? I'd have to check inside the magazine later.

"I have an idea," said El, rubbing her paws together. "When I call out, you shoot." She began to clamber up the nearest bookshelf, surprisingly agile, and after a few seconds, disappeared into the darkness.

"What if I hit you by mistake?" I called, but there was no response. Grimacing, I held the pellet gun at the ready, waiting for the signal.

"Here!" El's voice came down from above. "Gotcha—Gah!"

A shadow tumbled from the sky and slammed onto the ground right next to me. El was wrestling with a hefty tome, which flapped in a vain attempt to escape.

"Jesus, El! Let go so I can shoot it!" I aimed the pellet gun at the two shifting masses.

She released the bookbat, and it bolted upward to rejoin its fellows. I pulled a few shots and by dumb luck grazed the grimoire. It fell with a heavy thump, still flapping weakly.

"You should've booked it when you had the chance," I said, crushing it underfoot.

"Impressively corny," El commented from where she'd fallen. "Three out of five Schwarzeneggers."

"Everyone's a critic."

This second bookbat corpse was better preserved than the first, and we could clearly make out a page marked with the letter *X*. Placing the two side-by-side, we had *L* and *X*, in no particular order.

"Lox?" I asked. "Xtra-Large? Excellent? Excalibur? Expelliarmus?"

"Ex-Lax," said El.

I rubbed my eyes. "If it's meant to spell something, we're probably missing letters. Still, I'd like to avoid fighting more of these guys if we can help it."

Cross-referencing the ASL finger-spelling cheat sheet, I signed an *L* and *X* experimentally, in both orders. As expected, nothing changed.

It was almost by accident that I hit upon it. I was twisting my fingers through a mental list of words containing those two letters when, three letters into "luxurious," light flared out from my bracelet, resolving in a lantern flame that hovered on my hand. Its glow was cold and sterile, and it illuminated a hidden arrow on the floor that pointed to one of the room's exits.

"Lux," I said aloud. "Let there be light."

"Wow," said El. "God complex much?" She copied me, and a smaller lantern flame appeared in her hands. She danced it between her fingers, the light bouncing agreeably like a fairy sprite.

"How did you do that?" I asked. My flame remained stubbornly still, no matter how I twisted my hand.

"Must be a secret skill of press-titty-ficators."

We followed the line as it led us deeper through the library. I took the opportunity to pop the remaining two candies from the second floor into my mouth, one after the other. The green one was a shock, like last time, and a message appeared on my udjat eye.

You feel agile!

The blue one was comparatively mild, like soaking in a mint-fresh bath.

You feel mystical! Your magic has increased from Zilch to Nada!

With that, my lux-lamp seemed to expand outward by a small amount, and I grinned. **Nada** was the same level as my strength, and I supposed that meant it was better than **Zilch**. There was some correlation between these insulting ranks and numerical levels, I decided.

I was starting to put two and two together. It seemed to take multiple pills or candies to bring an attribute to the next level, and each level would bring a stepwise improvement to the corresponding abilities. So far, so good.

We followed the illuminated arrow to its end at a chamber, hexagonal like the rest, but with five crimson-colored walls. The sixth was covered in a kind of coarse parchment that shimmered with motes of light. I spelled *E-X* with my kada hand to Examine it, and my udjat lit up.

Spill my blot upon this page,
Find the way to your next stage.
I open doors with but a word,
They say I'm mightier than the sword.
What am I?

"'Word' doesn't rhyme with 'sword,'" I observed after a moment. "Bit of a stretch. And we need to find a pen."

"Imagine that," said El. "The king of pedants doesn't have a pen." With a flourish, she produced an elegant quill from her inventory. "*I* thought ahead and lifted this from the hotel lobby. Among other things." The kleptomaniacal raccoon sauntered up to the wallpaper and pressed the quill into it.

"You can hold a pen now," I said. "That's good. Is that part of your Aspect of Prestidigitation?"

"Probably."

The parchment drank in ink thirstily before blooming into a swirling design of its own accord. I gaped as lines and curves resolved themselves into a miniature semblance of a door, which swung open, leading into the page.

"Very cool," I muttered. "Very allegorical."

"I'm an artist," said El. "I create worlds at a whim."

"Good job. Now, let me see that pen for a bit."

"No." El clutched the quill protectively. "It's mine."

"Okay," I said. "Then can you draw me an exit that's not raccoon-sized?"

(Strive 4:1)

The paper door led to a tunnel that felt rough and drafty, as if the walls were unfinished, leaving sketchy holes for wind to enter. Our Lux spells cast an eerie glow on the sides of the passage. The narrow path twisted and turned and split, and without the light we would've been utterly lost. It was a relief when we finally stumbled out into an expansive cavern the size of a football field.

We stood at the edge of a small crater, a few dozen feet above the mirror-smooth surface of an underground lake. The light cast by our bracelets reflected off the water, illuminating an island in the center strewn with glittering rocks. That seemed likely to be our destination, but no footpaths led down to the water or the island.

Swimming wasn't my concern, although I wasn't thrilled about it. I wasn't scared to jump, either. Definitely not. It was more the fact that the mystery cave water could harbor any number of eldritch horrors in its depths, or even just good old-fashioned piranhas. It would be wisest to—

"Cowabunga!" cried El as she leaped off the ledge to splash down far below. She popped her head up and cackled in glee.

"You good down there?" I called. "No monster eels or anything?"

"Nothing. Water's clear and cool."

I stripped down to my boxers, stowing the rest of my clothing in my inventory where it'd be safe and dry. I stepped up to the edge, almost slipping on the moss.

Breathe in. Breathe out. Jump as far from the wall as you can. Stay vertical, like a pencil. Pinch your nose. Clench those cheeks so water doesn't get all up in your business. Three, two—

"Just jump already!" said El.

I pushed off the rock and fell for a long moment, then slapped down in the water. Every muscle in my body tightened, and I surfaced with a gasp.

"Clear and cool? It's fucking freezing!"

The raccoon paddled around me in circles, chittering with laughter. "That's right," she said. "Maybe try having fur like me."

But I didn't. The cold had me paddling like a madman for the island in the center of the lake. As soon as I touched land, I dragged myself ashore and lay there shivering. My Lux spell shone with a cold light, providing me with no warmth whatsoever.

My body was too drenched for clothes, but I was also freezing my balls off, so I compromised by donning the bathrobe Hilbert had placed in my storage. Now that I was dressed like a Cancun resort-goer, I was ready to explore.

Next to an arena, scattered with piles of metal cubes, a cheerful vending machine stood like a save point before a boss battle. The dispenser had a circular depression for my bracelet in place of a coin slot, and it chimed when I inserted my wrist.

Welcome, Xavier Shaw, to the Fourth Floor Vending Station. You have 1 free credit remaining.

I selected something called a Muscle Fiber Stick, which appeared to be a piece of red licorice, and put it in my mouth. As I chewed, I was rewarded with a taste of gristly meat and a surge of heat throughout my body that compressed all the pain of a weeklong fever into five seconds. "Geh," I said. Although the flavor and form factor were different, the effect was mostly the same as the red pill from the second floor.

You feel beefier! Your strength has increased from Nada to Zip!

I grimaced at that, but the next message brightened my mood.

Your strength and Corpus aspect have unlocked a new technique!

It almost made the pain worth it.

CHAPTER NINE

Copper Snakes and Iron Dogs

(Strive 4:2)

You've learned the basic technique *Harden*, a spell of ephemeral self-protection.
Energy consumption: Moderate.

"I guess we unlock stuff at certain stat levels," I mused as I scanned through the finger-spelling cheat sheet. "And the candies increase a stat, but sometimes it takes several bumps to reach a new level. That muscle fiber stick got me from Nada to Zip, whatever that means. I wish there was a way to see what the requirements are for each technique. We're flying blind here."

"Fingers crossed, I guess." El ordered a gummy worm called the **Bane of the Early Bird**. It plopped out of the vending machine with an electronic beep.

"Weird name," I said, glancing over.

"Yeah? Did you enjoy your *Muscle Fiber Stick*?"

I put my hands up in surrender. "Point taken."

El reached into the dispenser slot to retrieve the gummy worm, but it made a sudden leap out of her paw and began to escape, wriggling its neon-green body across the floor with surprising speed. She scrambled after it, stepping between two cairns into the circular arena, and a gong sounded. We both froze as the ground began to emit an unearthly light.

"Ruh-roh."

The scattered metal blocks levitated off the ground and began to resolve into two groups. The copper ones rotated in a massive circle, scraping the ground, before coiling together into a long chain. Each cube was about two feet to a side, and the effect of all of them joined together was like an enormous metal snake the length of a school bus.

Across the island, the iron blocks were stacking on top of each other, but at that point, the chain of copper hissed and slithered toward us. I jerked my fingers in a hasty gesture.

Copper Snake, a mini-boss. Loves hugs. Aim for the head.

Its copper cubes were joined loosely at corners and all spun against each other. Their sharp points left deep furrows as they ground into the dirt.

"This is fucked up," I said. No cube looked different from any other, but I had to assume the end coming toward me right now, kicking up a storm of dust, was the front part.

The Copper Snake lunged.

El dove out of the way, and I ducked to the other side. The front of the snake flew over me, but its other end whipped out and struck a glancing blow to my stomach. I let out a sound as all the air went out of me.

I gestured, and the letter *H* blinked on my bracelet, waiting for further input. Harden was both the name and the sequence of signs that would invoke my new technique. I had no way of knowing whether it'd be enough, but I had to cling to that hope. As I closed my hand into a fist, a shining *A* appeared next to the *H*.

The iron blocks had formed a quadrupedal creature that looked like a giant metal wolf, clanking as it chased El around the edge of the arena. El, in turn, was still trying to catch the rogue gummy worm from the vending machine. It was like a scene out of *Tom and Jerry* and would've been comical if it wasn't so dire. *H-A*, my bracelet winked at me in glowing light.

I managed to cross my fingers into an *R* before the blocky serpent lunged again and wrapped itself around my body. My vision blurred as the air squeezed out of my lungs. *Three more letters*, I thought. *Just three more. Please work . . .*

D. There was a loud crack inside me, and immense pain. One or more of my ribs, possibly.

E. I wanted to scream, but all I could do was open and close my mouth like a dying fish. The world started to turn black around the edges.

N.

A brilliant crimson light flared from my bracelet and shrouded my body. The pressure around my waist abated, and the air suddenly tightened around me as if compressed. But it wasn't a bad feeling; it felt like concentrated power, and I grinned wolfishly.

With a clenched fist, I struck a section of the snake, and my fist made a deep imprint in the copper like it was Play-Doh. The monster wriggled madly and slithered away from me. I was finally able to take a gasping breath.

Pain made it hard to feel too triumphant. I swung wildly at the snake, but it dodged backward. Worse still, my red aura had begun to blink, faster and faster. I had a strong suspicion that it was a warning—power-up time was about to run out. On the other side of the chamber, El was scrabbling at the floor, shoving something into her mouth, with the iron wolf closing in on her.

My shield blinked off, and in the same instant, the snake lunged at me.

I surprised myself by how fast my fingers could move.

The bloody aura roared back to life, and I grabbed the front copper block with both hands. It thrashed and spun at me with a metallic groan, but I folded it like a cardboard box. Before my ability could run out again, I stomped the head of the snake flat and dropped the body into the icy lake, where it sank like a rock into the depths below.

Good that I can reuse it, I thought, *because El's still in trouble.*

I turned and began to drag myself over to her, wincing at the pain in my ribcage. The raccoon was in a bad way, bloodied with bites from her looming opponent, which bared two spinning metal cubes like fangs. Her fur was matted, and she tried unsuccessfully to cast some new spell.

"I got something!" she cried. "I just need time."

My fingers made the word Harden as I stepped between her and the twenty-foot-tall metallic beast. It howled, and the twin drills of gleaming iron came down with a piercing whir. Behind me, I heard El cry out, and I closed my eyes.

There was an immense impact as my palms repelled the spinning metal. Wind gusted around me, smelling of blood and iron. Every moment I held off the beast, my energy seemed to drain. Worse still, my aura began to blink again, but my hands were occupied, and I couldn't recast the technique.

At the last possible moment, El vaulted onto me, then off my shoulder to tag one fang with a glowing paw.

One spinning cube vanished from existence.

It was simply gone, with a blue flash and a sound like a large bubble popping. The beast pulled back, roaring in pain.

"What was that?" I panted, my aura dissipating.

El gave me a feral grin. "Wanna see me do it again?"

A minute later, the now-toothless Iron Dog joined the Copper Snake in its watery grave, and we both collapsed to the ground.

"Fuck," I said.

"Yeah."

"Fuck," I repeated, putting a hand against my side gingerly. "I miss the puzzle floors. That snake broke a rib."

"I hate dogs," said El. "Loud, dumb, and smelly. A real trifecta."

"So . . . that new skill of yours . . ."

"*Pickpocket*," said El. "It lets me steal things and put them in my inventory."

I considered for a moment. "Useful. And kind of scary. Could you pickpocket my head off my neck?"

El perused the text in her udjat. "Says here it can't be living, or too big, or part of a continuous object, whatever that means."

"I guess we got lucky we weren't fighting an actual giant dog, then."

We lay there in silence until I groaned and pushed myself off the floor, brushing off rock dust that clung to my bathrobe. I limped to the other side of the island, where an intricate design was carved into the ground. Dozens of square depressions were etched into the stone, alternating brown and gray, the same size as the cubes composing the monsters we'd fought. They were arranged in a ring, and the center was inscribed with a spiral pattern. *It's almost as if . . . as if . . .*

I slapped my palm to my forehead.

"What?" said El.

"You like swimming, right? Cause we gotta go get those cubes back."

Over the next hour, we took turns diving into the icy water, retrieving cubes one by one, then dragging them to the matching divots. Thankfully, there were a lot fewer slots than cubes, so we could spare the ones I'd crushed. And El had the two dog-beast's fangs she'd pick-pocketed in her inventory, which meant two fewer trips to the bottom of the lake.

As soon as the final copper cube was in position, a low hum began to reverberate through the cave. The spiral pattern came alive and began to glow.

"P-portal," I said, teeth chattering.

"Don't have to tell me twice." El stepped forward, and as soon as her rear paws touched the light, she blipped upward through the ceiling. Holding my side, I shuffled in as well. There was a comforting warmth and a brilliant flash as the world went white.

CHAPTER TEN

A Lovely Place

Come on out, you wascally waccoon.

The trash bin jumped up and down, lid flapping like a cartoon mouth. With every bounce, it exhaled a scent of moldy vegetable scraps. I moved to open it . . . and leaped back, startled, as a sudden car horn blared from the freeway above. It was joined by a chorus of others that eventually faded into the normal rumble of late-night vehicle traffic.

Fucking A. Two-thirty in the morning and they're honking like it's rush hour in Midtown Manhattan. No wonder this apartment was so cheap.

I flipped the lid of the garbage can and caught the raccoon, its paws held up in surrender. In one hand, it still held a half-eaten chicken leg.

"Uhh," said the raccoon. "This isn't what it looks like?"

I leveled my pellet gun at the creature. "Gotcha now, you little asshole."

"Hey! C'mon, it's me!" the raccoon pleaded. "You know me."

The rifle shook in my hand. Why did its voice sound so familiar? I moved to set the gun aside, but a hand gripped it. My father stood next to me. "Do things in the way they should be done. Don't do things halfway," he said with a sneer, "like you always did with your life." I tried to let go of the trigger, but his weathered finger gripped mine tightly and forced it down.

(Strive 5:1)

Bang!

I gasped, bolting up amid fluffy white sheets. *A dream. It was just a dream.* My heart hammered in my chest, and I looked down at El's sleeping form, sprawled out at the foot of the bed like an overfed guard dog.

I crawled over and put a hand on her coarse fur. *Sorry,* I thought, feeling slightly foolish for apologizing to a raccoon.

She murmured in her sleep and a tiny paw pushed me away.

I got out of bed, rubbing cobwebs from my eyes. The portal from the fourth floor had deposited us here, in a plush hotel room with all the amenities we could've asked for—well-stocked minibar, coffee machine, and even a jacuzzi. It was sheer luxury.

We'd made good use of the showers, and I changed into one of the provided bathrobes. After that, even the combined aches and pains of all our injuries together couldn't prevent us from passing out.

My stomach rumbled, and I limped over to the minibar to Examine its contents. There were a few wafers my udjat identified as **Health Bars**, a suspicious jug of liquid labeled **Loose Juice**, and a dish chock full of button-shaped chewables called **Tastes of the Rainbow.**

I stuffed a turmeric-flavored health bar in my mouth and felt something twist inside my chest with a disconcerting pop. As I pressed my hand where the broken rib had been, only a bit of soreness remained. *Should've done that before sleeping,* I chided myself.

The Taste of the Rainbow was an overwhelming sensory experience. It was sweet, fresh, hot, and sour, like the taste bud equivalent of a seizure, or a really authentic Thai restaurant. That mixture of sensations began to trickle down my throat into the rest of my body, and I felt tears, sweat, and shivers come on all at once.

Flavor Town, baby. Population: Me.

You feel strong! You feel agile! You feel magical!

I'd take the system's word for it. Personally, I mostly felt like the roof of my mouth had been burned clean off. With a grimace, I pocketed half of the candies in the bowl, leaving the other half for El. The triple stat boost was too good to pass up, so it was going to have to be an acquired taste.

In the other corner of the minibar, the Loose Juice beckoned, but jars of radioactive-looking fluid were over the line for me. *Maybe I'll test it on an enemy*, I reasoned, stowing it in my inventory as I stepped outside the hotel room. *Or maybe El could hold onto it. She likes garbage.* Then I remembered her vomiting on the second floor and decided against it.

Our room stood at one side of a museum-like foyer with high ceilings. I hadn't had the energy to look before, but I did now. The centerpiece of the room was a glass display that held a miniature tower girdled by three sets of rings. Thin wires of various colors secured the tower to the glass at various points.

Model of Strive, not to scale, my contact lens told me.

I waited, but no more information was forthcoming. Puzzled, I flicked a gesture of Examination at a white strand of wire attached to the tower's midpoint, and more text illuminated my udjat.

Colored threads indicate external connections from tower.
White: Bidirectional
Blue: Outbound only
Red: Inbound only

I remembered the high-flying bridges I'd seen from the schoolhouse window, and suddenly shivered. The blue threads were worrying. Was every connection a bridge, or could they be subtler portals? What if I ventured into another tower and couldn't return to this one? Would I be aware of it if I had? So many questions, and this place didn't seem keen on feeding me the answers. I popped another Taste of the Rainbow in my mouth and grimaced. It didn't get any easier; that was for sure.

The door to our room cracked open and El padded over. "Find anything?" she yawned. "Why are you making a face like you gotta take a dump real bad?"

I flipped her a rainbow candy as the triple stat boost scrolled onto my display. "See for yourself."

The raccoon spat it out almost as soon as it touched her mouth. Her whiskers twitched in distaste. "The fuck."

"Goddammit, El." I had a sudden mental image of waves of monsters swarming and devouring her, leaving only a bare skeleton. "You're going to get left behind at this rate. Take your medicine."

"Why?"

I sighed. "Candy gives stats. Stats give levels, which give techniques, like your Pickpocket and my Harden. We need all the tricks we can get."

"They should make them taste better, then." She trotted to the wall and climbed up to another shelf, where a totem pole with three horizontal stripes stood. Sniffing at the art piece, she said, "Help me with something, would you?"

"What?"

"I need you to break that glass for me." She pointed at the display case the tower model sat in.

I sighed and summoned a red aura, striking the glass hard with my elbow. It shattered, and for a moment, I had the ridiculous notion that alarms would go off and Hilbert would come running, booting us out into the wasteland between the towers. *Apologies*, he'd say. *That's our procedure here*, before slamming the door shut in our faces, and shadowy legions dragged us to hell.

Nothing like that happened. El picked her way through shards of glass and leaped onto the podium where the model tower stood. She grabbed one of its floating rings and tried to yank it out, but it was stuck fast. Muttering, she made a sequence of hand signs, and the word *Pickpocket* spelled itself out on her kada.

Now, when she tagged the first ring with a glowing palm, it winked out of existence into her inventory.

She repeated this twice more, then returned to the totem. I stood by in fascinated silence as she summoned the rings back and looped them over the pole, with the largest at the bottom and smallest on top.

Clack! A woodblock sound rang out as the totem sank into the shelf, and two hand-sized slots appeared in its place. Golden text appeared on my display, reading: **Select one reward per player.**

"I'm a fucking genius," said El.

"Wow." I hadn't even realized it was a puzzle. "Do you want to do the honors, then?"

She rubbed her hands together. "Don't mind if I do." Leaping up to the left slot, she placed her kada hand into it. There was a long moment of silence, and she pulled it out. Her whiskers twitched in displeasure. "Useless," she said, moving to the other.

I tried the slot myself, and a display appeared.

Aetherphone, a gestural musical instrument.

This skill does not consume an aspect slot.

Download (Y/N)?

I raised an eyebrow. Just for good measure, I checked the right slot as well.

Airbrush, a gestural painting tool.

This skill does not consume an aspect slot.
Download (Y/N)?

"You go first," said El. "I'm thinking."

Without a second thought, I returned to the first slot and extended my thumb and pinky finger. The slot glowed, locking me in.

Downloading . . .
Download complete.
You've unlocked a new ability: _Aetherphone_.
Energy consumption: Negligible.

My hand was released, and I pulled out the slightly warm kada bracelet.

"You picked quickly," El commented.

"Ten years of piano lessons, you better believe I'm picking that one."

It took a while for me to twist my fingers through the long invocation. As I completed it, the word *Aetherphone* flashed once on my bracelet before remaining lit.

Suddenly, a piercing wail rang out from my kada, and I clapped my hands to my ears before realizing that only brought the sound source closer. El was yelling at me, but I couldn't hear her over the screech of my bracelet. It sounded like a dying cat amplified through stadium speakers.

A tiny legend had appeared in the corner of my display.

Open/close hand to control volume.
Hand position controls frequency.
Sign *X* to cancel.

I frantically curled my finger and the sound died away, echoes slowly fading in the reverberant space.

El lowered her paws from her ears. "I decided," she said. "I'm picking the brush one."

CHAPTER ELEVEN

(*Strive 5.2*)

After a final sweep of the floor, we made our way to the waiting elevator and rode up to the next one. But we emerged, impossibly, onto the exact same level we'd just left. The same posh hotel hallway, the same tiled flooring.

"This can't be right," I said, mashing the elevator button.

"It's not the same place," said El.

I stopped pressing the button for a second and opened my mouth to disagree. The appearance of the floor was undeniably the same as before.

And yet, there was a sense of wrongness in the air. The vibes were off, as the kids say.

My footsteps echoed as I turned to walk down the hotel hallway, El following close on my heels. Each of us jawed on a Taste of the Rainbow candy. My strength and magic had both reached **Unacceptable**, and my dexterity was apparently that of a **Worm**.

El refused to tell me the levels of her attributes, but she had at least started eating some of the candies, albeit complaining the whole time.

"It's like someone's watching us," I whispered.

"More than one," El said.

As we proceeded down the hallway, I stopped to look at a portrait hanging on the wall. It was some Victorian-looking noblewoman in a frilly dress, her hair pinned up in tight curls. She had a demure smile on her face, and her hands were crossed modestly. They were nice hands, except that the fingers were all twisted and warped. I spelled *E-X* to Examine it.

~~An ordinary painting.~~

"Hey—"

A six-fingered hand shot out of the painting and seized me by the throat just as the distorted text came up. Choking, I reached up to claw at the canvas in desperation, but the hand grabbing my throat extended, snake-like, and slammed me against the opposite side of the hallway. El hissed and leaped at the painting before she was seized by another twisted hand.

I managed to spell Harden on my kada, and the pressure around my windpipe lessened, repelled by the scarlet aura.

The woman in the painting unhinged her jaw to reveal teeth filed to points. She began to pull El into her mouth. Behind her, the background of the painting had morphed into bloody orange skies swirling with shadows. The raccoon thrashed and screamed in wordless animal fear as she was drawn into it.

Pushing against the force of the hand, I leaped forward and seized the edges of the frame, using the last of my Harden timer to tear the painting into two pieces. The hands retracted, and the ragged edges of what my udjat now called a **Painting Mimic** spurted dark red paint onto the carpet.

I gathered El's shaking form into my arms. "You're okay," I breathed. "You're okay."

She accepted the comfort, burying her snout in the crook of my neck. Something that I thought had long-since gone cold twinged in me. *How could I have ever wanted to shoot this helpless creature, as innocent as a child—*

"That fucking cunt of a painting," El said. "Let me down. I'll tear her to pieces, eat them, and shit them out. I'll piss on her corpse."

"Back to normal, then," I said dryly, and set her down on the ground.

Looking around, it was clear to me now that this wasn't the same place as the fifth floor. It was a passable copy, but everything was a bit wrong around the edges. Corners didn't line up right, and the repeating patterns in the carpet were a bit off. In truth, we were on the—

(Strive 6:1)

—sixth floor, whose whole job seemed to be to mimic the fifth. The fifth was the safe zone, and this was back to business. Which meant back to being afraid for our lives of what new threat lurked around the next god-forsaken corner.

I unholstered my pellet gun. Would the baseboards peel off the wall to tighten around our ankles? Would the sprinklers overhead shower us with a rain of blood? My throat tightened as I considered the possibilities. If an exit door presented itself to us, would it only drop us screaming into a trash chute? Or maybe the answer was *D: all of the above*?

It turned out to be *E: attack of the killer ice machine.*

The appliance lumbered into our path and sat itself down like a sentry, beeping once. A cheerful jingle began to play, rising higher and higher, as the lights on the front of the machine proclaimed: MAKING ICE . . .

"Get behind me!" I cried, throwing my hand up in a sequence of signs.

A flurry of frozen cubes shot out of the front of the machine, bombarding us like hail. They pinged off my aura shield, but the momentum still drove me backward. I dug my heels into the carpet and felt El's paws hanging onto me like a backpack.

Gritting my teeth, I pushed forward. Through the haze of frost and the red aura of my shield, I was nearly blind. I felt my energy sap as my defenses bore the continued assault. Harden didn't do anything for the cold, and I shivered. As I approached the source, the storm's intensity only increased, becoming a hurricane.

"I can't get any closer," I shouted, renewing my shield. "It keeps pushing me back."

El squinted around me, then ducked as a shard of ice grazed her fur. "Close enough!"

She clambered down my leg and darted forward along the ground. A moment later, she'd disappeared into the haze of ice, and then, without any fanfare, the attack simply stopped. The storm faded, and there was a final chunking sound as the machine's compressor snapped off.

El stood next to it, her paw glowing. "Used Pickpocket on its battery," she explained.

I dropped my shielding aura in relief. "You're a lifesaver."

We staggered to the end of the hall, where a small room held a sparkling treasure chest, practically begging us to open it.

"This is just obvious bait," I said, rubbing my neck. My vocal cords still felt funny from the painting's death grip.

Sure enough, my kada identified it as a **Regular Ol' Chest**, and I readied a Hardened fist. I punched a hole through the latch, and it popped open, fangs out and very dead.

"Good riddance," said El. She padded up and stuck her head and arms inside the chest. "Hey, free spellbook!" She held it up for me to see.

I was only mildly surprised when the book chomped me on the nose.

Folio of Flames, a minor spellbook. A consumable item that grants a fire attack spell.

"Who would've known?" I said. "Both a mimic and an actual spellbook. Seems pretty powerful, too."

"Mm," El said.

"You've got no attack spells right now. You should take it."

"Really?" El looked at me doubtfully. "You were the one who took the thing out. Got bit for your trouble, too."

I didn't need reminding of that, as my nose still stung. "I'm trying to give us the highest odds of survival here. Fairness doesn't come into it."

"If you say so," the raccoon said, before stuffing the book in her mouth.

By Examining the book, we found out that you didn't have to read the book to use it. In fact, the actual contents seemed to be just over four hundred and fifty pages of insane ranting about burning and destruction. All you needed to do was spell the sequence *U-S-E* with one hand while holding the book with the other. Unfortunately, even with her Aspect of Prestidigitation, El still needed both hands to sign.

So with the Folio of Flames clamped in her jaws, El used both hands to execute the signs. Her bracelet and the book each beamed out a pure white glow, drowning out the dim lamps of the room, as the new spell loaded into her kada. Then, as suddenly as it had started, the light faded, and the book crumbled into ash in her mouth.

The raccoon spat. "This whole system was clearly designed by someone with opposable thumbs." She produced a bottle of Fernet from her inventory.

"You stole that from the lobby!" I grinned. "I never even noticed."

El washed her mouth out with a generous swig from the bottle. "El Bandito strikes again." Her eyes unfocused as she read the spell description that lit up her udjat. "Oh, this is some good shit," she said, eyes glinting. "This one'll be a real blast, if you know what I mean."

CHAPTER TWELVE

Bones

(*Strive 6:2*)

El's paws came together, signing slowly and deliberately.

B-A-N-G

Her bracelet flashed blue, and with a spark and a loud crack, the wall exploded into scraps of sheetrock, a few meters ahead of us.

"'*Firecracker*, a basic explosive technique of the presto-didgeridoo aspect, yada, yada, yada,'" El read. "There's some more about energy usage, but the gist is that it blows shit up."

"Good." My mind raced. "Is there a maximum range? And how much energy can you put into it? In terms of TNT-equivalents, that looked like—"

El grabbed my foot with both paws. "You gotta calm down with this stuff. We'll figure it out as we go."

I sighed. If it was me with the spell, I'd be testing it all straight off the bat. Although, come to think of it, even with my Harden spell, I hadn't been experimenting much, so it was a bit hypocritical of me to push El like that. Hell, I had that new *Aetherphone* spell that I hadn't really used yet, either.

"Why not figure it out now?" I said. "I got a few things to try out, too."

"Alright, alright," El said as we advanced to the next room. It held a couple of vases, some couches, and a few tables with lamps. A cursory scan showed no sign of mimics, and I plopped myself down in a seat.

"Let's give ourselves half an hour," I said, before remembering I didn't have my phone or a watch. "Roughly."

El got to work blowing up the vases in the room while I turned on my Harden spell, beginning my investigation. Over the next few minutes, I learned a couple of things.

Number one. The spell lasted a total of ten seconds, beginning as soon as the *N* sign was formed, regardless of how long I took to spell the word, how aggressively I formed the signs, or any other factors I could determine. Warning blinks began after five seconds.

Number two. Recasting while the spell was active only refreshed the timer. The defensive effects didn't stack. I tested this by punching a wall repeatedly and rating the pain on a scale of one to ten.

Number three. The shroud of aura applied itself evenly to all parts of my body. I tried concentrating on my hand or my foot while casting, but nothing seemed to change. Likewise, the shroud didn't cover objects I was holding, such as my war plunger.

Number four, which I thought was the most interesting. The spell didn't seem to consume much, if any, of my body's strength on a passive basis. I only ever physically felt the drain when the shield was actually tested, a hunger and soreness like I'd done a mile run. I hadn't thought about it before, but this squared with what I knew about the conservation of energy.

Number five. All this testing was making me hungry.

I finished off my last few Tastes of the Rainbow while watching El test the range of her Firecracker spell. It was limited to her line of sight, but otherwise, she could hit things from surprisingly far away. The issue seemed to be more one of aim.

"Goddammit, El," I said, as a nearby explosion made my ears ring. "Be careful."

Next, I turned my attention to Aetherphone, my new musical instrument ability. Its combat applications felt limited, although maybe I could annoy enemies with it somehow. It almost seemed more like an Easter egg, and considering the circumstances in which El had found it, I figured it was more of an optional bonus than a strictly necessary upgrade.

I activated the ability and a whining pitch began to emit from my bracelet. I clamped my fist shut, and it stopped. I opened slightly and waved my hand around, making swoopy, slide whistle sounds. After a minute or two, I had enough control to play a recognizable, if somewhat detuned, version of "Mary Had a Little Lamb."

"Beautiful." El looked at me from behind some drawings she was scrawling in midair using Airbrush. "Are we finished?"

"More or less."

The exit door beckoned, and after checking it for mimicry, we went through. But instead of a stairway to the next floor, we found ourselves standing on a bare rooftop.

I wasn't naive enough to believe we'd reached the tower's peak already, but that was what it looked like at first. The kaleidoscope waste of the afterlife stretched to the horizon in all directions, towers sprouting up like far-flung trees in a nightmare savannah. Bridges long and thin as gossamer threads stretched across the ether, some of them connected to our tower, some crossing between unknown neighbors. Close by, an organic spire pulsed with a monstrous heartbeat, and I shuddered. The walls of our tower—if there were any here—felt as thin as single-paned glass, and I remembered Hilbert's warnings about the outside. *Only chaos awaits*, he had said, or something foreboding like that.

Next to us, a single golden thread descended from the sky. That seemed to be the path upward, and I grasped it. It felt disturbingly warm and a bit soft, how I imagined the entrails of an animal might feel, but as I pulled, it held stronger than any rope.

The landscape outside the tower suddenly receded into pitch black.

"That wasn't me, was it?" I said, letting go of the string.

"I don't think so." El's whiskers twitched. "Unless you're also in the habit of summoning schoolteachers."

I gaped as a familiar hooded figure emerged from the darkness, holding a red apple in one hand, standing in midair just outside the tower's margin. He placed a hand on an unseen barrier that seemed to prevent him from entering, knocked twice on it, and smiled at me. It was a charming grin or a snarling grimace. I couldn't tell. The invisible wall fractured, and a warning plastered itself over my entire contact in a terminal-like font.

Interstitial influence detected on the sixth floor.

"Oh, hell no," I said. "You can't make me go back there. Fuck your test."

The teacher from the schoolhouse peered at us with interest. He made no further attempt to break into the tower, just stared at us from the outer darkness. Then, he placed his palms outward, and the entire tower shook as he projected his voice into our minds.

I found you, Xavier Shaw and El Bandito, he boomed. *My wayward students.*

I stumbled backward and tried to push open the door we'd come from—locked. Next, I grasped at the trembling string. El was already scooting her way up it, and I started climbing behind her. I wasn't one for heights, but it seemed better than the alternative. Undeterred, the hooded being began floating up the outside of the tower alongside us. His cloak billowed in the outer winds.

No need to be so rude, Xavier. This is why you've always been lonely—you're constantly pushing others away. Like a carton of spoiled milk sitting in the refrigerator, wondering why no one will drink you. You think you have an old soul, but really you're just past your expiration date. He chuckled at his own joke. *You know who I am, don't you? You're a smart cookie. You knew as soon as you landed in my classroom after the truck crash.*

"So am I spoiled milk or a smart cookie?" My voice shook slightly. "You're mixing your food metaphors."

You don't have to say it aloud, said Death. *I can read your thoughts, even from outside the barrier of this Podunk little tower. Yes, right now, and stop thinking about weird Japanese fetish porn to throw me off. I don't want to see that.*

"Damn," said El. "Who knew Death could be so petty? You think he ever gets any grim reaping done, or does he just spend his time fucking around with assholes like us?"

"I think maybe this *is* the grim reaping," I replied, swatting El's tail out of my face. "Can you possibly go any slower? I feel like Davy Crockett with his coonskin cap."

"No one asked you to get all up in there."

Stop ignoring me, said Death. *I am Death, and you will come with me—*

There was a sudden sensation of overwhelming pressure and a blinding light as another presence manifested, this one inside the tower. I covered my eyes with one hand, then giving up on that, tried using the Examine spell instead. I could've sworn the figure reacted to my scan, turning its head in my direction, before nodding. Only then did my contact lens respond, letters appearing a fraction of a second later.

First Sender of the Tower Strive. The high authority of this tower.

Sender, said Death, his face cycling rapidly through moods and colors. *What a surprise. Aren't you going to invite me in?*

"This isn't going to happen to one of my climbers," said the being aloud. Looking at it was like staring at the sun, but its voice was male and surprisingly normal. "Not in my tower."

You stole them, said Death. *That was not part of the agreement.*

Agreement? I thought back to the beam of light that plucked us from Death's schoolroom. We'd escaped judgment for no reason I was aware of. Not that I'd say that aloud.

You see, said Death. *Even Xavier thinks so.*

Oops, I thought, trying to blank my mind.

As the two faced off, I felt like a kid watching an argument between divorced parents. The First Sender said nothing for a while, until Death opened his hands amicably. *What do you say we go halfsies? I'll take one, you take one. I'll even let you have first pick.*

Sender turned to look at us, and I finally found my voice again. "I'm enjoying not being dead, personally," I said, "and me and El, we're kind of a package deal, if that's okay."

Death boomed a psychic laugh that made the rope shake, and with a cry, El lost her grip. I extended a hand that barely caught her, my heart pounding. *'I-if that's okay?'* Death imitated me. *This is who you're going to all this trouble to protect? Come on, Sender. Hand over these two goobers.*

Sender's expression was obscured by the brilliance of his body, but I could sense the beginnings of anger in it. He held up a hand, surrounded by glowing white rings from wrist to shoulder, and said simply, "Not today."

Thick walls slammed down, layer after layer, enclosing the tower and hiding the darkness outside from view. Distantly, I heard Death's fading voice. *So be it, Xavier and El. But when we next meet . . . Well, let's just say make-up exams are only half credit.* Then, with a gentle laugh that was also somehow a scream of rage, he was gone.

"You just said no to Death himself," I said to the First Sender as the rope swayed. A question surfaced in my mind, and I voiced it to the being of light. If this was truly the entity that had saved us from that schoolroom in the afterlife, he'd know the answer. "Who are you? Why did you bring us here?"

"Onward and upward" was his only response as he fizzled into motes that drifted into nothingness.

We climbed in silence for a long while afterward, until gravity winked off and we began to float.

CHAPTER THIRTEEN

A Star String

(Strive 7:1)

Half of the sky above was the deep blackness of space. The other half was dominated by an enormous yellow gas giant. I felt small as the two of us floated weightless alongside the golden thread.

"Maybe Death's mad you ate his apple back in the classroom," I suggested to El, tossing a second floor token to propel myself in the opposite direction. "The fruit of street smarts or whatever."

"Of course it's my fault," El said, taking a soda can from her inventory and doing the same. She was drifting ahead faster than me, and I tossed two more coins to keep up.

"That's not what I meant," I sighed as my golden tokens flew off into the void. "I guess for now, all we can do is keep climbing—"

Gravity reasserted itself and we landed, or fell, in my case, onto a ring about ten feet wide that swept around the planet in a graceful arc.

I didn't know much about astronomy, but I didn't think this was how things were supposed to work. There was air, for one thing. And gravity was pointing the wrong way. And we hadn't exploded into goo from vacuum pressure. Also, for some reason, there was a piped-in odor of burnt steak, which made El's nose crinkle in distaste.

The darkness of space was dotted by bright specks. Unlike true stars, they shifted and swam around one another in chaotic patterns. We stood mesmerized by the display, but it wasn't long before our first enemy, a certain group of stars, descended from the sky and touched down on the ring facing us. Together, they looked like a squiggly fish hook.

Scorpio, an animated constellation.

As the cluster of stars landed, the space between them seemed to flesh out with interconnections of light. Sets of scuttling legs shot out from the sides. I could clearly make out a scorpion shape now, stinger and all. It let out an eerie synthetic growl, like a first-generation Pokémon.

"Here we go again." I glanced at El and cast Harden, stepping forward.

The man-sized insectoid skittered toward us, its stars burning white-hot trails in the air. Hologram-like lines connected the stars, which acted like joints. I wasn't sure if they were solid or not, but I hoped they were. Hard to fight something incorporeal.

Bang! El cast a Firecracker at the creature, but it flipped sideways dexterously and continued closing the distance. It'd reach me in a few seconds, before El could get off another attack.

But I'd miscalculated, still shaken by our brush with Death, and my Harden winked out before it got to me. I was bowled over by the constellation, and then jabbed by several scuttling legs in passing for good measure. They didn't break skin, but they were white-hot, and my skin was beginning to blister.

"It's solid," I groaned. "Don't let it touch you. Burns, too."

"No shit," cried El.

As I pushed myself off the ground, I saw the monster trying to use its long stinger to stab El, who was weaving between its legs. Whenever the stinger stabbed the ground, it sizzled and smoked like quenching metal.

The raccoon was more nimble, but she couldn't run forever, and she couldn't cast and avoid the thrusts at the same time.

"A little help here!" El cried as she ducked another swipe.

I stalked up behind the star scorpion and shaped my right hand into the Harden command as my kada ring glowed crimson. My body tensed, and I leaped forward with my hand outstretched.

My intention had been to grab the scorpion by its tail and yeet it into space, a la Bowser from *Super Mario 64*, but that wasn't what ended up happening. Instead, my spell-augmented hand crushed its tail like an empty beer can. The monster screeched and arched its body in pain. It wriggled frantically until the tail came off in my hand, and the rest of it scurried away into the night sky, back to being a regular constellation. Minus a couple stars.

I turned to El and grinned, holding the disembodied tail. "You're welcome."

The raccoon pointed behind me. "Let's not gloat yet."

Before we were through, we fought Leo the lion, Capricorn the sea-goat, and Libra, a floating set of scales, none of which were too challenging once I'd gotten in the flow again. They each dropped a Pill of Bursting Star, which looked suspiciously like a Starburst fruit chew. We pocketed those, and then a few fights and a brief trek on the planetary ring later, we spied a dinky little rocket.

"That floor wasn't so bad," I said as we boarded and took off, shuttling toward the next floor.

"How many floors do you think there are?"

"Huh." I scratched my head. "Somehow in between the slimes and the scorpions, I hadn't had time to think about it. A hundred? That's a nice round number."

El flattened herself against the floor of the rocket. "I hope it's less than that."

I watched meditatively as stars blurred past outside, then flinched as a living constellation thwacked against the window. There were no controls on the inside of the ship, just two cushioned seats. It brought to mind our floating journey across the wasteland from that terrible schoolhouse. Since then, it'd been one floor after another, with only one chance to relax. And then the brush with Death and the First Sender, whoever he was. *Whatever* he was.

Hilbert had said that the instanced levels, the ones where we were isolated, only went up to the ninth floor, and we'd meet other climbers afterward. That prospect sent a different kind of fear bubbling up inside me.

I twisted my fingers, gathering scarlet energy around a clenched fist. It was beyond pathetic to be worried about that old anxiety at this point. How could it be worse than Death?

No, a knowing voice said in my head. *They're different fears. In many ways, you're still the scared kid on the first day of school, eating lunch alone in a bathroom stall.*

But what else could I do? I still needed human companionship. Friends. Romance. I wondered idly what the dating scene was like in a magic tower of death.

Shadows passed overhead, interrupting my reverie. An enormous hangar bay opened and swallowed the ship, which docked automatically with a lurching motion. As our door irised open, arrows embedded in the floor lit up, pointing along a gangway to our next gauntlet.

(Strive 8:1)

We proceeded to the face of an enormous wall, the bottom of which exposed a hand-shaped slot. When I inserted my kada, my udjat display came to life.

Enter password: ______

"Password," I said.

Nothing happened.

"What?" El replied.

"Nothing. I'm trying to figure out this puzzle." I pressed my hand into a fist, and the prompt rapidly filled up with the letter *A*.

Enter password: AAAAA

Password denied.

"They want us to enter a password manually," I said. "Five characters."

"Probably find it there." El pointed.

There was a passage to one side of the wall, dark enough that I had to activate Lux to see more closely. Concerning growls and flickering lights emerged from it. It did seem like the tower intended for us to go that way, but as I pressed my kada's light forward, my eye was caught by a carving messily scratched into the metal—the single word *EPOCH*. I hurried back to the password slot.

Enter password: EPOCH

Password accepted.

With a celebratory chime, the wall split apart into two halves, creating a passage. *That was easy*, I thought, unsettled.

A large number flicked up to the corner of my display. It was in the low—I counted the digits—two billions, and advanced by one every second. Was it a timer? I knew there were roughly thirty million seconds in a year, so doing the math quickly in my head, it must've been counting up from something like seventy years ago, which would be the 1950's. *Very strange.*

Stranger still was the fact that the answer had just been right there for the taking. Maybe the instanced tower levels were reused, and whatever process scrubbed them had missed a hint left by a good Samaritan? The chicken scratch felt more organic than something the tower would generate. There was a hastiness about it, and I felt a bit guilty that I hadn't left any clues for those after me.

"Hello? Earth to Spaceman Shaw?" said El, waving at me.

I packed my thoughts for later and stepped forward. Turning around, I was about to make a snarky reply when the wall slammed shut behind me and an error flashed red in my eye.

Only one climber may participate in this challenge at a time.

CHAPTER FOURTEEN

Still Alive

(Strive 8:2)

A**Pill of Bursting Star** fell from my mouth as I read the error message over and over again.

Only one climber may participate in this challenge at a time.

I banged on the wall with a Hardened fist, but my aura dissipated uselessly against the cold steel. I imagined I heard Firecrackers bursting on the opposite side.

"Hey!" I called out, but the sound echoed and faded without an answer from the other side.

I was alone, in the dark and silence. More importantly, El was by herself, and even with her abilities, I couldn't shake the feeling that she was quite defenseless.

An array of fluorescent bulbs slammed on, bringing the space into harsh focus. It was white-washed and sterile, like a laboratory's test chamber. A slotted podium was the obvious focal point of the room. Other than that, the walls were bare except for a panel labeled #01. *Two digits,* I noted with dismay. *If that's the test chamber number, this could be a long trial.* I slid my hand into the receptacle, and a prompt appeared on my udjat, cursor blinking.

Enter current time: _

My kada hand locked in the slot, and I cursed myself. I could see the ten-digit number ticking up in the corner of my vision, but I didn't know how to finger-spell numbers. All I could do was twiddle my fingers ran-domly until I was released, my vision flashing with a red message.

Incorrect answer. Dispensing level 2 enemy.

I yelped as a glob of slime dropped from a chute in the high ceiling and splattered on the floor. It wriggled for a moment, then lay still.

"Hm," I said, my heart pounding. It was lucky the slime had died from the long fall. But even if it hadn't, it was no great danger to me at this point. All the same, I'd try to get the answer right this time.

With a flicked gesture, I retrieved the finger-spelling manual from my inventory. The numerals were listed next to the letters, and in retro-spect, the signs for one through five were obvious. Six to nine took a bit of practice, but when I had them memorized, I stepped back to the podium.

The nine-digit number in the corner of my eye continued to advance as I entered it, and the last digit slipped upward to six just as I spread my fingers, inputting five.

"Shit."

Incorrect answer. Dispensing level 3 enemy.

A flurry of pages sounded from the ceiling, and I groaned. *Bookbats.* Bookbats that wouldn't die to fall damage. And the level of the enemy had increased. Though a few Hardened punches made short work of them.

A few gestures later, I finally entered the correct number.

Correct answer. Dispensing reward.

There was a chime, and a smattering of red, green, and blue candy bars fell from the ceiling onto my head. With that, the prompt changed.

Enter current time with digits in reverse order: _

I grinned. Here was a slight challenge. Since the epoch crept upward every second, the first digit I entered would now be the first to change, long outdated by the time I finished. But thirty seconds of leeway should do it.

Adding thirty to the current epoch of—I glanced—2418822441 gave me 2418822471, and I started entering the sequence, back to front: 1-7-4. I took my time, signing a digit every few seconds. I waited until the number in my display matched my magic number, and blitzed out the last two figures, a four and two.

Chamber #01 cleared.

The wall in front of me opened with a triumphant fanfare. Unfortunately, the one behind remained stubbornly shut.

Before entering the next chamber, I ripped some pages from the dead bookbat and spread them out on the floor. I pulled my plunger, dipped its tip in slime goop, and scrawled on the paper "Learn ASL numbers!!" The acid left charred holes, but the sentences were still relatively legible.

I grimaced and wiped my hands on my bathrobe. Hopefully that was clear enough for El and whoever came after.

Chamber #02 held three doors. Above each was an icon—a music note, a paintbrush, and a skull. The last one was already open, while the first two were shut tight, even after I tried to force them with Harden.

When I activated my Aetherphone, though, the first door beeped and slid open, revealing not the entrance to the next room, but a ten-foot-tall Glass Golem that stormed toward me.

I disabled the whining instrument and brought up my shielding aura, just in time to block the golem's strike with an outstretched forearm. The impact reverberated through my bones like a gong. I counterattacked, but my Hardened fist bounced off its crystalline torso uselessly.

Why would the door with a music note lead to a combat encounter? I thought as I tanked another jarring slam from the golem. *Did they mess up?* It felt like this should've been the one behind the third door, the one with the skull.

While I was thinking, I'd disregarded my aura and it winked out. My stomach dropped for a second before the golem swung into me, knocking me clear across the room. I had never been hit so hard before, and I thought that without my Corpus aspect, I would've certainly died.

As it was, I saw blurred rainbows as the golem advanced, light prisming through its body and refracting onto the walls. With a desperate burst of energy, I rolled away from its immense fist as it struck the metal floor, hard.

The impact resonated with the sound of a struck carillon. For a moment, it staggered, confused, then realization dawned on me. *I've got it.*

Wind from the blow blasted me like the nearby passing of a subway train. I scrambled to my feet, twisted my fingers to refresh my red aura, then continued signing until a loud whine came forth from my kada bracelet. I turned my hand, slowly tuning the pitch with a savage grin.

The glass golem made a silent roar and stomped toward me. It loomed, then drove a monstrous foot down onto me. Thankfully, my Harden still remained in effect, and I was grateful I could stack it with the Aetherphone, something I'd forgotten to test before. *That could've easily been a fatal oversight.*

The golem's weight bore down on me as I rotated my wrist, seeking resonance. At a rumbling low tone somewhere between A and B-flat, I found it.

The glass pressing against me began to vibrate, even as my Hardening shield blinked a warning. *I almost have it*, I thought. *Just a bit more.* My whole body was bent double now, as I splayed my kada hand open-palmed on the golem's glass surface, conducting acoustic energy through it. It juddered like a lawnmower on crack, but still it crushed down on me.

Without warning, the golem's body shattered into a thousand shards. I squeezed my eyes shut as my shield winked out, and cuts lacerated every part of my body. I wanted to scream, but I gritted my teeth against the unending rain of glass.

When I opened my eyes, my hotel bathrobe was shredded to bits. Pinkish shards of glass lay in a pool of dark blood, my blood. With clumsy, sticking fingers and fading vision, I stuffed a health bar from the first challenge into my mouth, then collapsed onto the bed of crushed glass, relieved, at least, that El wouldn't have to go through this trial. She'd picked the paintbrush skill instead.

Chamber #02 cleared.

I startled awake to an insistent drone like an idling jet engine. It was incredibly loud and annoying, and seemed to be coming from my own wrist. My pounding headache didn't help, either.

Right, I thought groggily. *That's me.* Turning off the Aetherphone, I sat up. The million little scars across my skin were already fading to white, but unfortunately, my clothes were a total loss. *At this rate*, I thought, shrugging off scraps that had once been a bathrobe, *I might be making my debut to tower society buck-ass naked.*

My inventory was empty of clothes, but it still held a few more health bars and a single yellow Pill of Bursting Star. Downing my remaining pill in one swallow, I was informed that I now had a strength level of **Worm** and dexterity of **Give Up**. That made me snort. I wasn't going to give up, at least not yet.

As I pushed myself off the floor, worry for El gnawed at me. She'd shown she was adept at puzzles; hell, the reason I had my Aetherphone ability at all was thanks to her, but it was the combat I was more concerned about now.

The path to the next chamber stood open, and I made my way to it, picking up some more stat candies on the way. A ghostly #03 floated in the pitch-black room ahead. As I advanced, I spelled Lux with my kada hand, and a ball of light bloomed in my palm.

My lantern shone on a large empty space that extended into darkness. It was eerily quiet, with no sign of life. I crept forward, footsteps echoing on the metal. This would be easy enough—

The floor dropped out right in front of me, and I almost pitched forward into the abyss. I pinwheeled my arms and sat back, heart pounding. There'd been no warning, just solid ground one second and a bottomless pit the next.

I crawled forward on my hands and knees, and stars from the previous floor winked up from dizzyingly far below. As I looked across the room, I saw more of the same, missing patches of floor that dropped to nowhere. Even as I watched, another section of floor gave way to empty space.

With no time to think, I rose to my feet and started to run. There was only a thin strip of flooring now, surrounded by pits. I vaulted over a gap just as it opened up, and a chill wind blew up from beneath. I shivered and kept moving.

My light illuminated the door at the far end of the room. I jumped over the last small gap, but even as I hung in midair, the landing spot fell away, gaping open to swallow me whole. My hands flailed for the far edge, where the exit taunted me, now hopelessly out of reach.

This is some bullshit, I thought, as I fell headlong into the abyss.

CHAPTER FIFTEEN

Sequence Break

(*Strive 8:3*)

Wind rushed past me as I fell. The thought of death filled my mind with sudden clarity, and I twisted my fingers into the *Retrieve Item* command. As the hotelier's plunger materialized in my hands, I slammed it into the side of the chute with both hands. The rubber cup skidded against the wall with a screeching noise before it stuck.

My elbows jerked in pain as they took my full body weight. Everything wobbled, before slowly, gradually, settling into stillness. I took a shaky breath, my heart continuing to pound.

Curiosity made me peer downward to where the metal chute ended in a circular opening. Beyond that, there was only darkness and the yawning void of outer space.

Everything suddenly seemed upside down, and I felt like a frog at the bottom of a well, peering up at a circle of night sky. I squeezed my eyes shut as vertigo threatened to overwhelm me. The stars were supposed to be above my head, not under my dangling feet.

I looked back up (at least, the direction gravity told me was up) to find that I'd fallen just a few meters, but there were no handholds on the smooth steel wall I was adhered to. Only my new strength kept me hanging on. And the plunger, I supposed. And, to my surprise, the thought of my new raccoon friend.

If I fell here, my failure would be on me alone, and it'd be deserved, in a sense. But without me, El would be left to fend for herself.

I hated having others depend on me, and usually tried to avoid it at all costs. Yet somehow, I'd ended up in this situation with El. It was ridiculous. A few days ago, I would've happily thrown her into a fast-moving river. Now, I kept remembering that image of her snoring on a hotel bed, her tiny hand outstretched.

I struggled to lift myself to no avail. I swung my legs outward, but the other side of the shaft was too far for me to brace against. When I tried to use the plunger as a handhold, the soft rubber cup tipped precariously.

Fuck, I thought. *This really might be it—*

"There he is," came a voice from above. "Finally found you."

I craned my neck back in disbelief. "El?"

"In the flesh. How'd you end up down there? And why're you naked?"

"Glass golem," I said. "Jesus, am I glad to see you. Wanna help me get up?"

"I don't think I could lift you," said El dubiously. The shadow of her ears and snout poked over the lip of the ledge. "You're too far down. Unless . . ." El paused for a moment before she explained her idea.

"Are you serious?" I said. "Would that even work?"

"Hey." Her silhouette shrugged. "I'm all ears if you got anything better."

My arms were starting to ache, and sweat made my hands slippery. I heard a low clanking noise as another panel of the floor dropped away. "Fuck it. Fine." I dropped my right hand from the plunger to Harden myself, and the red aura flared to life. "Not in the face, alright?"

I clenched my kada hand, and the letter *S* appeared on my wrist.

"Ready?" I asked El.

A few moments later, she replied, "Ready."

"On my mark, get set, go!"

I signed *T*, and the Stow Item command sucked the plunger into my inventory. At the same time, El's bracelet flashed blue, and an explosion rocked the air under me. I was launched upward by the force of the Firecracker spell, popping out of the hole. Time seemed to slow as I rocketed up past the floor, past El, toward the top of the chamber, and I twisted cat-like to meet the ceiling with my limbs and push off horizontally. That move, apparently, used up my badassery quota for the day, as I landed in a sprawled heap on the dark room's floor, panting.

El let out a low whistle. "Pretty impressive for a two-legs."

Chamber #03 cleared.

The lights blinked on, and we were standing right by the exit.

"Appreciate the lift." I rose unsteadily as my aura shield dissipated, the red mist fading, along with wisps of smoke that came from my lower body. My ears rang from the concussive force of the explosion, but otherwise I was unharmed. "How'd you get into my test chambers anyway? I thought they wanted this floor to be single-player."

"A while after you left, the wall opened up and let me into the first room," El said. "Saw your note, but it all seemed like a real pain in the ass." She pointed her Lux lamp upward at a missing patch of ceiling that exposed a hidden crawlspace. "So I pickpocketed a couple ceiling panels to get up there, skipped the challenge room, then dropped down on your side."

It was the most raccoon approach ever, and I laughed and ruffled El's fur. "You know, I thought I was going to have to save *you*, but here you are, bailing *my* ass out. Shows what I know."

"Of course," said El. "Couldn't let you one-up me again. I already owed you for your help with that big iron mutt."

"True enough. Now, let's get out of here." We stepped through the exit doorway into a futuristic room with a chute that hung from the ceiling like a hamster's feeding tube, and my contact lit up.

Test chambers completed. Dispensing reward . . .

A buffet of multicolored candies rained down on us, dozens of them, too many different kinds to list. There were **Pills of Psychokinesis**, **Ballet-Step Bonbons**, **Lozenges of Ligament Strengthening**, and such an abundance of annoying alliterations that it started to kind of piss me off.

"'**Caramels of Constant Constitution**,'" I blinked at the words hovering in my display. "Who comes up with these names, Willy Wonka?"

"I decided," said El, "that the blue ones usually taste the best. Save those for me."

"If you say so." Despite the saccharine naming, I wasn't going to look a gift horse in the mouth. I scooped up some reds and greens and tasted one. The reddish Lozenge of Ligament Strengthening tasted sweet and spicy and oddly familiar. *Loquat syrup, maybe?*

At this point, the heat spreading through my body wasn't as unpleasant as before. It almost felt rejuvenating, like whiskey on a cold day, and I was rewarded with the information that I **felt strong!**

A large metal diving bell stood at the far side of the room. It hung from a thick metal chain that disappeared upward into a hole in the ceiling. It was clear that this was some sort of conveyance that would bring us to the next floor, and El and I stepped into it. The interior was cramped, with only a ring around the edge to sit on and a lever in the center. Small portholes looked out onto the room we'd entered from.

"Ready?" I asked, and El nodded.

Initially, the lever was too heavy for both of us. It was only after popping what felt like a million Lozenges of Ligament Strengthening and increasing my strength to Donkey doo-doo that I was able to heave it into the *ON* position. With a clinking sound, the chain went taut and began hauling us up to the next floor.

(*Strive 9:1*)

As we passed into the ceiling, the portholes grew dark, so our bumpy ascent was lit only by a single bare bulb that swung and flickered in the center of the diving bell. I wiped sweat off my face, wondering idly what the next floor would bring.

"Is it getting hot in here," I said aloud, "or have I eaten too many of these stupid spicy things?"

We passed through a current of flowing magma that cast the interior of the diving bell in a sinister orange glow.

"I don't think it's just you," El panted.

A moment later, we breached the surface, and the door swung open, a rush of hot sulfurous air buffeting us as we stumbled out of the conveyance. If I'd been wearing clothes before, I probably would've shed them here. Even breathing seemed to scald my throat.

We had arrived on a patch of ground in the middle of a magma-filled cavern. It reminded me of the fourth-floor arena where we'd fought the cube beasts, but with a lake of crackling molten rock instead of icy water. Swimming through that had been unpleasant; here, it would be fatal.

A spire of rock rose up into the ceiling of the cave, and I stepped slowly around it. Although it was thick enough to conceivably hold a spiral staircase, there were no entrances as far as I could tell. Likewise, there were no paths leading off the island. I wiped more sweat off my forehead. Damn, it was hot.

"Hey," El said, "doesn't it look like the lava's rising?"

Our island did seem to be shrinking by the second, now that I looked. The stifling air temperature climbed another few degrees, and my skin prickled with heat.

"It's actually called 'magma' when it's underground," I said informatively, as scraggly weeds near my foot caught on fire.

The raccoon's whiskers twitched. "I should've left you in that pit."

CHAPTER SIXTEEN

The Floor is Lava

(*Strive 9:2*)

I yelled as a spray of hot rock erupted from the magma lake. "The center of the island," I said. "That big rock column. Go!"

We scrambled away from the diving bell toward the stone spire. El took a running start and leaped onto it, scaling the rough rock to get to higher ground. I grabbed a starting hold and began to laboriously make my way up. Looking back, I saw that the magma had already begun to swallow the metallic bell.

"C'mon," El said, already far above me. "There's an exit up here!"

Unfortunately, I'd gotten myself stuck. My arms and legs were splayed out as far as they could, and my hands cupped small bumps that quickly grew slick with my sweat. I craned my head back, searching for the next hold.

There was only one, a shallow shelf about a knuckle deep, three feet above me. I made a very optimistic lunge for it with my right hand and missed. "Fuck," I cried, tumbling to the ground.

The heat was almost unbearable now, and a river of sweat stung my eyes. I clambered back up without looking back at the magma's progress. Not a moment later, it submerged the ground where I'd been standing. No more second chances, now.

I looked up and swore, realizing I'd climbed up to the same dead end. That same out-of-reach hold. It wasn't possible. Not with my current climbing ability. The red-hot liquid began to inch its way upward, and panic jolted me into action.

Retrieve Item. I twisted my fingers, and a candy from the last floor popped into my hand, a green apple flavored marshmallow that practically melted in the few seconds it took for me to open it. I had to scrape the wrapper to get it all, but I was rewarded by the shock of electricity coursing through my body and a displayed message on my udjat. **You feel nimble!**

I pulled another candy, a lollipop called a **Sucker of Strength**. I crunched it in my teeth and threw the stick into the rising magma. **You feel bulky!**

That's a start, I thought. *But not enough.*

From my inventory, I selected as many red and green pills as I could, and they materialized in a small pile in my palm. My stomach churned in anticipation, but a rumbly tummy would be the least of my troubles soon.

Grimacing, I crammed them into my mouth, wrappers and all. I chewed and swallowed, as quickly as I could, and my udjat came alive with a flood of updates. **You feel strong! You feel well-muscled! You feel agile! You feel quick! Your strength is now Bad! Your dexterity is now Dogwater!**

The pills blazed through my body like wildfire, and I was suddenly burning both inside and out. The shock almost made me lose my grip, but it was better than being swallowed by molten rock. Probably.

I crouched, then leaped for the tiny hold. This time, I caught it, swinging from three fingers on my right hand. Triumph and nausea mingled within me as I pulled myself up to a more secure position.

"Over here," El called, and I saw her looking through an exactly raccoon-sized hole in the ceiling.

"Do I fucking look like I'd fit in there? Goddammit, El, I swear to f—" I turned aside to spew a multi-colored sugary stream that caught fire as it descended into the magma, which now filled most of the chamber. My throat burned at the reflux, but what concerned me more was the messages that appeared in my display: **You feel weak! You feel weak! You feel clumsy! Your strength has decreased to Donkey doodoo!**

My muscles sagged as energy drained from me. Somehow, even though the messages indicated that I'd only returned to my previous strength, it felt like I'd ended up weaker than before. Throbbing with pain, I made my way over to the hole El was peering from.

"Back up," I said hoarsely, and twisted my fingers into the Harden technique. El's nose hastily disappeared from the hole.

A cloak of red aura blazed up around me, and I slammed my fist into the ceiling next to the hole. I squeezed my eyes shut as rock dust fell on me, and the opening widened a few inches. *Just a few more times*, I thought, as I pounded again and again, like the world's most insistent door-to-door salesman.

With a loud crack, a section of stone crumbled away, and I scrambled through the opening. The magma bubbled up to the hole mere seconds later . . . and simply stopped, as if deciding we weren't worth the trouble after all.

I collapsed on the floor in a pile of dust and sweat. "Fuck," I croaked. "I hate climbing. No more, please."

"At least there's a water fountain," said El. "Nice of them."

Raising my head, I saw through a haze of heat that El was right. In the midst of the hellish landscape of darkened skies and steaming fissures stood a metal drinking fountain. It looked bizarre, but I was grateful anyway.

I crawled over to it and washed the taste of acid and sugar from my mouth, then drank without any concern for dignity or decorum. It was only after a few hungry slurps that I realized it wasn't water. The taste was sweet, salty, and somehow familiar, and as I finished drinking, a message flashed up on my udjat.

Your energy has been restored!

What *was* that taste? Gatorade? No, but something close to that. It was on the tip of my tongue . . . I entered the Examine command at the fountain, hoping for a clue.

Fountain of Refreshment.

That unlocked something in my brain, a memory of pounding headaches and blurred mornings after. The liquid tasted almost exactly like Pedialyte, that electrolyte-replenishing nectar favored by toddlers and college students.

My cuts and bruises were still present, so it wasn't like a health bar, but I did feel a fog of tiredness lift from me. Whatever energy my spells consumed seemed like it had been replenished.

Sighing deeply, I sat down and pulled a candy from my inventory, the last red one. I fumbled and almost dropped it as a loud roar shook the earth.

"The fuck was that?" El asked.

"Just a volcano." A plume of smoke emerged from the distant mountain. Too far away for it to be concerning. Probably.

I turned my attention back to the pill I held. The sight of the neon-red **Mint of Might** sickened me, but I shoved it down my throat. A familiar burning feeling preceded the system message.

You feel strong! Your strength is now Bad!

Just like that, I'd regained the lost stat level. "They're color-coded, you know," I said to El. "Or flavor-coded."

"Hm?" The fur around El's mouth was stained blue.

"The blue ones, for example. I'm assuming they always give you a magic boost, right? They've all got wizard-sounding names like Pill of Psychokinesis or whatever. Based on their names and effects, those ones must increase your magic level." I pondered for a moment. "I've been taking them roughly evenly, but if you're going heavy on the blues, maybe it's better to balance things out."

"Or," El said, casually popping another blueberry-flavored Drop of the Deep Mind, "maybe it's better to do one thing well instead of being mediocre at everything."

"That's a fair point." I took a last quaff from the fountain. Since we were only one floor away from the end of our isolated tutorial, we might as well just wait and ask another climber. "Let's get moving, then."

The ground steamed and sizzled, but we hadn't been walking for too long when we stumbled upon a wooden sign. El scampered forward to read it, then turned to face me. A distant volcanic eruption cracked the sky.

"Well?" I prompted.

"The good news is we're basically at the exit," El said.

There was another loud boom above, but this one didn't sound like a volcano. For one thing, volcanoes didn't fly. Or beat the air with a sound like giant wings flapping.

"I take it the bad news is whatever's hovering above us right now?"

"Winner, winner! Chicken dinner."

It fell from the sky like a meteor, landing with an enormous crash that threw up rocks and dust. The drinking fountain bent and broke, and its liquid made a golden stream into the air that fizzled into steam. I backed away from the beast as one sharpened claw stepped out of the cloud of vapor.

"That's," I whispered. "That's . . ."

It stood statuesque, a creature of chiseled perfection, taller than me and three times as long. Its scales were like ruby-plated armor, covering its entire body, veiling its reptilian face. Waves of steam rolled off of it, making it appear to ripple with movement, even as it stood still. It roared at us, and two glands in the side of its mouth hissed with the scent of gasoline.

Baby Red Dragon, my udjat helpfully informed me. **A creature of strength and magic, with potent fiery breath. Its skin is coated with nigh-impenetrable armored scales. Its throat is its weak point.**

"It's a *baby*?"

The dragon fixed a malicious eye on me and reared its head back. A moment later, fire arced from its maw, and the world went white.

CHAPTER SEVENTEEN

Here Be Dragons

(Strive 9:3)

My fingers flew through a sequence of gestures, and the protective cloak of aura sprang up around me. For all I knew, the heat would scorch through my Hardening like a paper bag, but it was all I could think to do before the jet of flame reached me.

Then I was burning, blinded, and choked by fire and fumes, the last rags of my clothing burning away. The roar of it filled my ears, my nostrils, set every exposed orifice alight with pain, and I squeezed my eyes tightly shut against the firestorm. I thought I heard the distant *bang* of El's Firecracker spell going off, but I couldn't be sure.

The energy drain was severe, but miraculously, my shield seemed to be holding, given that I wasn't burnt to a crisp yet. The flames ratcheted up in intensity, as if the dragon had realized I was still alive and was eager to finish the job.

I dropped to the floor, where the heat was lessened, though it was like the difference between baking in the front of the oven versus the back. Either way, I was going to be cooked eventually. Something had to happen fast.

Adrenaline held the worst of the pain at bay, so I used the moment to recast Harden. Then, still lying in the white-hot stream of fire, I pulled up my inventory. Even with my eyes closed, I could see the interface glowing on the inside of my eyelid, white against dark red. The plunger would do no good, so I selected the only real weapon I had and felt it spawn into my hand.

My air rifle.

The toy gun felt dinky as hell in my hands as I blindly fumbled my way to the trigger guard. It was meant for hunting small game, not dragon-slaying. Regardless, I pointed the gun in the direction the heat emanated from and mashed the trigger like my life depended on it. *Its throat is its weak point.* I held onto that one thought. The rifle jumped sharply in my hand as pellets flew until it clicked, the magazine empty.

There was a choked growl that sounded disbelieving, and I felt the flames around me dissipate. I gasped in a lungful of air, finally able to see and breathe again. The dragon was roaring in its death throes, spraying flame as it gnashed and spun on the floor. Its tail and claws made deep furrows in the earth.

Finally, it spat something out with a clink of metal and fell still. My fingers seemed reluctant to obey as I cast Examine toward it.

Red dragon key. Grants access to the floor 9 exit.

I was too tired to feel triumphant. Hell, I couldn't even move from my prone position on the ground. Though the battle had lasted less than a minute, it was like I'd just run a marathon. The exhaustion from shielding the dragon's breath was unbelievable.

El came up and nosed my face in concern. "You okay?"

"Water," I croaked.

I half-crawled—and was half-dragged by El—to the broken fountain which still vented its contents up like a natural geyser. I stuck my face in the stream and let it soak into me.

Your energy has been restored!

It felt like being waterboarded with the nectar of the gods, and after choking and sputtering for a minute, I felt that whatever had been taken from me by my overuse of magic had been restored. So, it seemed like it was mana, after all. I flopped over and lay on the ground. Truth be told, I didn't really feel the need to rest anymore. It felt like I was badly sunburned, and that was it. Still, I *wanted* to lie there forever.

El was still looking at me with concern, so I reached out and tried to scratch behind her ears with a finger.

"Nah," she said, shying away from me. "Not a pet."

"Fair enough." I dropped my hand.

"A week ago, I would've bitten you for even trying that."

Rolling onto my back, I gazed up through the smoke-filled sky to where I knew the tenth floor was above it. Other people. "Your restraint is appreciated," I said, as the fountain dried up.

We were silent as another volcano boomed in the distance.

"Oh, alright." El twitched her whiskers. "Scratch if you must."

The red dragon key reflected its owner in that it was searing hot to the touch. I had to hot-potato it from hand to hand before stowing it in my inventory.

The signpost El pointed out had claimed there was a cave nearby that contained the exit, and after a brief search, we found an entrance in a rock wall that seemed promising.

We stepped into the cavern, casting Lux against the dimness. It was cooler in here, thankfully, and we soon encountered an ornate door built of red metal. I gingerly slid the key into the keyhole, and the door swung open on oiled hinges.

The dragon's hoard within was obviously never meant for the dragon itself. I couldn't picture it squeezing its bulky body through the narrow tunnels into this place. And even if it did, it wouldn't've had the dexterity to unlock the glittering chests of candies strewn about the room on heaps of golden coins.

In spite of the treasure, my eyes were immediately drawn to the podium standing at the center of the room. It seemed to radiate a haze of heat, but it wasn't painful. I flashed Examine, and the description appeared.

Red Dragon Upgrade Station. Augments strength and fire-based techniques. Once per player.

I raced El to the slot and beat her, inserting my braceleted hand. It locked me in, and my kada began to pulse.

Downloading . . .

"Not fair," said El, climbing up the podium. "You've got a height advantage."

Downloading . . .

"Skill issue," I replied. "And stop pulling on my hand, it's almost done."

Download complete.

I removed my wrist, and text scrolled onto my contact.

The *Harden* technique has been upgraded.

Impact and tensile strength increased.
Barrier temperature and heat resistance increased.
Note: Incurs ongoing energy drain.
Time limit removed. Cancellable by reversing the activation sequence.

After rereading the patch notes a few times, I slowly signed the spell with my kada hand, savoring the anticipation as each character lit in a burning red circle around my bracelet.

H-A-R-D-E-N.

The shielding aura flared out from me like wildfire before compressing to a thin layer against my skin. Seen through a red haze, the whole world seemed to burn around me. *Now this was power.* But then I felt the newly added energy drain, sapping my vitality.

I stepped away from the podium, reaching for one of the candies in the chests, and it melted from my radiating heat. Slowly, I signed Harden in reverse, expecting the aura to extinguish around me as it usually did when the timer ran out.

To my surprise, I exploded.

Not in a literal sense, with guts and gore flying everywhere in chunks. No, the compressed aura around me seemed to detonate, releasing a surge of energy outward in all directions. Coins and treasure chests near me blew away to clatter against the walls, some half-melted. Thankfully, I'd been far enough from El that the wind from the shockwave only ruffled her fur.

"The fuck was that?" she said.

"Oh, man." I put my palm against my face, suddenly drained. "That is going to be . . . a tradeoff, for sure."

This explosive deactivation could be a useful tool, but it would have to be worked around. First and foremost, I had to throw away my primary defense for a single shot at an attack. If that didn't work, I was up shit creek without a paddle.

And now, instead of only incurring an energy cost on impacts, the fiery component of the shield meant I'd be losing energy constantly. If there was a situation where I had to cancel the technique quickly, it would be downright dangerous to any allies who happened to be close to me.

Tricky. Potentially powerful, but very tricky.

"Maybe wait a sec—" I began saying to El, but she had already inserted her kada paw into the slot. I watched in silence as light flowed from the podium into her bracelet for a few seconds before she was released.

When she twisted her hands into the activation sequence for her Firecracker spell, there was a flash, followed by a chain of explosions in different colors across the ceiling of the chamber. Sparkling trails slowly descended around us like a fireworks display, and the room filled with their acrid smell.

"New *and* improved," El panted.

"Pretty," I commented, a bit jealous of the lack of downsides to her upgrade.

Although my explosion had liquefied the candies in the treasure chests closest to me, there was still a plethora of magic candies scattered throughout the room. I looted most of the reds and greens, and El stuck to her favored blues. She gleefully looted the coins as well, although I wasn't sure if they were more than set decoration.

I popped an Atomic Fireball of Force into my mouth and was rewarded with a scalded tongue and a level-up message from my udjat. We chewed as we walked deeper into the cave, where an especially ornate elevator waited patiently for us, with rising dragon designs on each side.

"This is it, then," I said as we stepped into the elevator cabin. "Our nine-floor-long tutorial is finally over." Looking vaguely upward, I stared at an imagined camera. "You know, Hilbert, usually the point of a tutorial is to allow players to learn the ropes in a friendly, low-stakes environment."

El scratched herself. "I'm gonna have some words for that smug prick next time we see him. Some claws, too."

"Fuck it," I sighed, jabbing the button that'd take us out of our isolated instance and up to the tenth floor. "Let's go make some friends."

CHAPTER EIGHTEEN

Cherubim

(*Strive 10:1*)

The elevator chugged along as I held El's bracelet in one hand and my own in the other. "Well, damn," I said. "You're right. Yours does look a bit bluer than mine. Must be responding to our attributes."

The roof of my mouth was burned raw from all the Atomic Fireballs I'd been scarfing down, but not for nothing. My strength stat had leveled up from **Special** to **Wee Baby**, and my dexterity to **Bad**. At least, I thought they were level ups. It was hard to tell when every tier was an insult. In any case, my kada was now tinted a light yellow that reminded me a bit of an underripe banana. I hadn't noticed before, so it must've been a gradual change.

"Not that it bothers me," El said, "but have you given any thought to your whole lack-of-clothes situation?"

I looked down. "We'll figure it out," I replied. In reality, I would've traded a hundred Pills of Girth Enhancement or whatever for a pair of pants right then.

Ding! We arrived at the tenth floor, and the doors opened to a view of lush greenery. The air was sweet with the thick and heady fragrance of wildflowers. Before us lay a narrow path—unkempt and grown over with weeds and moss, yet unmistakably a path—snaking between the trees before disappearing into the distance. Rays of sun came down in patches, casting light on overturned trunks and briefly illuminating small, quick things that darted away when I tried to scan them. The sound of a creek burbled cheerfully nearby.

Basically, it was downright pleasant after the hellishness of the previous floor, the infinite abyss of the floor below, the horrible mimics, et cetera. Someone had even left a jug of water and a bath towel on a nearby tree stump. Thankfully, although this would be the first floor with other people present, there was no welcoming party to see my nakedness.

"Well," I said, wrapping the towel around my waist, "it seems pretty clear where we need to go."

"What's that?"

I indicated the path between the trees. "Unless you've got a better idea."

"Right."

"Although," I said, "if I were a malicious person, I'd probably camp by the obvious path to waylay any new arrivals."

"They would've gotten us already." El seemed to only be half-paying attention, her gaze fixed on the trees, ears cocked to perceive the small noises around her. It was only with effort that she tore her eyes away and to the path ahead of us, and we began to walk.

"Something the matter?"

"Got this weird itch in my head. Feels like I'm remembering something, only I never knew it in the first place. Or like some part of my brain that I've never used before is waking back up." El sniffed at the ground. "But it feels comforting somehow."

It occurred to me that this might be the kind of place you'd see a raccoon in a nature documentary, living in a tree hollow with its raccoon family. "Though they've long made a name for themselves in pop culture as raiders of rubbish, a raccoon's true home is the forest," a David Attenborough-type voice would narrate. "It is the destruction of their natural habitats that has urbanized these resilient creatures. Their keen intellect, combined with a natural instinct for survival—"

Without a word, El bolted off the path, diving into the undergrowth. Moments later, there was a deep, subsonic growl that shook the earth.

"Oy!" I said. "Wait up!"

The air suddenly chilled, and a chorus of branches snapped. Everything felt darker, like a cloud passing over the sun. The forest fell suddenly silent except for the ominous growl that seemed to come from all around.

On second thought, maybe running's not such a bad idea, I thought as I clambered after El into the bushes.

My heart pumped as I ran, and I called out El's name. Soon the sun seemed to reappear, and the sound of the monster faded behind me. I turned to look hastily behind, saw nothing but leaves, then turned back forward, almost slamming into a stone wall. I only stopped myself from breaking my nose by throwing my hands out at the last second against the gray stone.

Taking a step back, I saw that the wall was part of a squat, weathered structure, pockmarked with the wear of ages and carpeted with lichen and moss so that it blended with the surroundings almost seamlessly. It was marked with symbols that felt discomfiting to look at in a way that I couldn't explain. It was a script made up mostly of dots stabbed into the stone, like reverse braille, and it somehow reminded me of punctured skin. Examining the symbols did nothing, much to my puzzlement. Neither did Examining the building itself.

I walked around the building until I saw a door, although maybe *door* wasn't the right word for it. It wasn't anything more than a human-sized hole in the wall, a threshold that led into the dark interior. There was a dark stain on the ground, and I Examined it.

Blood.

I shivered and looked into the hole in the wall. As my vision adjusted, I could see stairs spiraling down into the darkness.

"El," I called. "You down there?" *Please be okay.*

There was no response. My own voice echoed back at me from the inside of the structure, bouncing back out into the forest, and a few birds startled into flight. Cursing myself, I cast Lux and stepped across the threshold, following the stairs as they descended into the earth.

The stairs spiraled down seemingly without end, unlit except by my own magic lantern. There were no more bloodstains, though, and in fact it smelled almost sterile. I nearly tripped over my own feet when the steps abruptly terminated at the entrance of a room.

The room was filled with death.

At first I thought they were human knights. Though they were decorated in armor and armed with various weapons, within each suit was only a shapeless black mass. My udjat called them **Sentinels (Deceased)**.

Their corpses were strewn across the room. Most seemed to have been punctured multiple times by what looked like stabbing or cutting wounds from something very sharp. A few, oddly enough, appeared to have killed each other—one had its spear through another's gut, or where its gut would've been if it wasn't entirely made of inky slime.

A door led to another passageway at the opposite side of the room. I hesitated, looking back at the stairs that I'd descended from. It'd be a long way back up, but . . . *Better the devil you know*, I thought.

Before I could take a backward step, there was a muffled scream from deeper within the structure that rooted me to the spot. It was a human cry, a woman's, but it was wordless, with an animalistic quality of pain to it.

"Fuck me." I clenched my fists and ran forward through the chamber of dead monsters. "I must be fucking crazy."

I cast Harden as I entered a second room, this one built like a deadly obstacle course. Barely thinking, I circumnavigated spikes that jutted from every surface and jumped over seemingly bottomless pits. Crushing pistons were frozen in midair, and a boulder rested in a crater at one side of the room. It all seemed half-deactivated, like an already-cleared dungeon, and I felt a deep sense of unease as I followed the path to a third room.

There was the echoing sound of steel striking steel in the next room, and as I dashed through the doorway into the next high-walled chamber, I was met with the sight of someone far more skilled than me engaging in combat with something even they couldn't defeat.

A hulking automaton built of metal—*like a mecha*, I thought—swung its arm through the air, and wind gusted toward me. A slender figure with an emerald glow made a graceful dodging arc through the air, spun once, and slashed out with a dagger trailing blood. It was one slash, but there were three metallic pings of impact, and then five more, and then the figure was landing, only to disappear under the mech's stomping foot.

But she was on the monster's back now, driving the blade down with both hands. There was a frozen moment, and then it shattered with a horrible crystalline wail. She cried out in frustration, and I recognized the scream from earlier. Then the thing grabbed her and the scream became one of fear.

I'd thought I was frozen on the threshold, but my fingers were suddenly moving, and then *I* was moving, not getting the hell out of there as I'd planned, but lurching forward toward the base of the **Greater Sentinel** (very much *not* deceased), my udjat told me. And then I was slamming my Hardened fist into its metal patella, which was about as high as I could reach on the damn thing, praying that it'd break and not me.

To my surprise, its kneecap shattered.

The sentinel roared like a stuck gear from hell and began to sway. It seemed suspended for an everlasting moment before it toppled and crashed down on top of me like a mountain, muffling my explosion under its bulk.

The first thing I saw when I crawled my way out of the debris was a dagger pointed at my throat.

"Well, hello there," the woman said. Without the haze of her aura, I could see that she was short and slender, dressed in a set of fitted clothes that looked suspiciously like athleisure. Her hair was tied back in a long, single braid. Cute. But those were thoughts for later, what with the dagger she pressed against my neck and all. "It's good to finally meet my secret admirer. You've been following me for a good minute or two now, haven't you?"

"This seems uncalled for," I panted. "I just saved your life."

There was silence for a moment, then her hand snaked out to grip my kada with thin and graceful fingers. She seemed to Examine it for a bit, then let it drop. The blade remained against my skin, and I felt warm liquid drip from it onto me. "I don't recall asking for your help," she continued in a melodious voice, "and I'm in the middle of something important, so I don't have much time to chat. Who are you, and what's your reason for being here?"

"Name's Xavier. I just got to this floor, and I was run off the forest path by some huge creature. Stumbled onto this weird structure, and I saw blood on the ground." Somehow it seemed like a bad idea to bring up El. "I thought someone might need help."

The pressure at my neck might've relented just a hair. "Next question. Why are you naked?"

"Well, I'm wearing a towel," I pointed out. Miraculously, the thing wrapped around my waist had stayed on during the fight.

After another long moment, the dagger dropped. The hint of an amused smile played on her face. "Sorry about that." She sheathed the dagger. "One can't be too careful."

"So I take it you're okay, then," I said, rubbing my neck. "Well enough to threaten a passing Good Samaritan, at least."

"I am, thanks to you," she mused, tilting her head at me with an appraising look. "Perhaps we could help each other out here." She had a lilting accent that I couldn't place, but it wasn't unpleasant. Just different than anything I'd ever heard. Which was odd, since I had an ear for them. Her eyes, too, had a strange mixture of innocence and knowingness, sincerity and mischief.

I blinked. What was I saying? They were just normal brown eyes on a pretty face.

"Hold on a second." I sat down on the floor, leaning back against the sentinel's broken body. "What exactly is it we're trying to do here? Who are you? Are there other people around here?"

"You're right," she said, sitting next to me casually. "I apologize for getting off on the wrong foot. My name's Mia. I'm a treasure hunter—a solitary endeavor, most times. But often the most valuable things are guarded by more than just lock and key." She knocked on the sentinel, and it rang hollowly. "As you've already experienced."

"So there's a reward at the end of this . . . dungeon?" I said.

"I would not call it a dungeon," Mia said. "More like a series of escalating challenges and monsters with a treasure at the end."

"Right."

"In any case, I had thought I'd be able to surmount this gauntlet on my own, and I was doing well." She gave me a cheerful smile, dimples and all. "Until I wasn't. Clearly, I was outclassed by the previous challenge, and who knows what's coming in the next chamber. What do you say we see this through together, split the prize? Lord knows you've earned it."

"I don't know . . ." El was still missing, and dread was beginning to settle in my stomach. But I'd already decided to keep her a secret from this woman. El would have to be okay on her own for a bit. "Hold on, what even is the prize for all of this?"

She laughed, and everything seemed right in the world. I hadn't realized how lonely I was for human company. Even in my other life. "It's not," she promised. "It's a type of concentrated power called

Will. True power, not the whisper of it doled out in bracelets and confectionery."

"Alright," I said. "If it'll help us stay alive in this god-forsaken place, I suppose I'm game."

"Then let the games begin," Mia murmured, and there was the shine of excitement in her eyes.

A few unremarkable chambers later, the treasure rested on a podium in the center of a stark, open chamber like the nucleus of an atom, a glass-like sphere that sent pulses of light outward at irregular intervals. It reminded me of a Dragon Ball or a Materia, some legendary orb of power. I inspected the rest of the room, but I couldn't find any signs of traps or enemies. Didn't mean there weren't any, but it couldn't hurt to try.

It was like a chapel, with no ceiling as far as I could tell, just sheer white soaring up into eternity, a church with that treasure as its focus of worship, its holy relic. As the sphere's glow cast shifting patterns all around, I was hit with a certainty that this place was inviolable, sacred, and that we were undeserving of even stepping foot inside.

We shouldn't be here.

"A Willstone," Mia breathed. "Pure concentrated energy distilled into a physical form. It's beautiful." She didn't seem to feel the same repelling force I did, and I wanted to hold her back, but she stepped forward as if drawn involuntarily inward to the orb.

The moment she entered the room, a blaring klaxon shattered the silence, echoing off the walls in a way that made my head hurt. The podium extruded a set of metal brackets that swiveled into place, hiding the stone from view, and a countdown began in the periphery of my vision: **30s**. Thirty seconds.

"What does that mean?" I yelled.

In a flash, Mia was next to me, speaking directly into my ear to be heard over the raucous alarm. "You can open that thing, right? With your strength?"

"I think so." My fingers twitched in anticipation. "But it feels wrong."

"That feeling's the last challenge. Listen," Mia said, grabbing my arm. "It's important we don't damage the stone itself."

I eyed the counter—now reading **25s**—nervously. "What happens when the timer reaches zero?"

"What?"

"I said, what happens when the timer—"

"Oh. You don't want to know."

Cursing to myself, I advanced toward the podium, activating Harden as I went. The stone's enclosure was smooth, without any hint of a seam. I laid my hand on the metal, but my aura didn't burn hot enough to melt it outright. So, some force would be required, even at the risk of damaging the Willstone.

I wound my fist back and slammed it against the metal. My arm rang with the impact, and a moment later I felt the pain radiate through my hand. There was no evidence of any damage to the enclosure. Mia, standing far back from the heat, shouted something that I couldn't hear. I struck it again and again, to no avail, as the countdown continued. **10s.** Almost all of our time gone. And again the feeling of wrongness hit me.

This is not the intended path.

There was only one thing left I could think of. The explosive deactivation of my ability. It would take too long to explain it to Mia. I'd just have to do it.

I gripped my left hand around the metal enclosure as my right hand's fingers reversed their earlier pattern. Trembling, I misspelled it once, twice. My burning aura shrank to a moment of stillness as the last few seconds counted down.

5, 4, 3—

Ignition.

The whole room shook as my aura expanded outward at the speed of sound. A good amount of it went between the fingers of my left hand, into the steel as a reverberating shockwave that pinged out, a bright and airy ring that joined the cacophony of the explosion. When it all died down, the still-blaring alarm seemed almost peaceful in comparison.

The countdown had disappeared, leaving me wondering if it'd been imaginary except for the afterimage that still lingered, an indistinct blur of overlaid numbers followed by the letter *S* written in red on the upper right of my vision.

The enclosure was still intact. Despair washed over me as the exhaustion of using magic hit me in full force, and I leaned my body on the podium to steady myself.

The top half of the enclosure came clean off. Particles of light drifted out, carried on an unseen wind, rising to circle in the room in a lazy orbit. Mia stood with her mouth opened to the sky, and one of the particles diverted from its circuit to land on her tongue, melting onto it like a snowflake. The rest of the sparkling fragments began to follow, passing into her body. She seemed to begin radiating light, as well. She was taking it all.

Several of the particles jerked toward me, only briefly, before continuing toward Mia. Part of this reward had been promised to me, and I felt a flash of anger bolster me against exhaustion.

Mia turned to look at me for the first time since I'd broken the case, and there was an expression of amusement on her face. "These fragments respond to will," she said, "and mine happens to be stronger than yours. 'Might makes right,' and that's the way it's always been. Sorry, I don't make the rules."

Hot-blooded rage filled me. I wasn't so foolish as to be taken advantage of by an attractive face and a few sweet words. With that rising tide of emotion, the last fragments of the stream of light paused, seeming to hang in the air between us before slowly drawing closer to me. I relished the look of horror on Mia's face as the first one landed.

When it hit, it was like a stab in the chest with a hot knife. Then a few more, the final whispers of light, and silence.

She started toward me, but the whole place seemed to turn sideways. The sky roared apart. We were spat out into the forest unceremoniously, dumped into scraggly bushes and trees. The cool, dry air of the vault was replaced by warm dampness. The shaking subsided. Thin rays of sunlight filtered down through sharp-edged leaves, barely illuminating anything.

"Well, isn't this something," said Mia, her face half in shadow. "You managed to lap up some of the dregs of Will there. I'm almost impressed. Too bad for you, you're going to have to give it up again. Relinquish those parts of the Willstone you absorbed"—and here she pointed her dagger at a spot below my waist, whereupon I noticed that my towel had burned clean away—"or would you rather I relieved you of your other stones?"

We stood in a dense thicket of the forest, the leaves like sharp spines, pointed enough to draw blood. Her smile was sharper.

"I'm afraid I don't know how," I said, holding up my hands. "Honestly, I'm very confused why we had to fight at all. We were splitting it, weren't we? Or did you forget about our deal?"

"Here's the deal," she said in a voice like silk. "You hold still, and I cut the Fruit of Will out of you as painlessly as possible."

My fingers twitched, and my aura flared up. "I'll have to pass."

But I didn't want to fight her, either. I looked into her eyes, eyes that were at once knowing and innocent, sincere and mischievous, and found myself entranced by them. She was saying something to me, but I was lost in her gaze. I wanted to drown in those eyes that devoured me hungrily, a predator's eyes . . .

One of her eyes turned sapphire as her right hand moved behind her back. With a yelp, I signed Harden and jumped backward, my shield flaring around me.

The world shrank to a pinhole of light. As it expanded back, there was a moment of resistance before space seemed to *shatter*, and I was suddenly standing at the other side of the clearing from Mia, surrounded by shards of broken glass. The grass at my feet began to smoke from my aura, and through its red haze, it looked like the forest was stained with blood.

"You broke my canopic jar," Mia pouted. "Those are expensive, you know." She laughed at my expression, which must've been somewhere between shock and horror. "Still . . ." She looked me up and down, Examining my protective layer. ". . . it's pretty hard to do that. And you know what they say—a hard man is good to find."

"W-what did you try to do to me?" I stammered.

"That, my dear Xavier, is for me to know and you to f—"

A dark shape barreled into Mia from behind and tagged her with a glowing paw. A flash of light leaped from her bracelet to El's, as the raccoon rejoined me at my side.

"*Where the hell have you been?*" we both demanded at the same time.

After a pause, El continued, "More importantly, what's this thing?" She held up the item she'd stolen with the Pickpocket spell.

"It's a—oh," I said. "Oh, that is *fucked up*."

It looked like a big mason jar, tightly stoppered. The whole thing was stuffed with red and white with bits of pink, and I thought at first it was a strawberry yogurt parfait. But floating inside were shapes that reminded me of eyes and ears, and with horror, I realized that was exactly what they were. For still uncrushed, squeezed between layers of blood and viscera, I saw the scattered white points of human teeth.

CHAPTER NINETEEN

Savior

(Strive 10:2)

As I stared at the nightmarish jar of compressed organs, the grass below me began to smolder from my burning aura.

"Fuck," I said. "What the fuck." Not a question but a reflexive response. I couldn't even hazard a guess why she'd be carrying something like that around.

"Guess the cat's out of the body bag," Mia mused. "Pickpocket, huh? A spell that allows you to steal from people's inventories . . . That could be a useful addition to my collection."

"Who is this piece of work?" El said, crouching into a low stance. "You really know how to pick 'em, Xavier, I'll tell you that much."

Mia began to laugh, a light and carefree sound. "Xavier, you didn't tell me you had a pet. Must've slipped your mind, I guess. Maybe I'll keep it for myself."

El growled at the word *pet*, but that seemed the least of our concerns.

"This thing, this . . . corpse in a jar." I glanced at it and retched. "What did you do?"

"Rude," she said. "Didn't anyone teach you about not yucking other people's yums?" Casually, she undid a knot in her left sleeve, and a second bracelet fell down to her wrist. When she looked back up at me, her eyes had turned heterochromatic; each iris matched its kada's color, so that the left one was forest green and the right burned a deep indigo.

I hadn't imagined it after all.

"Whoever's body's stuffed in this jar . . . you killed them and stole their kada," I said. "Using your ability. You're able to teleport people across space. And you just tried to do the same thing to me before I shattered your jar."

"Not bad." Mia smiled prettily. "But it was *his* bracelet that had the teleportation ability. Honestly, he brought his fate on himself, the poor guy. All I had to do was encourage him. A sultry look and a warm touch . . . it wasn't long before he'd do anything for me. Even remove his bracelet in a moment of passion . . . Incidentally, he was guarding the entrance to the Willstone chamber, so really he did have to go."

Sickened, I realized that the bloodstain I'd seen had probably been from him. More than that, Mia was *enjoying* herself, I realized. She didn't have to tell us any of this, but she was luxuriating in it. Smoke curled from the bark of the tree behind me, and I shifted to avoid setting it alight.

"It's not quite teleportation, by the way. 'Immediately exchanges the positions of two living things, via an independent fourth spatial axis,' if I remember the description correctly." She paused.

"I saw it happen," El said. "It looked like you shrank and then grew back somewhere else."

Mia beamed. "Exactly! We can't see the fourth spatial axis, so that's how it appears to us. Shrinkage, followed by expansion. Now, here's a pop quiz for you." With a flourish, she pulled another jar from her inventory, with a small frog in it.

"This jar"—she rapped it with her knuckles, and the frog shied away to the other side, croaking silently—"is made of adamant-glass. Put against a normal human body, it'll win ten times out of ten. What do you think would happen if I swapped someone with this frog?"

El let out a growl and hid behind my leg. Rank-smelling steam rose up from the bottom of my aura.

"I guess that's too easy of a question," Mia continued when we didn't respond. "Canopic jars, I call them. The Egyptians used to preserve their pharaohs in them. Clever, isn't it?"

"Didn't work on me, though," I said.

Her left hand's fingers danced. "That's what the second bracelet's for, silly," she replied as her other kada glowed.

An aura the color of jade blossomed from her body, and she disappeared. I looked up and she was dropping onto me with her leg outstretched in an axe kick. I met it with a reinforced forearm, and the clash of our auras rang like steel meeting steel, before she flipped backward and landed with a gymnast's poise.

A crackle of explosions appeared where she was standing, filling the air with sulfurous smoke.

"Good one, El," I coughed. Glancing down, I saw that the raccoon's teeth were bared, her kada sparking with blue light while her paws held the last position of the Firecracker spell. But as the air cleared, there was no sign of the woman.

"As I was saying, nice try." Mia dangled upside down from a tree branch above, shirt dropping to expose her bare midriff. "Gotta be faster than that."

With a twist of her right hand, she vanished again. Then, I was the one in the tree, and not being as agile as she was, I fell out and landed roughly on the ground. I spun to see that she'd clutched El in her grip, holding the snarling raccoon at a distance from her face.

"You swapped us," I groaned.

"Sharp as a ta—ow!" El had managed to sink her teeth into Mia's hand. "Bad raccoon," she said, before flinging El's body against a tree with a sickening crunch. El fell senseless to the ground, and Mia raised her hand and grimaced at the bite marks. "Did you ever get that thing checked for diseases? Rabies is no joke."

The smoldering grass around me burst into flames. I ran at her, but she conjured a short blade and stabbed through my aura multiple times, her hand a blur of motion, before spinning away.

Stunned, I looked down and saw dots of blood. The shield had blocked the worst of it, but somehow she'd gotten through. I turned to strike her—

—and felt my vision go double and my joints stiffen. My knees buckled, and I sagged to the ground, suddenly weak. *El,* I thought. *Please be okay.*

"Feeling a bit woozy?" Mia asked, sheathing her knife carefully. "They call it belladonna. A good dose of it'll make you hallucinate, paralyzed and delirious. Fun fact"—and here she gave me a playful grin—"they used to use it as an aphrodisiac."

I stared daggers at her through the red haze of my shield as she shed hers.

She sighed and put a hand gently on my arm, or rather, on the part of my aura that hovered above my arm. "Come on," she coaxed. "Take it off already."

"If . . ." I fought against the poison to speak. The world felt wavy and indistinct.

She leaned toward me to hear, her chimeric eyes alight with interest. "If? If what?"

I moved my lips and fingers with effort. "If you insist."

My aura detonated right in her face, and with a roar the forest became a searing firestorm. I dropped to the ground, crawling under the smoke to find El. I picked her up, scooping the corpse jar into my inventory. My limbs didn't want to obey, but I forced them to move. Without Harden activated, I sweated and choked in the heat as I escaped from the clearing in a lurching run, not looking back.

Please be okay. With El cradled in my arms, I repeated the words like a silent mantra. *Please be okay.*

I don't remember how long I ran in that dim half-light, while laughing eyes seemed to lurk in the shadows, taunting me at every turn. My mind swam in the confusion of the belladonna poison.

I tried to shield myself again, but my fingers spasmed uselessly from the poison. Unable to cast Harden, I took more cuts—leaves and branches slicing like blades, *snicker-snack*—and began to bleed freely. Every so often, I had to stop to let out a hacking, smoke-filled cough. When at last I stumbled ungracefully from the darkness, and out into rolling hills and sunlight, I almost cried in relief.

The sun crested the horizon like a great breaching whale. A cylindrical city sat like a giant can of Chef Boyardee amid a grassland that gyred and gimbled. A squirrel periscoped its head up, then rippled nervously across the prairie. Trees dreamed their furious green dreams. All was vivid and bright.

"Beautiful," I tried to say, but coughed out silvery dust instead. I frowned. That seemed rather bourgeois of me.

Important-looking words swam up to my face, but they were all funny, like they had been written in that old font Wingdings. I waved them away impatiently. I didn't feel like reading right now. I wanted to rest by the trees and dream together, but as I stepped toward them, I almost dropped what I was carrying.

It was some kind of rodent, taking shallow breaths in its sleep. "It's okay, weird big mouse," I said, stroking its fur. "We're okay now. Everything's gonna be copacetic."

I collapsed with my back against an old oak tree, closing my eyes as it spoke to me.

"Yes," I said to the tree, "that's very wise."

Check your status, said the oak, rustling its leaves.

"I don't want to. I want to sleep."

An acorn fell on my head. I sighed and brought up my hand, then stared at it, stupefied. It was covered in red X's like a flunked school exam.

Another acorn fell on my head. *Check status. Examine.*

"Okay, okay," I wiggled my fingers, and words bloomed across my vision like red roses.

HP LOW BLD HALLU

The characters didn't make any sense. "Well, *HALLU* to you, as well, I suppose." I waved up at the oak, then squinted. Was it just me, or was the sky darkening? Hadn't it just been sunrise? But now it seemed like late afternoon, and that meant Mom was going to be home soon . . .

"Good afternoon, good evening, and good night," I murmured, as darkness overtook me.

"Xavier!"

My first kindergarten roll call with the warm and kindly Mrs. Grier, she'd had to call my name out half a dozen times before I recognized it. She'd looked at me with some concern before moving onto the next name, and I remembered wondering why she said it so strangely, so differently than I'd heard it from Mom and Dad.

Years later, in a college linguistics course, I learned that the phonotactics of my parents' native tongue—the sounds their mouths were trained to produce—precluded them from properly speaking my name. As a kid, I'd just been confused that they'd chosen a name for me that they couldn't pronounce.

In those good old days, I'd rush home after school and throw *Skies of Arcadia* up on the big CRT in the living room. I was too young to understand the gameplay, but I loved piloting Vyse's airship across the vast biomes of the world, feeling like a fantasy hero. The loyal crew, the feeling of freedom, the quest to save the world. All of that was an appealing escape from suburban mediocrity.

One afternoon, I heard the great droning sound from the garage door that announced my mom's arrival—much earlier than normal. Six was her usual time, but the microwave clock showed barely half past three. I scrambled to shut off the Dreamcast, flipped to a random page of the math textbook, and made myself look busy.

Maybe it was the somewhat frantic look in my eyes, or the fact my book was on a chapter we hadn't gotten near to covering yet. Whatever the case, she knew, as attentive parents always do. She reached under the Dreamcast console, and I cringed as her expression told me she felt the residual heat from my hours-long session.

"Xavier," she said. "You know our rule."

A mother's love made her hold back, but it still hurt as the belt landed on my rear with a thwacking sound. **HP LOW.** Meaningless words came to me from another reality, bizarre and disorienting.

I tried to harden myself to the pain as the blows rained down. **HP LOW. HP LOW. HP CRITICAL.**

She was yelling at me, calling me a sneak and a liar. But every time she said my name, Xavier, it sounded like the word *Savior* instead.

CHAPTER TWENTY

Second Language

(Strive 10:3)

Flashes of purple light woke me from the most comfortable sleep I'd had in a long time. Now that I was awake, everything hurt like a bitch. I could hear a man and a woman speaking to each other, but my eyes were sealed shut with dried blood. All I wanted was for the voices to shut up and go away.

"*Mmf,*" I said, my throat like sandpaper, and they stopped talking at once.

A woman's voice asked me something in a language that was just past the cusp of understanding, before cool water broke the seal of blood around my mouth. I drank thirstily. It was about all I had the energy to do.

"Death is out to get me," I mumbled, and one of the voices shushed me.

Someone's hand was on mine. Their fingers contorted my right hand into different positions. It felt wrong being manipulated this way, and I resisted briefly, but my muscles were like jelly. I was powerless to stop them as they forced me to pull up a system menu that appeared against the inside of my eyelids.

System Configuration Menu
BRIGHTNESS—50%
VERBOSITY—MEDIUM
FONT—14pt Arial
. . . MORE . . .

My brows furrowed as they made me scroll down to the setting labeled Font and changed it to Times New Roman. The woman spoke again, as though she expected something from me.

"What's wrong with Sans-Serif?" I asked hoarsely.

The woman's response was short and exasperated, but no more intelligible than before. It was only a moment later that I saw the next setting in my contact labeled Captions and realized what she had meant to do. Weakly twitching my fingers, I toggled them on, and text appeared at the bottom of my contact as the woman spoke.

Listening . . .

Language Identified: Sino-Tibetan, Sinitic, Old Chinese (~1000s BCE).

Hold for translation . . .

Subtitles began to scroll across my field of view a second later.

<<—hear me? Do you understand me?>>

"Wow. I read you. Yes." With awareness came sudden panic, and my voice cracked. "Where's El?"

There was an awkward pause before the next response. **<<What's an L?>>**

"My friend."

The two voices had a rapid back-and-forth exchange that eluded the translation software, as I teetered on the brink of consciousness. The last thing I saw was the message **<<They're taking you to the hospital. I've healed the worst of the injuries for now . . . I'm sure we'll find your friend.>>**

I was being moved now, lifted like a child. I tried to protest, but the rocking motion lulled me back into a deep sleep.

When I woke again, it was to the smell of rubbing alcohol.

A cheap, foam-tiled ceiling hung above me, the kind they use in places like dentists' offices or cubicle farms. The tiles sagged slightly, giving the whole thing the effect of a giant sheep's stomach pressing down from above. I giggled, then slapped myself. Mia's poison was still working its way through my system, making me feel strangely giddy.

Lying here, I could almost believe that everything since the night of the truck crash had been a bad dream. The classroom and the magic tower with its deadly floors. Yes, it was all too absurd to be true. I was in a regular hospital now. Someone had washed me and dressed me in starched linens, and even the thousand cuts on my skin had disappeared. But my hopes were dashed when I looked down and saw the pale-yellow stone bracelet on my wrist, the color of raw sulfur.

The room didn't seem to have any traditional doctoring equipment in it, just a few cots that were empty, besides mine. A single skylight cast a square of sun onto the table next to me, where a glass of suspicious orange liquid sat.

My kada informed me that the contents of the glass were a **refreshing drink**. Remembering the sequence of gestures to reach the system configuration menu, I had just switched the font back to Arial when a man in a tunic entered. I didn't understand the words he spoke, but my contact evidently did.

Language Identified: Early Anatolian, Hittite (~1700s BC).

As I stared, words of a long-dead language winked to life in my field of vision, scrolling across the screen.

<<You gave us quite a scare out there . . . What's the matter? Do I have something on my face?>>

"No," I managed. "It's just . . . you're from almost four thousand years in my past. And the lady that healed me, too . . ."

The man nodded. **<<That's right, you wouldn't know. The tower accepts people from anyplace, anytime, any species of adequate intelligence, for the most part—>>**

I bolted upright. "Where's El?"

<<The climber? No one's seen him in years.>>

"Him? Years?" My mind was fuzzy, but something scraped at the corners of it. "El's a female. We were together through the first nine floors. I was holding her, but we must've gotten separated somehow."

<<That doesn't sound like the same person.>>

Gotta find her. I struggled to get out of bed, and he barred my way. **<<No can do. You need to rest. And drink this glass.>>**

"I need to find her," I said, reluctantly accepting the drink. It was a sugary-salty beverage similar to the fountain on the previous floor, and I felt better after a sip. Before I'd finished drinking, another voice boomed from the next room, and my udjat lit up anew, before the source of the sound had even entered.

Language Identified: Balto-Slavic, Old East Slavic (~1000 AD).

The po-po, the fuzz, five-o, whatever you wanted to call it . . . I knew it when I saw it, even without the badge and blue uniform. The man who entered the room moved with the slowness that comes from utter confidence. His features seemed to be chiseled from rock, unkempt stubble only accentuating his sharp chin. He wore an X-shaped emblem pinned to his lapel, and on his wrist, a kada bracelet with ruby-like luster.

<<Who wants to know about El Bandito?>> drawled the man.

"Please," I said. "She's a raccoon, about this big. We were both injured . . . and there was a man who'd been killed, squeezed into a jar, I think . . ."

An odd look on the man's face made me conscious of my jabbering, and I trailed off. He spoke again, ignoring my question.

<<You have taken something that doesn't belong to you. Where have you put it?>>

"What?" I said. "Where's El?"

<<Not to worry. You'll be with the raccoon again shortly.>>

The prison smelled dank, not in the good way. There was definitely black mold in the walls, and I tried to hold my breath briefly before realizing how ridiculous that was.

El's complaining voice reached me long before I saw her, echoing off the hard stone walls. My heart swelled, and I was surprised at how relieved I felt when they threw me into her cell.

"Nice of you to finally show." El sniffed at my legs. "They kept asking me about some rock or something. Obviously I had no idea what they were talking about. Did you know there's another raccoon named El Bandito?"

"I remember Hilbert saying that." I began to lean up against the dungeon wall, felt wetness seep through my thin linens, and thought better of it. My head started to pound again. "We have some catching up to do."

"Right, so basically, after the big goon in the forest stopped chasing me . . ." I listened patiently as El recounted a mostly uneventful story in the forest, doing things like chasing bugs, harvesting nuts, basically just raccoon things. It sounded quite nice. ". . . and then, right when I'm in the middle of washing some acorns, everything starts shaking like the world's gonna end, and this big hole opens up in the ground. And when I look again, there you are, getting your ass handed to you by a little girl. So of course I gotta come in and bail you out, as I always do."

"I seem to recall that you then got knocked out," I said, "and I rescued both of us."

El plowed onward. "Anyway, I wake up and see you beat half to death. I go off to find help, and somehow, there's a bunch of people passing by. I manage to wave them down, but one of them starts asking me a bunch of questions about a glowing rock which I've never seen, and then they throw me in here. But I manage to tell them where to find you." El rubbed her paws together in satisfaction. "And then I just chilled in here for a while. And peed on that wall." She indicated the damp wall I'd sat back against, and I moved over to the opposite side of the cell.

"This rock," I said, taking off my shirt. "Did they call it something specific? Like a Willstone or Fruit of Will or something?"

"That's exactly what he said. Said our greed had doomed us all or something. I couldn't really make heads or tails of it."

"Hmm." A sinking feeling grew in my stomach. "That can't be good."

The raccoon sniffed at the barren corners of the cell. "By the way, you wouldn't hold out on me if you had some food in your back pocket, would you? Some spare candies? Normally I'd be more picky, but I'm *starving*."

"Wouldn't dream of it, compadre."

Our kada bracelets, along with the inventories they stored, were on a shelf across from our cell, tantalizingly close. I thought I might still have a health bar in there, and to be honest, I was getting the munchies, too, now that I wasn't tripping balls anymore.

"Hey!" El banged the cell door. "What's a raccoon gotta do to get some grub around here?"

There was no response.

I sighed. "Look at us. Ten floors of hell just to end up locked in a dungeon. How long do you think they'll keep us here without talking to us?" I hoped it wouldn't be long; they hadn't questioned us about our crimes yet. But did they even have due process here?

Thankfully, only half an hour had passed before our cell door swung open with a click, revealing a rough-looking man wearing the same X-shaped lapel pin.

"Bossman wants to see you." He paused and sniffed. "And get yourself cleaned up. Smell like animal piss."

CHAPTER TWENTY-ONE

Grandmaster

(Strive 10:4)

The guard took us from the cell up a series of winding stairs, holding our kadas loosely in one hand. El stared at the jangling bracelets while she rode on my shoulder, and I shook my head vehemently, putting a hand on her back just in case she had a mind to spring for them. No way would that end well.

My chest tightened with a sense of impending doom. So far, a fair number of the people we'd met inside the tower had been assholes, but maybe we'd get lucky here. I remembered vaguely the purple glow of someone healing me from near death. At least one person had been kind.

We must've been far below ground, because the spiraling steps seemed to go on forever. Slowly but surely, we left dim corridors lit only by flickering orbs to enter brighter halls. I never thought I'd be so glad to see windows and feel fresh air on my skin—I only hoped it wouldn't be the last time.

The guard escorted us to a large wooden door, opened it slightly, and passed our bracelets through the gap to someone inside. He indicated that we should enter without him, so we stepped through the threshold, the door slamming shut on our backs.

For some reason, I'd been expecting an opulent throne room where some mighty lord would pass judgment on us from on high. But really it was a modest space—just a few chairs and a rug for comfort, and a fireplace that crackled with warmth. Two men faced us, one seated behind a desk almost submerged in paperwork, one hovering above in an advisory position. I wished I wasn't wearing thin hospital clothes. They made me feel like I was at a severe disadvantage.

The seated man did have something lordly in him, but it was an old, weathered authority, like a gunslinging sheriff of the Wild West. He was dressed pragmatically in a shirt and pants, no stiff ruffled neckwear or luxurious robes. If he wore a kada, it was hidden by the long sleeves of his tunic.

The other one was the harsh-looking man who'd arrested me, gripping our bracelets tightly in one fist. His own kada was deep red, like blood or anger. The seated man whispered something to him, and he responded in a low rumble without taking his eyes from El and me. He dropped the bracelets on the table and indicated that we should take them.

"You're giving them back?" I asked, surprised.

"The guildmaster instructs me to do so," said the man with obvious disdain.

It felt good sliding the kada on again. My wrist had felt empty without it.

The seated man spoke aloud, in a surprisingly erudite voice, and thankfully in English, unlike his counterpart. "You don't much look like your last name's Shaw, if you'll forgive my saying. And you"—here he glanced at El—"don't seem like our El Bandito. Aside from the obvious similarity."

I cleared my throat. "Family name's originally spelled *X-I-A*. I changed it—wanted to make it easier for people to pronounce."

He looked thoughtful. "Indeed. I'm a Shaw myself. Convergent evolution of names, I suppose."

"And I *am* El Bandito," snapped El. "What, is there a trademark on it?"

That brought a small smile to Mr. Shaw's face. "So you are, so you are. And I am Jacob Shaw, at your service. You've already met Artem." I glanced at the policeman, who scowled in greeting. "You are currently in the headquarters of Uomo Universale, of which I am guildmaster."

I had no idea what any of that was, so I just said something vaguely polite in response, although I took it as a good sign that this man wasn't overtly aggressive toward us. There was a brief silence before he spoke again.

"Might I have permission to scan you?"

Supposing that he meant Examine, I saw no reason against it. "Go ahead."

His fingers suddenly moved as though they were searching for something, his right eye flashed white, and I felt a disconcerting pull, like someone had put a fishing hook on my arm and yanked. Transparent images of the contents of my inventory moved to float in the center of the room in an accelerating cascade. My kada projected three symbols—a shroud of fire, a ball of light, and a musical note—that began to revolve lazily about my wrist.

"Cool," said El. "What's that light coming out of you?"

A pulsing light that looked like the Willstone's glow was strobing from the center of my abdomen, not the bracelet. Artem looked like he wanted to rip my throat out, and Mr. Shaw put a hand up to calm him. Then, he redirected his searching hand to El and did the same. Although the raccoon had secreted a huge number of items in her inventory, she did not exhibit the same Willstone glow as me.

"As Artem suspected," he said, turning to me, "you are in possession of roughly one-tenth of the Willstone. What have you done with the rest of it?"

Finally given the chance to speak, I explained as best I could how I'd been tricked by Mia, duped into being an accomplice to her heist, and how she'd betrayed me, taking the lion's share of the Willstone for herself. How we'd fought her in the forest, escaping by the skin of our teeth. When I finished, Artem was sneering.

"You believe this?" Artem said to the guildmaster, who looked at me with a measured gaze.

"I'm as of now undecided," said the guildmaster.

"Let me help you decide." El leaped onto the desk and made the signs to retrieve an inventory item, and the bottle of Fernet from the lobby appeared in front of her on the table.

"If this is a bribe—" Artem began.

"Sorry, I fat-fingered that," said El. "Here."

The jar containing the poor guard's remains landed on the desk with a thud, and the guildmaster flinched back from his desk. It was subtle, but I saw it. Even stoic Artem took a step back. Bile rose up into my mouth at the sight of it—here, in a civilized room, its presence seemed even more macabre.

But El was triumphant. "Neither of us has an ability that would allow us to do that. Scan me if you don't believe me. There must have been a third party involved."

"How was this done?" The guildmaster looked at the jar. "Teleportation magic? No . . . I recognize this spell. But no glass that we know of could hold up to the forces involved."

"Adamant-glass, she called it," I said. "Against a human body, it'll win ten times out of ten, she said."

Artem shot Mr. Shaw a look, but his face was unreadable.

"What?" I demanded. "And can you please tell me what's so important about this stone? I'll give it back; just teach me how."

"A myth," Artem said, ignoring me again. "Adamant-glass doesn't exist—"

"Look in front of you, Artem." Shaw put a hand against the glass gingerly. "There are other towers besides this, where what to us is myth happens every day. In the Tower Eramai—"

Just then, the whole world began to shake. Books toppled over, cabinets fell out of drawers, and papers went flying. I held onto the sturdy desk with one hand and grabbed El with the other until the shaking subsided.

"Two quakes in one day," said Shaw ironically. "The same day our Willstone is stolen. Imagine that."

CHAPTER TWENTY-TWO

Towerfall

This is a world in between," Shaw said. "Between reality and unreality, life and death, order and chaos."

We were all seated around the guildmaster's desk. The mess lay where it was, papers scooted into an untidy pile as far away from the hearth as possible. The mood in the room felt darker than before, and Artem's glowering was half-hearted at best. El lounged on a table, but her ears were perked up, listening.

At least, I thought, *if he's explaining this to us, he probably doesn't consider us enemies anymore.*

"Have you heard of the principle of entropy?" Shaw continued. "The natural tendency of the world is to decay, to become disordered over time. All things shuffle slowly toward the grave. Here"—he smiled without humor—"you could say we have one foot already in it. It requires a great amount of energy to stave off that inevitable end. That's where the Willstones come in."

I thought back to the view outside of Death's schoolroom, that unfixed twilight world, and a sudden surge of vertigo hit me. Those towers I'd seen felt like twigs jutting out of cracked mud, thin and vulnerable, able to be blown over by the slightest breeze.

"Each tower is a bastion of order in this fundamentally chaotic realm, sent up by an authority with the strength to bend the world to their desired shape. And when I say 'strength,' what I'm actually referring to is, of course, Will."

"Do we really have time for this?" Artem said.

"We must," said the guildmaster. "And in the meantime, we should provide these two with translators as well. The visual captioning they've been relying on is unworkable in the long term."

"Why would they need—" Artem froze. "Surely you don't mean . . ."

"Oh, but I do," said Shaw. "I am quite serious about it. Unless you have any better ideas?"

Artem glared at the guildmaster before storming out, slamming the door behind him and sending the papers on the floor into flight. Shaw watched impassively as one drifted into the fireplace, denaturing quickly into ash.

"I'm starting to get the picture," I said. "Will is the energy that binds a tower together. Without it, everything falls apart."

"Not just energy. You see, unfocused energy is the very definition of disorder. A tornado tears apart, a flood uproots and washes away . . . a fire burns. To serve order, that energy must be brought to bear on something—call it a principle or a desire. That purity of purpose is what elevates mere energy into Will." The guildmaster steepled his fingers. "Our tower's authority is the First Sender, and his principle is Strive. He has encoded that principle into anchor points—the Willstones—and secreted them in various places across the tower. One of which we were charged with protecting."

El twitched an ear. "So that girl removed one of the pillars holding this place up. Sounds pretty bad."

"Correct," Shaw said, "and now you know why its removal has caused these . . . instabilities in the tower. If a second or third is taken, well . . . we are all going to be quite permanently dead, or wishing we were. Entropy will win."

My gut wrenched with guilt as I realized the enormity of what Mia and I had done. She had deceived me, but I had been the one to destroy the stone's defenses.

Shaw stood up from the table and walked to a curtain-drawn window, throwing it open. I blinked as sunlight and noise suddenly flooded in. I had thought we were in some isolated decrepit building somewhere, but we were two or three floors up from a bustling city square.

"The guild quarter of our city," Master Shaw said. "Home to tens of thousands of souls. And not the only city in the tower, either. All sheltered by the Will of the First Sender."

Glints of wrist bracelets flashed up from people as they walked to and from places. It was not unlike cities I'd lived in before or been to. Montmartre in Paris or somewhere like that. Cobblestones and hills and cute little shops selling—well, I guess I had no idea what they'd sell here, actually.

"I think I'm going to throw up," I said.

"Good," said Artem behind me, making me jump. "Maybe the Willstone will come with it. I should feed you syrup of ipecac . . . In any case, I've brought the translators as you requested, Master Shaw."

"Thank you, Artem." The guildmaster took two small white earpieces from him. "All our devices, our kadas and udjats and translators, draw power from the same Will that holds up Strive. A few hours ago, every single magic item and spell in this tower lost approximately five percent of its power output. Even without the towerquakes, it was immediately obvious."

"But what does Mia have to gain from all this?" I asked, somewhat desperately. "I mean, she's in here with us, too, right?"

Artem barked a laugh. "Not for long. I imagine she's on her way to the nearest tower bridge forthwith."

"The adamant-glass was all the confirmation I needed." Shaw stared hard at the grisly jar. "It's Eramai-made, no doubt. We don't have access to such materials here or the means to shape them. No, your mystery girl is not from this tower, and she is certainly not planning to suffer the ill effects of this. Her powers have a different source."

"What if she steals another Willstone?" I asked. "She could gain even more power and bury us behind her. Two birds with one . . ." A glance at Artem prevented me from finishing my sentence.

"She very well could," Master Shaw said, "and we'd be right fucked."

I put my head in my hands. "I didn't know."

"That ignorance is the only reason you're still alive," Master Shaw said mildly. "Well, that and the fact that you've only retained a small fraction of the Willstone, a pittance really. We could dissect it out of you, but it's almost not worth it. The problem would remain—your Mia has absconded with the lion's share of the power."

El growled, and I felt a rush of sudden anger. "So why are you wasting time giving us the third degree? Seems there's bigger fish to fry. If you really don't need our 'pittance' of the Willstone, as you put it, we'll be heading out. Good day to both of you." I snatched up the earpieces and our kadas from the table and stood to leave.

Shaw gave a sudden, humorless chuckle.

"What's funny?"

"Xavier Xia," he said, as if speaking to himself. "Xavier Xia. Kind of a superhero name, isn't it?"

"Or a supervillain," I replied, and Artem snorted in disdain. *Can't butter me up that easy, old man*, I thought as the door closed behind me.

CHAPTER TWENTY-THREE

The Tower Origins

(Strive 10:5)

Reddish-gold afternoon light burnished the walls of Uomo Universale in a kind of shabby grandeur. A beacon like an artificial moon shone from atop a hill at the center of the city, and a thin cable next to it shot upward to the next floor. Surrounding it was a crown of fine castles, contrasting the rows of houses and rough cobblestones of our current avenue.

<<Step aside, please.>> The text flashed into my peripheral vision as a shoulder checked mine. Lowering my eyes, I saw that we stood in the middle of a bustling crowd—people on their way to and from one place or another—and quickly stepped aside. My heart was still beating rapidly, and I couldn't quite believe the guild had let us go like that. Part of me still expected a hand on my wrist to grab me, pull me back inside to those dungeons.

El looked miserable as she hid behind my legs, backed against the wall. "Let's get the hell out of here," she said. "Too many people."

We ducked into an alley—I guessed every city, even a fantasy one, needed somewhere to dump their trash—and emerged onto a quieter street. It was jarring, I thought, to go from isolation back to society, and every time I saw movement, my fingers wanted to twitch and throw up that protective shield, but it was invariably just some innocent passerby, with only the flash of their kada to let us know that we weren't in Kansas anymore, proverbially speaking.

"Those two," said El. "Who do they think they are? We almost died while they were sitting pretty in their castle, scared to death of a little shaking."

I gave a noncommittal grunt. If what Master Shaw had said was true, there was reason for all of us to be concerned. I looked up at the red-gold sky again. Hard to believe that was painted onto a ceiling, mounted on walls. But if those walls fell . . .

We stopped dead in our tracks. The road ahead of us was blocked by a mass of people, craning their necks to look at something and talking in hushed whispers. Fearful anticipation weighed on me as I pushed forward through the crowd, making my way to the front of the lolly-gaggers, and my vision was overwhelmed by dialogue pop-ups from my udjat furiously translating. I could barely see.

Grimacing, I screwed in one of the earpieces the guildmaster had given us, and my udjat lit up, overlaying the translations with glowing text.

Registering new output peripheral . . .
Sync with Babelfish-110 OK . . .
Automatically disabling visual captioning . . .
A female voice spoke a single word in my ear: "Connected," and the hubbub of the crowd suddenly shifted into focus.

"—how awful—"

"—heard the sound of it crashing down—"

"—move, asshole!"

The last was directed at me, and I blinked as I stepped aside. None of these folks had been speaking English before, yet now I understood them perfectly. It wasn't that the earpiece translated their words on receiving them; the words now emerged from their mouths as Standard American English.

"How is that possible?" I wondered aloud.

"What?" said El.

"I can understand them now." I was awestruck. "I don't need captions anymore. This is amazing!"

Some folks glanced at me curiously as El replied, "Good for you." She made no move to insert her own earpiece. "And that's special because . . . ?"

"Wait a second." Realization dawned on me. "You never needed—"

"I'm a magical talking raccoon," said El. "English ain't special. But listen, they're saying someone's trapped in that building ahead."

My blood ran cold. "What do you mean? Who?"

The front of the crowd was a few paces away from the ruins of a building. "What happened?" I asked someone nearby.

"An old smith lives there, name of Kieran. Couldn't run out in time before the building caved in, I guess, from the shaking earlier. We heard his voice earlier calling out, so he's probably still alive."

"Isn't anyone going to help? What is everyone waiting for?"

This led to an outbreak of arguing about whether it was safe or not, which ability would be best, and a lot of jargon that went over my head, but my understanding was that no one felt confident they'd be able to move the rubble without crushing the poor soul trapped inside.

My fault. The words voiced themselves in my head, as much as I tried to suppress them, and I'd been trying since the meeting with Master Shaw and Artem; but they finally burst through the dam, resonating as I stepped numbly forward to the edge of the rubble. How many scenes like this were there, across the city? Across every floor of this place?

I reviewed my limited options. *Maybe Harden could break through, but it'd cook the survivor inside like a pizza in a brick oven. Did El have anything? Pickpocket wouldn't help. Firecracker was too risky. There had to be something.*

"What are you doing?" A voice called from behind me. "It's too dangerous to go in there."

As I turned, I saw a sea of faces looking at me. God, I hated being the center of attention. But that wasn't what made my stomach lurch suddenly. My guilty conscience read something other than concern in all those eyes, and I wondered what they'd think of me if they learned what had happened in that chamber far underground, if they realized that I was the cause of it all. I wanted to be like El and live in the forest, far from any accusing eyes. I wanted to become invisible.

I willed it to happen.

The crowd began to murmur, too low for my udjat to pick up. But as I looked down, I saw with a start that my body was fading into nothing. I began to sink into the cobblestones for a moment, then steadied.

"What the hell?" El tried to grab onto my leg with her jaws, but she chomped down on empty air. "You're disappearing!"

I hadn't made any signs, and my kada floated dark and inert on my transparent wrist. This was some other kind of power. It was clear now that the Willstone had reacted directly to my desires. I reached for the rubble again, and the space where my hand would've been passed right through it.

"This might work," I said. "Stay here."

Be a ghost. Be intangible.

My whole body was light and airy now. Feeling emboldened, I stepped forward and passed into the destroyed house like a ghost.

It was tricky work. Every step, my foot sank into the ground like the paved streets had become a muddy bog, and I had to consciously think of the solidity of the floor. But then when I did, I'd end bashing my invisible shin against the next piece of rubble. My sight had darkened, too, and everything seemed to be visible only from a great distance. I was too afraid to focus my vision, worried my eyeball would rematerialize only to be pasted inside some piece of masonry. El's voice faded into the background as well.

"Who's there?"

The sound that came from nearby was barely a whisper, and I realized I'd passed into a hollow within the collapse, tall enough to stand in a crouched position and a few feet wide. I let go of the thoughts of invisibility and my body slumped, held down suddenly by the weight of matter.

The man—Kieran—lay there, his lower leg bent in a way that made me queasy. He looked unkempt with a scraggly beard, as though he'd lived in this rubble for weeks, even though I knew that couldn't be the case. The air was stale, although I felt a slight breeze from gaps in the fallen brickwork.

"I'm here to help," I said, kneeling down awkwardly in the tight space. "We're going to get you out of here."

He made no reply, so I maneuvered myself in front of him and slung his arms over my shoulders. Turning to face the direction I thought I'd come from, I thought as hard as I could.

I don't exist.

Nothing happened.

Do not perceive me.

Still no dice.

"Shit." I paused in an awkward half-crouch, not wanting to move and disturb the man on my back. "I don't suppose you have some kind of heat resistance?"

There was only heavy breathing for a second, then he spoke laboriously, between coughs. "This forge goes up to 3000 Kelvin. What do you think?"

"Step back!" I called.

The last bricks pushed aside as we broke into open air, sweat and fumes pouring from my aura. Taking a step forward, I gently lowered the smith to the ground. True to his word, he hadn't even been singed.

It was darker now, and my red glow cast long black shadows before me. The crowd that remained was silent for a moment, then one man yelled something, and then all of them were cheering and hollering. That was a blessing; I didn't want to know what they said anyway. All I felt was tiredness and shame. And I would've stayed to tell them to knock it off, but I had to find somewhere safe to deactivate my shield first.

"El?" I called.

"I'm here," replied El, a small shadow hunched over away from the crowd. "Just didn't want to be too close in case you blew up."

"I'm going to head outside the city to detonate," I yelled. "You're welcome to follow. There's a lot of people here."

"Okay," said El.

As I walked away, her shadowing me from afar, I was conscious of other stares on my back, stares from everyone I passed. Burning red, I led us from one winding street to another, until we stumbled out onto a wide thoroughfare. On one side, the road rose up out of the ground, turned to an endless stair that ascended to that hill in the city's center, where the bright beacon shone and the skywire reflected the light faintly. *Then the other way must lead outside.*

We set the beacon at our backs and began to walk. My energy was sapped by the heating element of the shield; it was a constant drain, and my vision blurred. I hardly noticed as I stumbled out the city gates. Where before there'd been handsome walls and awnings on each side of me, now there was only grass. The path beneath me had vanished as well.

"Hang back behind the gate for this part," I warned El.

"Don't need to tell me twice."

I put a few more paces between myself and the city walls, and my fingers twitched loosely.

The world went white with a roar, then settled. A radius of destruction surrounded me, grass turned into a pit of dirt. I swayed, then buckled to my knees. It was only with effort that I prevented my eyes from closing. Turning, I made to wearily trudge back to the city, but seeing it in truth for the first time, I stopped short.

The face of the city wall loomed before me, alabaster white, almost geological in scale. But while a mountain had crags and faults and spines, this was all one smooth piece, soaring up to a predetermined height before terminating smoothly. Set into the midpoint of the wall were arched alcoves, windows into the interior, and the glow from the city's central beacon leaked out from them like a lighthouse.

"Tens of thousands of people could easily fit in here," I said. "Hell, millions."

"It's a lot of people," El agreed with a twitch of her whiskers.

A pang of guilt cut through my tiredness, followed by a flash of anger at Mia. But what could I do? She was probably long gone from here, long since moved onto another floor. *And how easily you say, 'Not my problem,'* part of my brain whispered to me. *Almost like you've had plenty of practice doing it.*

There was a ruffling sound of cloth on cloth, very near, distracting me from my stupor, and El cursed. Someone else was there.

CHAPTER TWENTY-FOUR

Instruments

(Strive 10:6)

Away from the gate to the city, slightly off the path, the ground lifted slightly into a dark mound. In the darkness, I saw the flash of white robes standing there. Cautiously, I approached, my signing hand at the ready.

"I'm done with people for today," El whispered. "Let me on your shoulder, and I'll pretend I'm asleep."

As I bent down to let her up, a mournful note sounded, shattering the quiet and making me jump. The woman (I could see now) was playing an ancient-looking flute, facing away from me and the city. The city's bright beacon lit the back of her blue robes, her waves of black hair, and her bracelet, which shone a deep amethyst. Her song was floating and melancholic, and its last note lingered like an unanswered question as she set the flute down.

"So," the woman said without turning around, "is Death still out to get you?"

Death is out to get me. It was something I'd mumbled in my delirium earlier. "It's you," I realized. "You were the one that healed me."

She said nothing.

"I'm surprised you remember me saying that," I said after a moment. "The thing about Death. My head was pretty messed up at that point."

"With that much blood loss, it's no wonder. But you were right in a way. Sooner or later, Death comes for us all."

"I wasn't really being figurative," I said. "He's pretty mad I got away from him the first time."

"Is that so?" She finally turned to look at me. The purple of her bracelet was mirrored slightly in her left eye. She was pale and slender, younger than I expected from her voice and posture. Her robes were unadorned but draped in a way that reminded me of flowing water. She held the flute loosely with graceful fingers, and there was a sadness in her face that matched the sound of her song. "I hope you haven't brought him with you to Shinar."

"Shinar?"

"This city," she said, waving a sleeve behind me. "Its name means 'ten-place' in my language. Whoever chose the name wasn't blessed with creativity, I guess. 'Ten-place,' the city of the tenth floor."

"Ah," I said, and then because I couldn't think of how to respond, "I'm Xavier, by the way."

"I know." She inclined her head. "Selene."

After an awkward pause, I noticed that she was staring at El's prone form draped over my shoulder. She was still playing dead. "This is El Bandito the raccoon."

"Raccoon," she said, as if the word were foreign to her.

"What was that song you were playing? It's beautiful."

"It's only one half of a duet," she said, almost apologetically, and lifted the wind flute to blow a few hollow notes. "There's supposed to be a harmony part."

"Could you teach it to me?" I said. "I've got something of a music background myself."

It was the wrong thing to say. I cursed my eagerness as she gave me a sharp look that told me I'd overstepped.

"No," she said shortly.

There was another long pause, then she turned her back to me and knelt to the ground. The darkness obscured her motions.

"What are you doing?" I asked, wondering if she'd forgotten I was standing there.

"Burying a friend."

"Jesus. I'm sorry." She seemed to be struggling physically, and I figured with my foot already firmly in my mouth, it couldn't get any worse. "Is there any way I can help?"

Selene went still for a moment, then turned around, holding something out to me. "You can help by opening this for me."

My stomach dropped. It was the third time today I'd seen that grisly jar.

Night fell.

Pale light from the city's strange beacon filtered down through awnings and walkways, throwing patterns across the paving. Most of the windows were darkened, although one in every few flickered with dim candlelight and the drifting murmur of conversation.

"What are you going to do now?" I tried to ignore the taste of bile in my mouth. As grotesque as the jar was, at least when it had been sealed, that grotesqueness had been contained. We'd had to open it to return his body to the earth. The sound the contents had made as they slid out . . .

"Master Shaw told me about the one who did this. I'm going to find her, and I'm going to make her suffer." Her violet eye flashed, and my heart did a backflip.

How much had Shaw told her? I wondered. "You're going alone?"

She shook her head. "The constable of Uomo Universale, a man named Artem. Of course, he is more concerned about taking back Shinar's Willstone. That's understandable." She paused to wipe something off her sleeve. "Some things taken can yet be returned. Others can only be repaid."

It's my responsibility. I'll come, too, I wanted to say, but I choked on the words. "When will you go?"

"Tomorrow. As soon as my work allows—"

She stopped speaking. A figure seemed to be approaching us from the direction of the city's gates, making a beeline for me. As he came closer, I saw that he was a short, soft-looking man with a pale-blue bracelet. El twitched restlessly on my shoulder. I couldn't blame her; this was getting to be too many introductions for so late at night.

The man stopped in front of us, peering at me closely. "It's you, isn't it? The one who saved the smith."

"Ah, I suppose."

My tone might've betrayed my tiredness, but the man either didn't notice or chose to ignore it. He beamed, grabbing my hand in both of his to shake it effusively. "Florian, at your service. The whole guild quarter's been talking about what you did. A bona fide hero, that's what you are."

I looked at Selene for assistance, but she stood back with an inscrutable look on her face. "I'm really not—" I started.

He cut me off with an exaggerated wave of his hands. "Nonsense. If you need a place to stay, I have an open bedroom. Nothing fancy, but it's the least I can do." He looked at me with eyes that seemed hopeful I'd take him up on his offer.

". . . actually, that would be appreciated," I said, stroking El's fur. "It's our first day here, and I—"

The man held up a hand. "Please, no need for explanations. I'm sure you're exhausted. Come this way. Your friend is welcome to stay as well."

But Selene had already disappeared.

Eramai

(???)

In a far-off, green-peaked tower, there lived a prince and a princess who loved each other dearly. They spent many happy seasons together in their high solaria until one day, the princess was abducted by an evil tyrant.

The prince sought her out, but her kidnapper had covered his tracks well, and he did not know where to begin. He remembered then that at the uppermost reaches of his tower, there resided a sibyl, an oracle who had a reputation for deep wisdom. So he journeyed there and asked her where his princess might be.

The sibyl opened her eyes from a deep meditation. "I'm sorry, my prince," she said. "If the princess yet lives, it is not within these walls."

"Then what shall I do?" cried the prince.

Pitying him, the sibyl said, "I shall grant you a small boon of wisdom to aid your search." And she touched him on the brow. A star grew there, and his thoughts quickened. He knew then what he must do.

The prince crossed over to another tower to begin the ascent anew. This time, it was not an oracle but a sculptor that he found at the top.

"Haven't seen 'er," the sculptor responded brusquely, chiseling at a marble block, for that was what he did, day in and day out, crafting ever higher and more beautiful floors for his tower.

The prince was tired from his climb, and he asked if he might rest there for a while. The sculptor gestured to an unfinished marble slab, perhaps intended to be a bier or a coffin. So the prince lay on it and slept little, for the stone was rough and cold on his princely skin, which was indeed more accustomed to goose down and silken sheets.

In the morning, the prince found that the floor had been completed around him (the slab he'd been lying on turned out to be a bench) and went up a new staircase to find the sculptor already hard at work on the next floor.

"If I only had your fortitude," the prince marveled, "I should be able to find my dearest easily."

The sculptor took pity on the lad and lay his hand on the prince's chest, shaping something within him. When it was done, the prince found that the very walls now lent their hardness and strength to him. He bowed and left, feeling very thankful.

In the next tower, the prince fought through floors of scorching heat to ascend to a cosmic forge, where a smith hammered steel upon an anvil made of stars. The smith did not know of the princess's whereabouts, but he too had a gift for the prince. The smith struck him once, twice, three times on the breastbone, and after the pain subsided, the prince found that his chest had become like a great bellows, and every breath pumped him full of vigor. "My utmost thanks," said the prince, kneeling in respect.

The prince's heart was weary as he climbed a third tower. Here he found a young sender, who was impressed at his prowess and skill. But the sender could not help him, as he was still busy climbing the tower himself. Still, he was fairly certain no one had come this way. He gave the prince a sidelong smile and said, "I'm sorry, but your princess is in another tower." And he gave no aid to the prince.

Many towers the prince scaled, and many blessings were bestowed on him, except that which he most desired, which was the return of his beloved. One day, as he was wandering the land-between-the-towers, almost in despair, he happened upon a small cottage. His heart leaped, for it had been constructed in the style peculiar to his almost-forgotten homeland, which is a triangular sloped roof around an open courtyard.

When he entered, he knew that it was her, somehow escaped from the tyrant's grip. Though her dress was simple, her scent filled his mind, and the look of her filled his heart. All his senses delighted, and he moved to embrace her.

But the thousand blessings, augmentations, modifications, and enhancements, all in the service of his quest, had changed him into what appeared to her akin to a monster. She did not know him, and she screamed.

At this, the prince, scarcely knowing why, reached inside himself to seize his own heart and planted it into the earth. There was a deep rumbling. Out of the floorboards of the cottage something grew, with all the feelings enmeshed within him as the seed. The earth trembled and shook for many hours, and when the air had stilled, the cottage, the prince, and the princess were nowhere to be seen, and in their place a new tower reached to the heavens above.

Yet, that part of the world was never truly still again, for from the moment the new tower appeared, it thrummed with a beating rhythm that was both more and less than human.

And they called the new tower *Eramai*, for in the language of that prince's people, the name meant *He loved* . . .

CHAPTER TWENTY-FIVE

Hero

(*Strive 10:7*)

I woke from uneasy dreams of suffocating under others' expectations, only to find myself choking under a different kind of weight. El lay spread-eagle on top of my sternum, and she yowled as I pushed her off.

"Good morning to you, too," I told her. I hadn't realized she'd warmed enough to me to do that, but it didn't seem entirely a bad thing.

I was pleasantly surprised by the accommodations. The bed was certainly on the firmer side, but free of lumps. A desk stood in the opposite corner of the room. The only strange thing was the complete lack of dressers, wardrobes, or any kind of storage whatsoever, though when I thought about it for a second, maybe it wasn't that surprising after all.

I raised my right hand in front of my face, staring at the bracelet that never came off anymore. The kada's weight still bothered me in moments of calm. *A literal golden handcuff*, I thought wryly. And then there was that other power, the fragment of Will inside me. I couldn't feel it at all now, although I knew it slept somewhere under my breastbone.

I cast Aetherphone with a twitch of my fingers and searched my memory for the tune Selene had been playing last night. To my surprise, it was already lodged firmly in my head. There was an inevitability to the notes, each one following the last like a river running downstream.

"Do you mind?" El's muffled voice emerged from under a pillow. "I'm trying to get a few more minutes of sleep in."

I let my arm flop down to the bed, and my mind wandered to our meeting last night. Why hadn't I been able to tell Selene I'd go with her? I'd stood there like a mute idiot, let myself be called a hero. She had looked at me. Said nothing, only looked, but there'd been judgment in her eyes, or was that my imagination? Did I truly want to go, or was I too afraid?

"El," I said. "What do you think of all this?"

"All what."

"Everything." I rubbed my eyes. "Mia. Selene. Willstones and cities and guilds. Feels like everything's gotten ten times more complicated since we landed on this floor."

"Too many people." El remained stoically under the pillow, but her tail shifted slightly. "People always bring problems."

"What if we were to leave the city?"

Her tail stopped moving. "And go where?"

"After Mia. At least for a while. You heard as well as me what Selene and Artem are planning. With the Willstone gone, I'm not even sure it's safe to stay. Somebody has to get it back, or at least stop her from getting her hands on any more of the things. And I can't help feeling like it's the right thing to do. For me, at least."

"Alright."

"Just like that?"

"I told you, there's too many people here." El twitched her whiskers. "What's that smell?"

The scent of bacon had wafted upward into our room from the stairwell, and El quickly threw off the act of tiredness and scampered downstairs, leaving me to change into the day's clothes.

After a disappointingly normal breakfast, our host told us that the man I'd saved from the day before wanted to thank me in person.

"You really don't have to come if you don't want to," I said to El, but she remained sitting on my shoulder as we walked down the busy street.

Thus, we found ourselves paying a visit to the smithy again. The debris had been cleared, and a fervent haze billowed from a makeshift chimney. We opened a door and a wave of hot air blasted out at us. I almost threw up my shield on instinct.

The gray-haired man—Kieran—seemed none the worse for wear after yesterday. He stood in the center of the room, his kada burning blue, and his udjat also glowed, giving him a slightly crazed look. The source of the heat was a long weapon that he held with an evil-looking curved blade at one end. Power seemed to flow from his bracelet to the polearm, and the air shimmered with excess energy.

Then, in an instant, it all stopped, and he wiped his brow and swigged from a glass.

"Whew." The smith wiped his brow. "More and more orders nowadays. I'm grateful for the work, but still. Not as young as I used to be."

"The place looks good," I said, looking around. Dirt and loose rubble still littered the floor in places, but otherwise it was surprisingly neat. Thick steel beams had been installed vertically to serve as makeshift supports. "Is everything okay?"

"Okay?" He fixed me with a stare that, while no longer blue, was still unnervingly intense. "No, it's not okay. It's wonderful! People have been so shaken up recently, no pun intended, that they've been coming in droves for weapons and upgrades. It's the most business I've had in years! A dozen customers already today, and can you believe I had to turn some of them away?"

"Oh," I said. "I see. And your leg is healed?"

"Indeed it is!" He clapped and danced a little jig. "And it's thanks to you, good sir!"

It's my fault that you got hurt in the first place, I thought guiltily. "There's really no need—"

"Ah, but there is! Allow me to show my gratitude with a custom job for you. Obviously an accomplished fighter like yourself already knows this, but I can improve any weapons that you'd like." Without warning, he tossed the polearm at me, and I caught it. Only then did I notice the blade at the end seemed to warp the air around it like fabric. "I imbued this billhook with the ability to tear space. Fun little project."

I slashed with the polearm, and a cut filled with dusky shadows opened up in the room briefly before fading away. "How does that work?" I asked as he took the weapon back.

"The client who brought Ripper to me carried her for a long time," he said, laying the weapon down fondly. "My magic works best when there's a strong connection between wielder and weapon."

I pulled up my inventory and scrolled through. The only thing I saw that qualified as a weapon was the air rifle from Earth. I cast *Retrieve Item*, and it appeared in my hand. El looked at it sourly.

"What in God's name is that?" Kieran stared at the gun as if it were a particularly unsavory insect. "A toy?"

"It's a gun," I said. "It fires pellets at the speed of sound."

"No." Kieran shook his head. "I don't think it'll work. I'm sorry, but I need something simpler if I'm going to work on it. Do you have a sword or a lance or something?"

"He has a plunger," El snickered.

"Shut up."

Kieran raised an eyebrow and, rolling my eyes, I brought it out.

"Oh," he said. "Oh, but this has some potential now."

"Does it?" I said doubtfully, handing it over to him.

His eyes gleamed at it, the udjat seeming to glow brighter than ever, reflecting in the plunger's brass haft. "Yes, this is the one." He held it carefully, not like a person holding something dirty, but as a cherished and priceless artifact. "You've wielded it well, but it's lacking a little something."

"Like what?"

"A name, a name! For names hold power, and that which we call a rose, by any other name . . . might smell like feet!" He boomed an unnerving laugh—for effect, I hoped. "If you're not up to it, would you allow me the honor?"

"The honor of naming my plunger?" Self-consciously, I looked around, wondering if I was being punked. "Um, sure, I guess."

Kieran's fingers twitched and his udjat-eye burned blue again, giving him an unhinged look as he intoned, *"Usage begets familiarity, Familiarity begets understanding, Understanding begets naming, A name begets power."*

As he spoke and signed the last word, the plunger turned bright in his hand and trembled. Heat began to rise, slowly but surely, then dissipated. An oily coating seemed to peel off of the plunger, leaving it shinier than before, but otherwise exactly the same.

"What did you do to it?" I asked in a low voice.

"Examine it," he said, and I knew he didn't mean with the naked eye. As I shifted my fingers, the plunger's new description burned in my udjat:

Purgator.

This is a Named Item. It was originally a Fancy Plunger.

Ability: Remove status effects. The activation command is P-U-R-G-E.

"*Purgator*," he pronounced, taking another swig of his beverage. "That which purges, or that which cleanses. Not bad, eh?"

I passed the plunger to my left hand and signed with my right. As the characters scrolled around my wrist, a mote of violet light traveled through the air from my kada to the plunger and hovered, revolving around it in a slow orbit.

"How does this work?" I asked, swinging it back and forth, the light following lazily.

"Same way you use a regular plunger," said Kieran. "Your friends get poisoned or something, stick 'em with the business end."

It didn't seem the most sanitary, but I wasn't about to complain about gaining an unexpected new ability. Not only that, the plunger had acquired a new balance in my hand. As I gave it a few experimental swings, it felt like an extension of my arm. "I don't know what to say," I told him.

"My good man, say nothing." He extended a hand to shake, and I took it. His grip was powerful and sure.

I stowed the plunger with a flash of my fingers only to see El rolling on the floor in laughter. "*Purgator*," she howled. "En garde! Have at ye! Taste rubber, villain! For my plunger hath a name, and it is *Purgator*!"

Even the smith had to crack a smile at that.

CHAPTER TWENTY-SIX

Inside of You There Are Two Wolves

(*Strive 10:8*)

Let's take a breather to consider the idea of the lone wolf.

I'd be the first to admit the concept has a certain mystique. A silent killer, seeking company only when it's advantageous, stalking the land, solitary and proud.

But what if he's more like an outcast, driven out from society, forced to wander alone, taking food and warmth where he can? And was it one of those lonely strays who first sold their dignity to man in return for meager scraps of meat and affection?

These thoughts and others ran through my mind as I stared at a braceleted Pomeranian standing in the street. It yipped at El, while the raccoon hissed and turned sideways to present a larger profile. The toy dog's owner, a fashionable dark-skinned lady with a pink bracelet, apologized and scooped it up in her arms, turning away from us.

Everyone we passed had kadas, but their colors were pallid and weak. The people of the city were all pastels—peaches and lilacs and chartreuse greens, nothing more saturated than that. If my understanding of the correlation between attributes and color was correct, that seemed to indicate that no one was much stronger than El and me, which suggested one of two things.

Option one: Stat candies, the items that gave rings their hue and people their power, were much harder to acquire after the tutorial.

Option two: These people just did not get outside very often. Which I could sympathize with.

Asking would probably be rude, I thought.

Looking out the window at the high stone walls of the city, the second seemed more and more likely to be true. I had zero problems with that. Having made it this far, the people here had built a semblance of a working society, and they were entitled to their happiness. I looked at the people milling about, spell-sun reflecting off their bracelets, and felt a semblance of resolve harden in me.

It must've been a market day or something; the main boulevard was awash with people. Vendors spread their wares on rugs and tarps, hawking all kinds of fruits and vegetables. The raucous cries of merchants and the scent of ripe produce filled the air, and we had to fight through the crowd until we finally reached an area where the masses of market goers thinned out. We soon came to the front of Uomo Universale.

Squat as it was, the guildhouse seemed to loom over us, and my throat tightened. Were we really walking back into the same place we'd been arrested literally yesterday?

The door swung open to reveal Artem, standing there with his broad face and dark uniform. His ruby-red kada gleamed, more deeply colored than most in the city by far. He greeted me with his characteristic scowl.

"I want in," I said. "We want in."

"Into what?"

"You know. Mia, the Willstone."

Artem only continued glaring at me.

"It's important to me," I pressed. "To set things straight. I got wrapped up in this from the beginning, and I'd like to see it through to the end."

Artem folded his arms. "We're not looking for volunteers. If you'll excuse me now, I have to return to my preparations."

"Hold on!" I wedged my foot in the door. "Is that what Master Shaw decided?"

"I speak for him."

"Right. So when he went to the trouble of getting us these"—I indicated my earpiece translator—"that was just an act of generosity? Artem, he wanted us to work together. To communicate. I know you think this is somehow my fault, and trust me, I feel the same way. I can't live among the people here knowing that my actions have hurt them, even by accident."

"You'll figure it out, I'm sure," Artem said. "Good day."

The door slammed shut, leaving me standing alone. After a brief pause, I grinned. While I'd distracted Artem, El had slipped inside right under his nose.

Master Shaw, Artem, El, and I sat in the guildmaster's room, engaged in a heated discussion as the fireplace crackled.

"Selene told me she's part of this team," I said. "I don't see why we can't be allowed to join. All we want is to help."

"Every party needs a medica." Artem replied to my words, but his eyes were busy glowering at El for sneaking by him. "And she's proven herself skilled and trustworthy."

"Selene is a known quantity," the guildmaster admitted. "She's been one of the top healers in Shinar for years. And Artem won't say it himself, but he's quite the pugilist. I'm not against the idea of a larger party on principle, but I have to say, I'm left wondering what the two of you bring to the table."

"Maybe we should take this outside," El said, staring back at Artem.

"What El means to say," I added hastily, "is that neither of our abilities are very well-suited for an indoor demonstration."

Artem cracked a slight smile. "I have no objections. And before you say anything"—he looked at Master Shaw, who had a finger in the air—"you told me to organize this expedition however I liked. That includes the criteria for admitting participants."

The guildmaster folded his arms. "Fair enough. I did say that."

"That's that, then." Artem seemed in good spirits, which worried me. "How about a friendly sparring match?"

We were atop the roof of Uomo Universale, standing on that giant emblem of the guild. From up close, it was clear that the cross shape on the roof wasn't an X at all, but a roughly drawn image of Da Vinci's Vitruvian Man. I looked across at Artem, who stood on the other side.

In the light of Shinar's beacon, his kada gleamed vermilion opposite my washed-out yellow. Master Shaw stood at the side of the ring as arbitrator. El sulked on the sidelines—she had wanted to fight, and I'd had to talk her down and convince her it was too dangerous.

"So we've agreed," Master Shaw said, "Xavier versus Artem, one-on-one. If you win this bout, you will both be qualified to join the party.

Victory will be decided by knocking the other outside of the largest circle marked on the rooftop."

"Way to hog the fun," El said to me. "Knocking this guy out would be its own reward."

"Knocking out of the *ring*," Shaw emphasized. "And no weapons."

I nodded at Artem. "Ready when you are."

"Begin!" called Shaw, and with a familiar gesture, Artem's aura flared around his large frame, red like dark wine.

That pattern of signs . . . I knew it all too well.

It was the same spell as mine, Harden, from the strength line of the Aspect of Corpus. He lumbered toward me slowly, not bothering with a fighting stance. Torrents of energy shrouded his eyes, but I saw his lips curled in a smile.

I started to cast Harden—

He sank a fist into my stomach before I could finish the gesture, and I spat blood. Before I could catch my breath, he slugged me with the other fist, then the first again. If I hadn't had my augmented body . . . Looking up, I saw no compassion in his dark eyes, and a great deal of enjoyment. He wasn't trying to win the contest. He was using me as a goddamn punching bag.

"Dammit, Artem," roared Shaw. "This is supposed to be a test, not a massacre. Show some restraint."

Artem removed his fist, and I collapsed to my knees.

"Apologies," he rumbled. "It won't happen again."

I propped myself up on my elbows, and El tapped me with a health bar in her hands, probably stolen from somewhere.

"Is—" I couldn't speak, but El caught my meaning.

"Hey, ref. Is this allowed?" She waved the item at Master Shaw.

"As long as you stay inside the ring," he replied dryly.

I grabbed it and wolfed the thing down, and my organs lurched back into place.

Now I was pissed off.

The hell if I'd let that prick push me around this way. I'd win just to spite him. And if he really was that much stronger than me, well, I'd win a different way.

Deliberately, I shifted my fingers into the same six letters, and hellfire enshrouded me.

CHAPTER TWENTY-SEVEN

Hardboiled

(Strive 10:8)

I kicked off the ground at Artem as he refreshed his Harden spell with a twitch of his fingers. That meant he didn't have the same burning variant as me, since mine lasted until deactivation.

The inferno around me blurred my vision, and through it, Artem's own aura made him dark and indistinct. *It's a shame,* I thought, *that I won't get to see his expression when I kick his teeth in.*

I swung a fist at him, and he didn't even bother to block, tanking the blow on his wide chest. I had a moment to gape in surprise before he backhanded me across the arena, my body skittering across the roof like a stone on a pond. *Five skips. Impressive.*

As I lay there looking up at the burning sky, Artem said something I couldn't understand and laughed. With a start, I realized that my translator earpiece fizzed and crackled a few feet away from me, utterly broken. *Not good. I'll have to get that replaced.*

My opponent's strength clearly far outstripped mine, so attacking head-on wouldn't work. There was, however, one way in which I might have the advantage. I groaned and pushed myself to my feet.

"Get his ass," El cheered.

Artem's shadowy figure put out a hand and beckoned. This time, when I rushed at him, I didn't punch—I went low and wrapped my arms around his torso.

He seemed to be confused why someone half his weight would want to grapple, but my burning aura soon enlightened him. As for me, it'd been clear since the ice machine fight on the sixth floor that thermal resistance didn't come standard with the Harden spell. And it was lucky that he hadn't acquired it some other way, like the smith had.

Artem tried briefly to break my hold before he came to the same conclusion I had a few seconds ago: It's pretty hard to wrestle someone who's on fire. He settled for elbow drops to my back that felt like the stomps of an elephant. But I held him tight and pushed, and unbelievably, felt his weight shift back slightly.

With a roar of indignation, he lifted me bodily off the ground, ready to toss me from the arena. This was it. I had a few seconds before he threw me. Squinting my eyes closed, I reversed the signs of Harden. *With his defensive abilities, he'll be okay, right?*

My aura detonated, and the world went white.

When the smoke had cleared, Artem remained standing, his hands and waist slightly charred, but otherwise unharmed. He was at the edge of the circle, but to my dismay, still comfortably within the boundaries. With a start, I realized that spectators had gathered on nearby rooftops, cheering and booing in turn. Someone had even set up a deck chair and a bucket of popcorn.

"This is more public than I'd hoped," muttered Master Shaw. To us, he called out, "Good to continue?"

Artem said something and wiped his hands on his pants. I didn't speak Old East Slavic, but that didn't sound like a no.

My stomach sank. My trump card hadn't been enough.

"One sec." I pulled up my system menu to toggle captions back on, and text scrolled across the bottom of my field of view.

Listening . . .

"Alright, I'm good."

"Go," said Shaw, and we dashed forward to meet in the circle's center.

This time, Artem actually bothered to dodge my claw-handed strikes, and I counted that in itself as a minor victory. Still, I was flagging, while he seemed inexhaustible. His elbow strikes had taken an immense toll on my energy, and my knees threatened to buckle under my own weight.

My left leg trembled, and Artem seized the opportunity to deliver an open-handed palm strike that launched me to the very edge of the circle. He strode up, ready to deliver the final blow.

He spoke a contemptuous word and struck out with a lazy fist.

"No thanks," I said, dodging and grabbing his unprotected arm. Only then did the translation of his statement scroll onto my udjat.

<<Weak.>>

Artem yelled as steam rose from his skin, striking me repeatedly with the other hand, but I latched on stubbornly. His punches crashed through my barrier, and blood ran from my nose and mouth, but I held on. He stopped pounding me to refresh his aura, and I used the chance to maneuver myself onto his backside, putting him against the outside of the circle, all the while signing *N-E-D-R-A* . . .

I released his arm, holding two fingers forward, and for the second time that fight, blasted him with a wave of concussive force.

There was a series of explosions like fireworks, and Artem flew off the rooftop entirely, landing with a crash below. There was a startled scream from below, then silence, before I heard Artem bellow something that sounded impolite. My translator declined to comment.

"Who's weak now?" I said in a low voice.

An immense shout rose up from the spectators, in a cacophony of languages that I couldn't understand, and some of them even tried to leap over to Uomo Universale's rooftop before Master Shaw waved them off. My vision was overwhelmed by dozens of translator notifications, and I had to toggle the feature off just to see. As the black dialogue boxes cleared, I saw a ghost of a smile pass over Master Shaw's face.

"The animal interfered," said Artem. "I saw its kada activate, clear as day, right before I fell off the roof."

I tensed. El had interfered, but I'd been hoping he hadn't noticed.

"Artem," Master Shaw said finally. "You have quite a head start in the advancement of your kada's abilities. I know it was against the stated rules, and it's only my opinion, but I would say the playing field was even."

"Basically, he's saying 'get bent,'" El chimed in.

"No," Master Shaw emphasized. "That's not what I'm saying at all. And I should remind you, your inclusion in this matter is still very much at Artem's discretion. I might act a bit more diplomatically if I were you."

Artem gritted his teeth and closed his eyes. He stormed up to me, daggers in his eyes, and thrust his hand out. "I, at least, am not one to violate my word."

I clasped his wrist. "Excited to work with you, too."

Our kadas clanked against each other, and then Artem stepped back.

El coughed. "Aren't you forgetting someone?"

"I am not shaking hands with an up-jumped street rat," said Artem, "especially one who delights in cheating and insulting me without provocation."

I'd never seen El speechless before, but she was then. "*Without provocation?*" she finally said. "I'll show you provocation!"

Her paws met to start casting Firecracker, but I grabbed her before she could finish. "Chill out," I said. "We're part of a team now. Time to start acting like it."

As the four of us looked out over Shinar, the beacon at the city's center captured my gaze. It was especially clear tonight, and the shadows of the city radiated outward like spokes on a great wheel. Lowering my eyes to the cobblestones, I thought of the life I'd left behind and realized I didn't miss it at all. There simply wasn't anything to miss. I'd rather Artem punch me in the gut a hundred times than have to look at another Excel spreadsheet.

No relationships to mourn, no roots to uproot. I wasn't a sentimental person at the best of times—there were no scraps in my scrapbook, as the saying went.

"So," I said, "when do we ship out?"

CHAPTER TWENTY-EIGHT

Embarcadero

(Strive 10:9)

The target is in all likelihood headed back to Eramai," said Master Shaw. "Now, I have never met someone from there, but you should know that they are said to utilize a different sort of magic which does not involve bracelets and contacts."

I blinked. "But she had two kadas. One she took from the guard, Selene's friend. What about the other?"

Master Shaw sighed. "You know as well as I do where she must have borrowed the other one from."

"Some other poor schmuck from around here donated it to her." El gnawed on a leg of chicken from the guildhall's kitchen. "Rest in peace, anonymous guy."

"Eramai, the place she's from—what's it like?" I asked. "What powers do they have?"

"It's supposed to be quite beautiful," said Master Shaw. "I've heard it called the Tower of Roses, a place where the flowers always bloom."

"The land of milk and honey," muttered Artem, "but the milk is laudanum and the honey, poison. One sip of that draught, and you forget everything else, content to languish there for eternity."

Master Shaw rose from his desk and retrieved a hefty tome from the shelves. "According to the stories, the people of Eramai are invariably beautiful. One wonders if that might be their native magic."

He flipped to a page showing a sketch of a dancer in a loose, flowing garment, mid-twirl in the center of a ballroom. The nobility all appeared transfixed, and I thought back to my meeting with Mia, how her laugh had made everything seem right in the world.

"Yeah," I said. "That seems about right."

"Did you get a good look at her?" Artem said. "We should know what she looks like—"

The door to the rooftop of Uomo Universale opened, and Selene emerged. "Thank you all for waiting," she said. "I just finished with my last patient." Her eyes fell on me. "Why is he here?"

"You've come at the perfect time," said Master Shaw. "Xavier was just about to describe our quarry. But perhaps we should retire to the sitting room where it's more comfortable."

"She was . . ." I paused. Trying to recall Mia's appearance, it suddenly felt like all I could think about was comparing her to the woman who sat in front of me. Mia was dark while Selene was light. The first was petite and doll-like, the other willowy and slender. Their personalities were opposite, too. It was uncanny.

"Long black hair," I said, "tied behind in a single braid. When she was using her kada powers, her eyes were two different colors—one blue, one green. Tight-fitting clothes, athletic wear. The body type of a gymnast, slim and short, and very light on her feet. Her skin's about as tan as mine, maybe a little darker."

"You remember a lot," Selene observed. *Was that an accusatory tone, or was I just imagining it?*

"What about personality?" Master Shaw prompted.

"In our brief interactions, she was very forward and flirtatious." I hesitated. "Maybe even playful? Like the whole world, people's lives and everything, was all a game to her—I'm sorry, I don't want to go into more detail than necessary." I glanced at Selene, whose gaze was studiously neutral.

"Continue," she said.

"The one thing she was serious about was getting that Willstone. She was practically salivating over it. After that, when we fought, she seemed to be having fun, if anything. I don't think there was a moment she was taking things seriously, even up to the point when I blasted her point-blank."

Selene folded her arms. "When we met last night, it didn't occur to you at all to mention that you'd been in contact with the killer, this girl from Eramai? How curious."

"I know. I should've said something. It just didn't seem like the right time for it, and you disappeared right after . . ."

There was a long silence, during which I could've easily summoned up the Will to become invisible.

"Anyway," said El. "The girl nearly killed us both. We got away by the skin of our teeth."

"You were very lucky," said Master Shaw. "She has her native powers, two kada bracelets, and the better portion of a Willstone."

You crafty old man, I thought. *You were planning this from the outset.* Aloud, I said, "So is there some way that we can know where she is? With her teleportation, she could be anywhere by now."

"*Interchange*," said Selene, "not teleportation. I'm quite familiar with the spell. It requires lifeforms to switch with, which slows her down. Not a lot, but slightly."

"And she may be seeking the other Willstones of the tower," said Master Shaw. "They are not straightforward to find. So while she's puttering about, you all may be able to recover some ground. As for tracking, well . . . I take it you haven't seen Selene's abilities other than her healing."

"I don't have the necessary materials," said Selene. "I'll have to acquire them in the field. But my preliminary reading is that she's several floors above us at the moment."

"So be it," said Artem. "The builders are holding back the towerquakes on our floor, but the signs of instability continue on all floors, above and below. The way things are going, it's only a matter of time." He didn't elaborate on what would happen after "a matter of time," but I had already seen some of the effects.

"Let's get the hell out of here, then," said El. "We've got an elevator to catch."

There was no fanfare to send us off, no farewell parade. And yet, I couldn't help but feel some kind of strange energy stirring in me. El sat on my shoulder, and though she didn't say anything, I could feel her trembling with fear or excitement. It was like we were setting out on a quest.

Somehow, the knowledge that we were finally doing the right thing cheered me up immensely.

We stood at the central plaza of Shinar's Hilltop District, where the city fell away in every direction, shadows stretching away from us.

"There's someone up there making the light," El noted.

"That's Paul," said Master Shaw. "Solid spellcaster."

I turned and waved up at the artificial sun, and the caster of the Lux spell waved back, then made a hand shadow puppet of a dog, whose silhouette loomed over the plaza.

"Dammit, Paul," muttered Artem. "And you, don't encourage him."

The commissary from Uomo Universale outfitted us with a whole army's worth of necessities—food, waterskins, toiletries, sleeping bags, tents, ropes, stakes, etc. It would've been a ridiculous amount to carry if it weren't for our dimensional inventory systems, which now spanned several pages.

I remembered the people I'd met, the music I'd seen, and the small kindnesses I'd been shown during my brief time in Shinar. Looking out on the well-lit city, I had the sense that, as Master Shaw had said, this was a place worth protecting.

We made our way to the building that held the next floor's entrance, where an elevator thrummed gently, a low contrabass note. Fear and apprehension mingled with a hint of excitement as the guard read a list of our names aloud.

"Bandito, El."

"That's me."

"Bykov, Artem."

"Present."

"Shaw, Xavier."

"Here."

"Wang, Mingyue."

". . . here."

I felt a new kinship with the white-robed woman. Mingyue to Selene. Xia to Shaw. It wasn't so different.

"All set, then." The guard looked up from his sheet. "Y'all ever been out of the First City before?"

"Yes," said Artem, Selene, and El.

"No, you haven't," I said to El, "and neither have I."

"Yeah, whatever."

The guard turned to El and me. "Floor eleven usually has a pretty cheerful beach theme. Don't let your guard down, though. Don't get in the water unless you have a real good reason. Towerquakes make big waves, and here there be monsters, as they say. There are floor-specific tokens that can be redeemed at an arcade for equipment. Very handy. Also—"

"We don't have time for the whole spiel," Artem said curtly. "We'll have to cover it as we go. Apologies."

He strode into the elevator cabin, followed by Selene, neither of them looking back. I gave the guard an apologetic look, then El and I stepped forward as well. The doors closed, and with a wrenching sensation, we flew skyward, up toward the unknown.

CHAPTER TWENTY-NINE

Azure Blue World

(Strive 11:1)

W e'll need to get off the beach as soon as we can," said Artem as we rode upward in the elevator. "Giant crabs burrow under the sand, and they're unfriendly at the best of times. When the towerquakes rile them up . . ." He left the sentence unfinished, but I could guess.

"Crabs sound good." El spoke with her mouth stuffed with blue candy, courtesy of Master Shaw. "All these candies . . . blue raspberry, blueberry, peppermint—you know, there's not that many blue flavors. Gets dull real fast."

"No one told you to limit yourself to those," I said, chewing on a Peach Ring of Power that flooded me with vitality. "Artem, is it better to go wide or deep, stats-wise? El says deep, but I beg to differ."

"If you don't stop talking with your mouths full, both of you will be six feet deep," Artem rumbled.

"I didn't know they had that expression where you're from."

"They don't," said Artem, "Unfortunately, my mind has been polluted by modern vernacular through the dubious magic of cultural exchange." He raised his pure-red bracelet, and it flared with an aura of power.

"We're unlocking a whole new side of you, Artem," said El. "Used to think you were a humorless asshole, but now I see I was only half right." She chittered in mirth, but in spite of the jab, I noticed she'd waited until after she swallowed to speak.

Meanwhile, Selene kept her eyes pinned to the floor indicator with the patience of a long-suffering commuter. As the elevator slowed its ascent, a beam of light swept down through the crack in the doors. Unlike Shinar's magical beacon, this was harsh and searing, like an equatorial sun at noon.

"I already hate it." El covered her eyes.

Ding! The doors opened, and I was blinded by the sudden glare. A rush of warm air brought the tang of salt and the sound of waves. Stepping out of the elevator, my foot sank into what felt like fine sand. My eyes began to adjust, and I saw the sky, impossibly vast and blue, and a coastline girdled by an expanse of sparkling water. On the other side, the sand turned to rocks, sloping up into a jagged line of cliffs.

The elevator line ended unceremoniously in the middle of the beach, its dial all the way to the right. It sat unmoving, seeming almost embarrassed to spoil paradise with its gaudy modernity. As I looked closer, I saw that what Hilbert had said was true: This was the first elevator with a down button.

Artem and Selene wasted no time, making a beeline for the rocky cliffs. After a moment's hesitation, El and I followed.

"What's the plan after we make it off the beach?" I asked. The sand made it difficult to move quickly, and I felt like I was already sweating. "Just head toward the next floor elevator?"

"Yes," said Artem, at the same time Selene replied, "No."

They glared at each other, or rather, he glared at her while she looked calmly back at him. "We need to first determine where the next floor is," she said. "These worlds change as swiftly as water, and the exit will have already moved somewhere else."

"Fair enough." Artem folded his massive arms. "So what do you suggest?"

"Use my powers. Provide me with the raw materials, and I'll divine the path forward and find out where our target is. In other words . . ." Selene's violet eye flashed in the sun. "Let's go crab-hunting."

Artem volunteered himself as bait, pounding the sand with an aura-packed fist, and I welcomed the opportunity to see more of his abilities in action. His left hand twitched and the bracelet sparkled garnet-red, before he slammed his right down with an immense thud, throwing up a blinding cloud of sand that suggested his fist weighed about as much as a falling semi-truck.

"So there's no time limit on this ability, Power Strike?" I asked, covering my face. "It just makes your next attack stronger, but how does it determine what constitutes an attack?"

"Good questions." Artem sounded surprised. "There may be hope for you yet. No time limit. Activation merely requires a certain threshold of muscle contraction to be met."

I thought for a moment. "Could I make *any* muscle execute a Power Strike? The tongue is a muscle."

Artem stopped punching the sand for a moment to reply. "That is, quite possibly, the stupidest thing I've ever—"

The sand erupted underneath us, sending both Artem and me flying. I landed on my hands and feet, while Artem dropped heavily on his side. Nearby, Selene and El rushed over in preparation for combat.

The armored crustacean was huge, built like a tank, and it snapped mean-looking pincers at me. I wondered if a Hardened fist would get through its shell. Still, I cast the spell on myself as a protective measure. The burning aura actually seemed to insulate me from the tropical heat.

"Plan?" I asked Artem, who was pushing himself off the ground.

"Hit it hard," he grunted, and rushed at it with his fist raised. His fingers twitched, and a blood-red aura enfolded him, before a second darker one wrapped around his fist. The crab swung a greatsword-like claw, but it clanged off his aura and bounced back, throwing the crab off-balance. Artem started to swing his fist, and halfway through the motion, his fist *cracked* forward impossibly fast, tearing a hole through the crab's carapace. The crab jerked away, scuttling sideways toward Selene and El.

There was a series of small explosions as El's Firecracker popped near the crab's face. Most of the explosions missed, but one of them took out the crab's eyestalks, and the monster ran right between the woman and raccoon, colliding with the cliff wall. Its mouth foamed as it clamped its claws blindly, tearing at the rock wall as if it were trying to burrow into it.

"You." Artem pointed at me with an arm covered in yellow crab gunk. "Finish it off. Don't damage its shell too much."

"I'll try," I said dubiously. "I don't have that Power Strike ability, though."

I approached the wounded crab, my aura burning around me. Its flailing limbs made me cringe, but I reminded myself that they wouldn't penetrate my shield and pressed forward. At an opportune moment, I ducked under its shell and threw an uppercut to the bottom of its carapace. Hot crab innards spilled out on me, sizzling against my fiery cloak, then I was pelted with an array of what felt like both candies and small coins that adhered to the crab glue. Gagging, I tramped off toward the water to clean myself off.

"No!" said Artem. "Avoid the water. They hunt in packs. Stay on the rocks."

"Aw, hell," I said. "You mean I can't rinse this off? I smell like the dishwashing station at a Red Lobster."

"You'll have to bear with it." I could've sworn Artem cracked a slight smile, that fucker.

"Well, I need to detonate my shield, at least, so I'll be right back. If you hear a big explosion and see crab parts flying everywhere, don't be alarmed."

After ducking behind a rocky outcropping to deactivate Harden, I found that our commissary-supplied expedition kit included a trusty bath towel, and I was able to get myself somewhat cleaned up. The candies that had fallen from the crab and onto me were entirely melted, but I pocketed the floor eleven tokens. They looked similar to the second floor's vending machine tokens, and the elevator guard had mentioned we could use them at some sort of arcade here.

On my return, Selene was sitting next to the crab's shell, performing a long sequence of hand signs that wrapped around her wrist in ribbons of text. The white characters formed a full sleeve on her arm before flowing into her upturned palm.

"Scapulimancy," said Artem. "Better known in some places as oracle bone divination."

With an azure spark in her right eye, she slammed her hand down on the crab's carapace.

There was a hot blue flame and a loud crack. The monstrous shell jerked as a network of deep cuts suddenly spiderwebbed across it, forming something that looked like esoteric writing. Selene traced each line with her finger, gazing at the shell intensely, her eye alit with an inner flame. The slashes on the crab felt uncannily like language, but their interpretation was out of my reach.

Her brow furrowed with each line she read, and her mouth moved silently. Then, her blue eye dulled, and she sagged back. Artem caught her and lowered her gently to the ground, retrieving a refreshing drink from his inventory.

"It's not good," she said, holding the drink with both hands.

"What do you mean?" El asked, looking like she'd been the one the crab spilled its guts on.

Selene took a long sip, then coughed. "First off, my readings indicate our target's not on the floor, which isn't unexpected. But this second part is new. It's saying the entrance to the twelfth floor . . . it's that way." She pointed past the beach, at the endless expanse of water.

CHAPTER THIRTY

Midway

(*Strive 11:2*)

I tried to help Artem build a raft out of palm timber and fronds, but after he pronounced me useless for the fifteenth time, I decided to demote myself to tree-cutting duty. Well, it was more like tree-punching, *Minecraft*-style, since I didn't have a machete or cutting tool. All in all, I found it therapeutic and enjoyable, and fortunately, we weren't bothered by any other crabs.

"That seems like enough logs, don't you think?" Selene's voice came from behind me.

I turned to see her standing there with El snoozing on her shoulder. She looked calm as ever, running a hand over the raccoon's back absent-mindedly. Behind her, a swath of dozens of felled palm trees littered the island. Artem was lugging one over to the raft, which seemed almost completed.

"Guess I overdid it." I gave her a rueful smile. "You know how us industrialists are and all that." I cringed inwardly. *What was I saying?* I still didn't fully know how to act around her, this pretty young woman who by all accounts should've been grieving. If her composure was an act, she could've won an Oscar. "How are things with you? Is everything okay?"

Her eyes met mine, and she tilted her head slightly. "You mean regarding Yao's death?"

Yao. That was his name. I opened my mouth and closed it. "You know, you're pretty direct, for a fortune teller. Yeah. I'm just—I mean, in your place, I feel like I'd be . . . less alright, somehow."

Selene was quiet for a moment. "I just don't see the point," she said. "What will be, will be. What has happened, has happened. We do the best we can in the reality that remains."

"Yeah, but . . ." I hesitated. Who was I to try to convince this poor lady to mourn? It wasn't any of my business. "Never mind." I quested for a more neutral subject. "So where in China are you from? My parents are from—"

Artem hollered at us; it was time to board the boat. We walked across the sand, careful to step lightly to avoid waking any crabs.

"The twin city of Fenghao," she said, so much later I'd almost forgotten I'd asked. "I worked at the royal residence there as a shrine maiden."

"Fenghao?" I wracked my brain. "I haven't heard of it."

"That's alright," she said, stepping over a piece of driftwood. "I'm told it doesn't exist anymore."

Bolstered by his aura, Artem launched the boat, while I climbed aboard. Selene and El already stood atop the deck. As the vessel began to float, we vaulted aboard to join them, and I had to admit that for all his faults, Artem was a deft shipwright. The knots were lashed tight, the logs packed into neat rows. There were even two benches for us to sit on, and notches for oars carved from scraps of palm. It was awkward for El to hold the oars, so she appointed herself ship mascot and moral support.

Slowly, our little party rowed the boat away from shore. The lowering sun cast the sky into layers—deep blue over bands of blushing pink and orange, all resting on red firmament. Without a moon to make tides, the sea sat silent and still as blackened glass, except where the ripples of unknown creatures disturbed the surface.

"What do we know about M—about the murderer?" I asked.

There was silence in the boat for a while, aside from the rhythmic sound of rowing.

"With one of her bracelets, she's a Corpus user," said Artem, "but focused on agility more than strength. That path's equivalent to our Harden ability is an aura called Quicken."

I remembered the green of her own bracelet and the speed of her movements, and decided that checked out. "So, in addition to that, she has a second kada with Interchange. Is that it?" I asked. "One aspect per bracelet?"

"No one has found the method to gain a second aspect on a single kada," Selene said. "We know there's a slot for it, as it's part of the standard introductory spiel Hilbert gives new climbers. But how to obtain one is an open question. For now, we're limited to the one we selected in the Room of First Principles."

"So much of this tower is unexplored," Artem growled. "The theoreticians in their labs can try to reverse engineer the kada's inner workings all day, but in the end, they're just twiddling their thumbs." He slapped his oar down harder than necessary, and the boat jumped. Then, it jumped again. The water around us became suddenly turbulent with bubbles.

"These quakes happen a lot now, huh?" I said.

"Uh, guys." El looked down into the frothing waters. "Something's coming—"

With a roar, the surface was breached by a sparkling behemoth, a translucent whale that shone in the colors of the sunset. It seemed sculpted from ice, but it moved like a living thing, slipping through the water with great agility. The boat rocked as it slapped its tail down on the water, sending waves in all directions. The thing was massive, staring at our ship with smooth, featureless eyes.

"Get down!" Artem threw aside his oar and sprawled.

The ice whale roared, and from its mouth came a rain of icicles. We all ducked, and I watched as the shards of ice thunked into the wood, points protruding into the interior of the boat. Almost immediately, water began to leak through the holes.

El cast a Firecracker at it, which chipped some ice off the whale's surface, but it only seemed to anger it further. "Looks like another job for the Human Torch," she said.

"I don't know how I'm supposed to do that without burning the boat down." I gripped the side of the vessel with one hand as it rocked in the waves. "Okay, I do. But it sucks." I told Artem my idea, and he gave me a nasty grin.

"I like it," he said, which is how I knew it was a terrible idea.

"Let's go," said Artem, straightening. He moved his fingers through the hand signs of Power Strike, and his kada flared red, reflecting off the facets of the icy whale. "No time to waste."

Taking a deep breath, I stepped onto his interlaced fingers. "I trust you," I said untruthfully. "On my count. One, two—"

With a great shout, he flung me like a rocket into the air.

"Fuck you, Artem!" I cried, but the howling wind ate my words. My hand moved, and I became a fiery missile, burning across the reddened sky. Now I could see that Artem's aim was true, and I would come down exactly where the whale's blowhole would've been. The bastard even gave me some spin, like a football. I tucked my arms and legs in and braced.

Then came impact, like slamming into a wall. My body drilled through the ice with the enthusiasm of an Alaskan oil baron, and although the friction slowed my rotation, I had already penetrated the outer shell, and my overflowing heat did the rest. I melted a thin, claustrophobic channel through the body of the whale. As quickly as the ice melt filled the tube, it vaporized from my aura and turned to steam. When I couldn't bear the feeling of being trapped any longer, I detonated.

Cracking ice sounded like a glacier cleaving in two, and suddenly I was falling through the blue and white to splash down into water. I gasped, opening my eyes, and beheld an underwater city.

There was no seabed. The water somehow ended below us, and below that was Shinar, visible beneath the floating ocean. The spell-moon glinted with a dull pearl-like luster, a round clamshell of high walls enclosing it. For a moment, it brought to mind that other submerged city, Atlantis, and I wondered if I swam down far enough, would I fall out of the sky and onto the floor below?

Then I was back above the surface, gasping for air. Floes of ice surrounded me, as well as multi-colored Swedish Fish candies and small golden tokens. Then I saw the boat a distance away, rowing slowly toward me. I turned over onto my back and floated, watching the stars wink on one by one, while I imagined myself beating the shit out of Artem.

We made landfall just as the last blot of red was fading from the sky, near a rocky mountain and the thunderous roar of a waterfall. There was a pool under it, but no sign of the way to the next floor. It was too loud to speak, as the falls drowned out our voices, but I could see the worried look on Selene's face even as the sky darkened. She and Artem made a few quick hand motions back and forth that eluded me; Selene's were fluid and graceful, while Artem's were rigid and harsh.

Then, Selene's fingers danced, and an orb manifested above her like a miniature moon, casting a brilliant white glow over the whole area. It was her Lux lamp, I realized, and it made mine and El's look like children's toys. *Probably because her magic ability is higher.*

Even so, we didn't see any signs of the way upward. While we searched the area, El washed her candies in the pond. I stood next to her to peer into the depths of the water. Nothing. Then I looked up at the waterfall, squinted, and grinned. *Of course.*

I turned to the party. "I know what this is. I've seen it before!" I yelled, knowing they couldn't hear me over the roar of the water. "Oldest trick in the book!"

They looked at me bemused, but I was too giddy to care. Holding my breath, I ran toward the screaming torrent and plunged in headlong. The immense pressure pounded down for an instant, then two, before the pounding abated.

I pushed wet hair out of my eyes to reveal a large cavern decorated with torches on both sides. Brightly painted masks hung on the walls and thatched grass covered the ceiling and floor, framed by bamboo and rattan, like in a tiki bar. I moved deeper into the cove until the roar of the waterfall became muted behind me and triumphant text lit up my vision.

Secret location discovered: Atlantis Resort!
Sublocations are as follows.
Atlantis Resort Lodging: Free use of rooms to rest!
Atlantis Resort Restaurant: Exchange tokens for delicious tropical food and beverages!
Atlantis Resort Arcade and Midway: Use tokens to play games with unique and powerful prizes!

"Thank God there's something back here," I muttered to myself. "That would've been really embarrassing otherwise."

CHAPTER THIRTY-ONE

Tilt

(*Strive 11:3*)

The passage opened to a small chamber lined with racks of fresh-smelling towels. I tied one around my waist, grabbed a few extras, and went back to fetch the others.

Leaning against the wall by the waterfall, I watched as El leaped through the curtain of water, sputtering and swearing. She looked about half the size she normally did with her fur matted down. A red glow resolved into Artem's shape, and he emerged, completely dry under his shield.

Would've been nice if I could do that without blowing the cave to bits, I thought with more than a hint of jealousy.

"How did you know?" he demanded. "That this place would be here."

"It's a bit of a trope," I said. "Kind of a stereotypical thing in games. Always check behind waterfalls."

"Good way to slip and crack your head open."

A second later, Selene appeared, her robes soaked through, and I averted my eyes as I handed her a towel.

"In any case," I said, "this area seems safe enough. We're close to the next floor's entrance, and that means there's a field of safety, right?"

"It doesn't always work that way," Selene said, wringing her hair out. "In fact, that's likely one of the reasons Shinar was settled on the tenth floor. That being said . . ." She looked around at the merrily dancing torches on the walls. Three doorways, when we Examined them, indicated that they led to the lodging, restaurant, and arcade, respectively. "This does seem reasonably safe. And the floor shouldn't shift while we're here."

El yawned. "In that case, I'm going to get some food. Restaurant sounds nice."

"Hold on," I said, turning out a couple dozen floor eleven tokens from my inventory. Both the giant crab and the ice whale had literally showered me with them. "Let's split these four ways. We'll need them to pay for the amenities here, at least the restaurant and arcade."

After I gave her the tokens, El decided to visit the restaurant, and surprisingly, Selene joined her, which left Artem and me standing awkwardly in the towel room.

"I'm going to go check out the arcade," I said.

"Lead the way," he said. Somehow it irked me not to be able to explore on my own, but I began walking and Artem followed.

The passage to the arcade was cavernous and dark, but before I could light my Lux spell, I noticed a glow and motion in the wall around us. It was a glass tube, teeming with cave fish, and their shadows seemed to make the ground shimmer. As we walked, it grew brighter and brighter, and with a crescendo of jangling noise, we emerged into a room filled with flashing light and a cacophony of sound.

I flashed a few tokens to my palm and made an effort to smile at Artem. "Now this is more like it. Welcome to my world."

"Not a fan so far," he rumbled.

The arcade was decked out in the same Hawaiian theme as the entryway; even the game machines had hula skirts. The wooden clacks of drums and twang of ukuleles filled the air as all the devices looped through their attract mode sequences. The first aisle had all the old classics—Skee-Ball, hoops, some kind of drum machine, and a game where you knocked down teeth in a cartoon clown's mouth.

But the machine that caught my eye was one I'd played countless times at the local bowling alley as a kid.

The backbox art depicted a buxom woman casting a silver ball at the player, surrounded by images of doves, tigers, and playing cards. Across the top, in red and gold lettering, were the words *Theatre of Magic*. The British spelling gave it a little old-world flair, though I knew Bally-Williams was an American company through and through. Midwestern, even. I hummed and popped a cinnamon-flavored jawbreaker in my mouth as I approached the pinball machine.

The playfield was all purples and reds and golds, decked out with ramps, wire-form rails, and flashing arrows. As I popped a token in and pressed the start button, red-gold text sparkled in my right eye.

Prize awarded at two billion points.

I shook my head as a carousel appeared on the LED display, blinking through three options, and fired the plunger just as it read *Advance Clock*. Two billion was a lot, even as inflated as the scores were in this game.

"What's *Advance Clock* mean?" Artem's harsh voice came from right next to me, and I jumped as the ball drained down the center. The machine mercifully returned my ball, allowing me a second chance.

"It's the award you get for hitting the magic trunk," I said, tapping on the flipper buttons. "The clock starts at noon, and six o'clock earns you an extra ball. Which is good, because the goal of the game is to avoid losing your balls." That earned a grunt that might've been a chuckle.

I plunged the saved ball and hopped it over the center gap, trapping it in the crook of the left flipper. "This is called a cradle." With an early flip, I bounced it back over to the right flipper. "And this is a post transfer. It doesn't work on every machine, but—"

"Just play the damn game," Artem said.

"You have the magic!" cheered the magician lady from the pinball machine.

So much for being a helpful teammate. "Yessir. Yes ma'am." With a tap of my right hand, I sent the ball around the left orbit. As with many pinball games, what the machine wanted you to do wasn't the best strategy. You were supposed to bash the magic trunk repeatedly to start illusions, but that was an easy way to lose your ball. I preferred going around the outer loop, racking up free points. It was safer. Until it wasn't, as a bad ricochet off the captive ball sent me down one of the outlanes.

"Your turn," I said.

Artem sighed, but he stepped up without arguing. His first bat with the flipper sent the ball straight into the trunk to start the *Levitating Woman* mode. "Levitate," cooed the floating woman, her wink and seductive pose reminding me of Mia. "Levitate." As with many beginners, Artem mashed both flipper buttons whenever the ball came close to the bottom. But his aim was good, and he hit the trunk almost every time.

Despite the fact that the goal of the mode was to shoot the center stair-case, he kept wailing on the fixed target, his eyes intent.

When the ball inevitably rebounded and drained down the center, he lifted the front legs of the machine and dropped it with an enormous crash. There was a blaring alarm as the machine ended our game prematurely, the word *TILT* flashing on the LED display.

"Stupid fucking game," he said, stomping off as I put in another token.

Unfortunately, his slam had damaged some mechanism in the machine. As I started the *Metamorphosis* mode, I realized the left flipper now juddered, making the required ramp shot impossible. My mode timed out, and I was left to play out the rest of my balls unmetamorphosed. Overall, I scored less than a billion points.

I was inspecting some type of rhythm game when Selene returned with El draped around her shoulders, sipping on a drink with an umbrella in it.

"What?" she said, looking at me.

"You look very glam," I said. "Where'd you get the fur shawl?"

"She likes me." Selene reached over her shoulder to pet El, who stretched like a cat.

"Unbelievable, El. No loyalty at all."

"I heard an awful slamming noise a few minutes ago," Selene said. "Is everything okay?"

I turned to look at Artem, who was whaling on a punching bag game like it owed him money. The display read "999" and candies were starting to overflow the dispenser slot.

"Yeah, we're good," I said. "Check this out, though."

My udjat had informed me earlier that the device in front of us was a rhythm game, but deductive reasoning told me something more specific. The top of the platform was square, divided into a three-by-three grid by long grooves. I could recognize a *Dance Dance Revolution* or *Pump It Up*-type game when I saw one—those arcade games where arrows flew up the screen to the pulsing beat of Eurodance or J-pop. I was pretty damn good at them, too.

I stood in the middle of the platform and pressed three tokens down into the circular depression. There was a loud click as they were whisked away, and text bloomed on my contact.

Prize awarded based on number of hits.

Twin pairs of thick bamboo rods rose up from the grooves in the platform.

"Interesting," said Selene.

"Ah . . . this is not what I expected."

"Now I know some funny shit is about to go down," El said, as the rods swung together and smacked my ankles.

You achieved an overall rank of C. You were hit fifteen times. Ouch!

I groaned and bent down to feel my ankles, which were already bruising.

You received a reward: Scroll of Fuse Weapon.

Combines two random weapons in your inventory with unpredictable effects. Single use item. Use by signing *U-S*.

That seemed a surprisingly good reward for a rank of C. I'd have to think carefully about how to use it, which weapons to use it on. I could probably game the system by dropping all but two weapons, forcing it to be used on them. *Just imagine all the weapons you could craft*, I thought. *Fire sabers. Gun swords. Ice spears.*

"Hey!" I yelled at Artem. "Come check this out! Wait, what the—"

The scroll flashed hot white, and then crumbled to dust. I checked my inventory, and nothing seemed different. It was mostly full of supplies. Then I realized that my pellet gun had vanished. Only Purgator, my ridiculously named plunger, remained.

Artem jogged over, covered in a sheen of sweat. "What?"

"I was holding this scroll, and then as soon as I asked you to come over, it consumed itself."

It made no sense. All I'd done was beckon him over—extend my hand in his direction, two fingers out, and then close those fingers to a fist . . .

The kada reads all your hand movements as potential inputs, Hilbert had warned us. *Accidents happen.*

"Shit," I said. "I think I accidentally used it."

CHAPTER THIRTY-TWO

Purgator

(Strive 11:4)

I turned my plunger, Purgator, over in my hand, and saw that it had been newly augmented with a trigger on the handle. Bizarrely, it was also now equipped with what appeared to be a safety switch. Other than that, it looked almost the same as ever, gaudy and ridiculous, with its brass handle and gem-encrusted suction cup. Clearly, the Scroll of Fuse Weapon had combined my pellet gun and plunger. But what exactly did that entail?

I toggled the safety to the Fire setting, placed my finger on the trigger, and pressed it down.

With a *thwip* sound, the plunger's cup ejected upward, spun through the air, and stuck to the ceiling of the arcade far above us. We all craned our necks back, dumbfounded, especially Artem and Selene, who'd never seen the plunger before.

At first, I wondered how I'd get it back, but then I saw that the cup trailed a nearly invisible thread behind it. As soon as I released the trigger, the line began to reel itself back in like a tape measure. But instead of the plunger cup returning to me, the handle yanked me up into the air.

The floor rushed away from me as I clung onto the plunger's handle. The ceiling approached quickly, and I switched hands on the plunger to hastily sign Harden. Aura flared about me a moment before I slammed into the ceiling, with a speed that would've pancaked me.

"You okay up there?" called El, her voice small and far below as my ears popped.

Both of my hands were white-knuckled as I gripped Purgator's haft. "Obviously not," I said, as the ceiling started to blacken from my coat of flames. "Why does this keep happening to me?" I looked down, then back up again, and in a lower voice muttered, "I hate heights."

The safety switch on the plunger could be toggled between Fire and Release. It seemed pretty clear what the second option was for, but dangling this far above the floor made it seem like a bad idea. The ceiling suddenly sagged as it continued to burn.

"Y'all probably want to move," I said.

"What?" bellowed Artem. "Speak up."

"I said—"

There was a crack and a stretched-out moment of falling, and then I crashed down on top of a Galaga machine, turning it into scrap metal that immediately burst into flames. The others backed up as my heat spread through the room, setting grassy ornaments on fire.

"Be right back," I said, as I ran from the arcade, leaving a trail of smoke and flames. I dashed through the cave's entrance and plunged through the waterfall to splash down with a cloud of steam in the rocky pool outside. Then, I waded out and went another few meters for good measure before I detonated.

With an enormous bang, an eruption of sand and rocks flew everywhere, and I ended up standing in a dug-out half-sphere, sand slowly pouring back in to bury me up to my knees. I sighed and decided to stay outside for a bit, and without intending to, dozed off to sleep.

"That was something else." El's silhouette was next to me, and I startled awake.

"Sorry. That tail-end explosion tired me out more than I thought." I paused. "How long was I out?"

"A few hours. The big one went to sleep, says to be up by twenty. I don't know where the lady is."

Twenty meant twenty-thousand on the epoch timer, I supposed. I took it as a vote of confidence that they knew I'd be fine. "You should sleep, too. I wanted to practice with Purgator a bit more."

"You know raccoons are nocturnal, right?" El twitched her whiskers. "But I get it. Oh, by the way, there's a back entrance to the resort. So you don't have to get soaked every time." She padded off across the sand.

Then I was alone, seemingly for the first time in a while, with only the occasional *thwip* of my plunger breaking the silence of the night. By the beach, the stars were twinned in the glassy ocean, making the sky seem twice as tall as it should've been.

I shot my plunger for a while before growing bored and heading over to the other side of the waterfall, stepping lightly to avoid waking any crabs. As El had said, there was another way in, a small aperture that led to a rocky tunnel. No pounding waterfall guarded this entrance, only dense shrubbery that obscured the opening.

Outside the passageway, Selene sat with her arms wrapped around her knees, chin tucked to her chest, her slender figure almost swallowed up by the moonless night. I thought about leaving her be, but she'd see me if I walked past her to the entrance. I approached and sat down beside her in the sand.

For a long time, we were silent, and I didn't think she would speak. She didn't acknowledge my presence in any way, just stared out at the sea and the stars. Then she said something in a quiet voice.

"I'm sorry, I didn't catch that," I said.

"You need to work on your finger independence," Selene repeated.

"Um." I had heard the words correctly the first time, but it was so out of left field that I hadn't parsed them.

"Practice with me." Selene turned to me with surprising intensity in her eyes. Her fingers flashed before me, and a small flame flickered. "Copy me. You don't have this spell, but copy the motions."

I did my best, signing laboriously. It wasn't a sequence of letters I'd practiced. I formed the letters *T-H-E-R-M-O-S*. As expected, nothing happened, but Selene was looking at me oddly. "You can't follow my signing, can you? You're guessing."

She made the signs slower, and this time I saw that the sequence was *T-H-E-R-M-E*.

I felt foolish. I'd relied on context clues and a faulty memory instead of using my eyes. Carefully, I formed the signs. *Therme.*

"Good, now this one. As fast as you can." *Cryos.* She signed this one slowly for me, and I had an odd realization.

"It's odd that it's American Sign Language specifically," I said. "Shouldn't there be multiple different systems?"

Selene just shrugged. "You'd have to take that up with the one who created this place. But it's not so difficult to memorize. For now, there's no need to focus so much on the *why*. Let's first worry about the *how*."

I snapped back into focus. *Cryos*, I signed quickly. She nodded and continued.

After some time, my fingers were moving a bit easier, and I wondered if my dexterity stat had anything to do with it. Or maybe those long-lost hours of tickling the ivories had been useful after all. Finally, she dropped her hand to her side. "Practice left-handed, too," she said. "It might come in handy someday."

"Thank you," I said. "You teach well."

She gave me a smile that made my chest tighten. "Helping you helps me." Then, she looked away, back toward the water.

I'd lost friends before. I knew something of grief and the relief that distraction could bring. I wished that I could help more, say something more. But everything I could think of, any insight or comfort, seemed comically small, almost insulting. I suspected her dead friend had been more than a friend, and if Mia had seduced him, wouldn't that constitute a kind of betrayal? And then for him to just be gone, not giving her the satisfaction of an explanation, argumentation, or even empty excuses. Hate them? Avenge them? I couldn't imagine the storm of emotion going through her head, and her face gave me no hint of it.

So I did what I could, which was sit there by the well-hidden passage with Selene and her well-hidden pain. The sea was like glass, and together we watched the turning of the mirrored stars, above and below, clockwise and counterclockwise, like an old cassette unwinding the night, unspooling dawn.

CHAPTER THIRTY-THREE

¡Arriba!

(Strive 11:4)

Piña coladas from the resort's breakfast bar helped wash the cloying taste of advancement pills from my mouth. My strength was now at Mediocre, and my dexterity at **Una Poca de Gracia**, courtesy of the Swedish Fish looted from Moby Dicksicle. My magic continued to hover at **Unacceptable**, since I always passed those pills to El.

"What's with the level names?" I asked Selene, wrapping kalua pig and loco moco in banana leaves and stowing them in my inventory. "It's like they're all insults."

"Sender's sense of humor." She piled rice noodles onto a plate. "People usually don't go by those. If you're being technical, people will use decimal RGB or gem names."

"What do you mean?"

"See the color of your bracelet?" Artem jumped in. "With decimal RGB, we define each color component as varying from one to one hundred. Your levels stand around 20-20-5, in red-green-blue order, which tells us you are primarily focused on strength and dexterity."

"What about gem names?" El asked.

Artem sniffed, and Selene smoothly responded, "Visual descriptors. So yours would be around 5-5-25 in decimal RGB, but it could also be described as azurite."

"A bit needlessly poetic," Artem said.

"Still," I insisted, "the official names are the weird ones, right?"

Selene shrugged. "He may have created the system, but that doesn't mean we can't have our own interpretations."

"As expected of a pagan," muttered Artem. "You should have more respect for the creator—oy!"

El swiped a roll from Artem's plate and ran outside, chittering. I rubbed my eyes. It was barely light out, and the last five digits of my epoch timer were just over twenty thousand. Doing some mental arithmetic, that meant we'd slept less than three hours. *Well*, I reminded myself, *we're not on vacation here.*

"So what's your strength at, Artem?"

He paused. "It's 'Nothing to write home about.'"

"Seriously?"

We finished our meal and packed up, which meant stripping the place bare of anything that'd fit in our inventories. The arcade machines wouldn't go in, but the decorations and towels did, as well as ample food and drink and our winnings from the arcade, mostly a large haul of stat candies.

"Keep some health bars and refreshing drinks outside your inventory," Selene said. "Easier access."

"I'm not a kangaroo," said El. "No pockets, unfortunately."

Luckily for us, the supplies from Shinar included a couple straps and bits of cloth, and Artem was able to fashion a makeshift holster that fit around a raccoon-sized waist. El was able to carry a few items this way, and to my surprise, took to it rather well, carrying them around like a little backpack.

"Man, I wish I had my phone camera," I said. "This would do numbers on social media."

"Piss off."

"My reading had the next floor's entrance slightly northeast of here, at a substantial elevation," said Selene. "It should be up the cliffside by the waterfall. Our target will have already ascended by now."

"Let's roll out, then," said Artem.

"Aye-aye, captain."

We set off in the direction Selene had pointed, Artem in front, followed by her, with me and El taking up the rear. All of us chewed on various candies as we went. Mine was an Atomic Fireball, since I was trying to push my way to the Power Strike skill.

The path upward was steep and winding, one side exposed to a long drop with jagged rocks below. We tried to advance slowly and steadily, but it still felt sketchy as hell. Once, during the climb, I slipped on a patch of moss and almost fell, taking El with me. She decided to give me more space after that.

As we walked, I spent some time testing Purgator's new capabilities. Last night's practice had improved my aim somewhat. On the beach, I'd been missing more shots than I was hitting, even on stationary objects. But now, after a few attempts, I managed to stick a seagull in midair. It dragged the line around like a kite until I flipped the safety to the *Release* position and let it flap away, squawking indignantly.

It was midday when we came upon the chasm. Artem and Selene waited for us at a ledge where a rockslide had demolished a good chunk of the path, leaving a gap where the cliff plunged down to the sea. Artem eyed the far side, a good thirty feet away.

He thrust his hand into a series of gestures, and his bracelet flared crimson as he slowly knelt down into a racer's starting position. He was going to use Power Strike on his legs.

A moment later, Artem exploded off the ledge, tearing chunks of rock away from the cliff. He hung above the gap for a moment before coming down in a roll on the other side. Pebbles tumbled down to the surf below.

"I could make that, easy," said El.

"No you couldn't. But maybe I can." I backed up a few steps and unholstered my plunger. "I'm going to try something."

Eyeing a rocky outcropping above, I fired the cup. It stuck, and the trailing rope went taut. I leaned back experimentally, letting the line take my entire body weight, and Purgator held fast. I jumped up and down vigorously, and the plunger never moved.

"I don't know about this one," said Selene.

"Me neither," I responded, and jumped.

Wind rushed past my face as I swung through the air like a janitorial Spiderman. *Don't look down*, I told myself. *Don't fucking look down.* I pinwheeled my feet for what seemed like an eternity until they met solid rock again, then retracted the plunger. It snapped back to me, jarring my hand.

I was across.

Artem stood next to me, eyeing me with what seemed like slight respect. Or alarm. "Big risk for a small reward."

"Says the one who jumped." I gave him a grin, slightly crazed with adrenaline. "How long do you think we'd have been stuck here if I shoved candies down my throat till I unlocked Power Strike?"

Artem grunted, then jerked his head over at El and Selene on the far side. "What about them?"

Images of Tarzan and Jane clouded my head for a minute before I dismissed them. Hefting the plunger, I aimed it at El. "I have an idea for this one, at least."

"This is fucked up," El complained, dangling above the abyss. Recovery items spilled out of her harness as she slowly rotated.

"Sorry," I said, "but this is the only way." I hoisted the raccoon up, and she scrabbled onto the solid ground.

Selene called something, but her voice was too quiet to hear. She repeated herself.

"What is she saying?" I asked.

"She says, 'Hold it tight,'" Artem rumbled.

"Oh," I said. "Sure, we can do that—ow! El, what the fuck?"

El released her teeth from my ankle. "Maybe do a little brainstorming next time before sticking me with the dirty plunger. That thing's been in a lot of places."

"My bad," I said, firing the cup at Selene's side of the gap. She picked it up and pressed it down to the rock, stepping on it a few times to ensure it held fast. I walked backward until the rope went taut. "Artem, can I get some help?"

Wordlessly, he grabbed the rope and pulled back, and we watched as Selene made her way across elegantly and hopped down onto our side. A second later, I realized that a towerquake just then could've been disastrous. The thought must've shown on my face.

"What?" said Selene.

"Nothing. Let's go."

Further walking brought us to a place where the wall of rock on our left fell away, turning our path into a thin ridge like a dragon's spine. Dry brush and craggy rock shot down steeply to water on either side. The sky was painterly with pinks and oranges to the west and blues and grays to the east.

I noted that I wasn't breathing heavily at all. I hadn't been particularly fit before the tower climb, but even with my strength stat sitting at Mediocre, a steep multi-hour hike felt like a walk in the park.

The calls of the seagulls and the ocean breeze made everything feel strangely peaceful. Things were simpler here in Strive. Yes, there were homicidal bookbats and giant enemy crabs, but those were simple problems, in a sense. Hit them with a stick enough times and they went away.

Lost in daydreaming, I stumbled over a rock, and something whizzed past me, right where my head had been. It splatted behind me, and I caught a whiff of coconut.

"Shields," cried Artem, and I ran forward before thrusting my hand into the six signs that would surround me with flames.

Another coconut slammed into me, cracking on my aura. It smelled amazing for a moment as it toasted, then burned. Looking up, I saw a monstrous palm tree the size of a building. It had been motionless a second ago, but now it swayed back and forth unnaturally as it flung the heavy fruits down at us like cannonballs. A face that had opened up on the tree's trunk blinked at me with a surprised expression, as if astonished I'd blocked the attack.

As I advanced, the palm began pelting me with a machine-gun barrage of coconuts that pushed me back with its sheer volume. Each fruit burst against me, showering me in a way that felt somewhat not-safe-for-work.

A sharp series of cracks signaled that El had arrived, but as the tree swung out of the way, her Firecrackers went wide. I turned back to see Artem shielding Selene, while a stream of violet energy—black in my red-filtered vision—connected them. But they were pinned down; it wasn't like Artem could abandon her to go on the offensive. With an unexpected pang of sadness, I realized that my burning shield could never be used to protect others. Even now, El was out in the open unguarded, hopping back and forth to dodge stray coconuts.

"Hit the middle of the trunk," Artem yelled. "As low as you can. That'll disconnect its circulatory system."

"Easier said than done," I said under my breath. With a gesture, I summoned Purgator and fired it at the tree, but the cup was knocked astray by a well-aimed coconut. Gritting my teeth, I retracted it and fired again. This time, the tree leaned out of the way of my shot with incredible elasticity, and it landed in the bushes behind it.

"Motherfucker," I said, yanking the rope back. "Stay still, you sorry excuse for a tree."

El shot a series of explosions that made the palm focus fire on her for a bit, and that gave me the opening I needed to land a plunger shot with a satisfying *thunk*. I jumped at the tree and yanked Purgator toward me. The momentum of the retracting rope catapulted me forward as the world blurred past.

I smashed through the trunk and burst out the other side in a shower of splinters, leaving behind a me-shaped hole. "Oh, yeah," I cried, landing on the ground. "Shit, that felt amazing—"

The entire remaining crop of coconuts fell on top of me as the tree shook them off in its death throes. It was too much for my shield to bear, and the aura winked out as exhaustion and toasting coconuts buried me.

Muffled voices came through the pile of coconuts, before a pinhole of light appeared. A flash of purple light peeked through, and I felt soreness and pain vanish. But I still had no energy to move, and I had to wait until a pair of thick arms reached in and yanked me out.

I rolled over onto my back, then choked as refreshing liquid was poured down my throat. "Okay, okay, I'm good," I sputtered, turning away from the stream.

"You don't look good," Selene said.

"That hurts," I said. "Looks-wise, I'd consider myself at least a seven out of ten."

"Not with that coconut shell on your head," Artem replied.

I laughed, brushed the fragment off, then coughed again. *Was that humor? From him, of all people?* "Well, at least we know how to turn off my shield without the explodey side effect," I said. "I just need to run myself completely dry and pass out. That was a joke."

Artem had a thoughtful look on his face I didn't like. "Harden doesn't consume energy passively, but your variant must, to give off so much heat. Even though the human body stores over a hundred thousand calories of energy, the kada system only has access to some of it. Prevents things like ketoacidosis. So burn through your allotment, and there's no more energy left to combust. What?"

I was staring at Artem.

"I was a doctor before." He shrugged his massive shoulders. "A well-rounded education is important."

"Fainting is not a strategy," I said firmly. "That's even worse than exploding. Let's move before this tree tips over on us."

"With each second, Mia only gets further ahead," Selene agreed.

The palmón—that's what the udjat called it, anyway—was almost fully blackened, with the me-shaped hole still burned through the center of it. Some of the coconuts had spilled stat-augmenting candies instead of juice, and we took a moment to loot these before moving to the other side, where a cliff awaited. A barrel hovered a few inches off the ground, pointing into the horizon.

Twelfth floor barrel was the description, and I had a distinct feeling this mode of transportation was cribbed from *Donkey Kong Country*. That meant I knew exactly what to expect when the barrel launched me into the sky, and I definitely didn't scream like a little girl.

CHAPTER THIRTY-FOUR

Flush

(*Strive 12:1*)

Three-of-a-kind." Grak turned his cards over and laid them on the table with a toothy grin. "Read 'em and weep."

"Flush." Krogz kept his face carefully composed, but the slight rise of one corner of his mouth betrayed his satisfaction.

"Motherfuck." Grak pushed his remaining chips across the table brusquely. "Got me on the river, you lucky bastard. I'm tapping out. Enjoy yourselves." He moved to stand.

Complaints rose up around the smoke-filled den. Security detail was always drab, with long stretches of monotony punctuated by rare moments of excitement. Gambling was one of the few ways they had to amuse themselves. Well, it was almost better to be trudging around the dank halls, skewering rats and making idle passes at the ladyfolk, than to be getting cleaned out of your whole paycheck by the likes of Krogz. Sometimes, you just had to know when to quit.

The obligatory accusations—being a pussy, lacking balls, et cetera— followed Grak as he retrieved his spear from the wall rack and stepped out into the hall. He flared his nostrils, snuffing deeply of the outside air. It was fresher here, away from that pipe smoke. Grak had never taken up the devil's lettuce the same way most of the Sector B crew did. The way it smelled, it was more like the devil's armpit, as far as he was concerned.

Grak had grown to manhood here amid the twisting steel corridors. They shifted and rerouted themselves on occasion, but that was no matter to him. His feet always knew how to carry him from his quarters to the mess hall or to one of the scattered security rooms that monitored the live feeds. They were supposed to be scanning for intruders, but there hadn't been any for a long time, so they mostly ended up playing cards instead. And smoking the devil's armpit. *Heh, I'll have to write that one down.*

Grak was congratulating himself on his wit when he found himself tumbling suddenly onto the floor. *Hmm, that's odd*, he thought. *Who is that in front of me, and where'd their head go?*

With sudden horror, he realized that the well-muscled body in front of him was his own. He could see the ancient scar across his back, his own hand still gripping his well-loved spear. Blood spurted noisily from the stump of his neck. Three humans were there, and a small gray-furred creature that was unfamiliar to him.

The muscled man in front wiped black blood off his fist with a fluffy white towel. He seemed like the leader, as he was the largest of them, and likely he'd been the one who'd decapitated Grak. Next to him stood another male, this one with softer features. He leaned on what looked like a plunger, seeming queasy as he spoke something in the human's strange, rounded language.

A female who looked similar to him said something in response. Well, all humans looked similar, but this one was maybe of the same . . . clan? Tribe? More similar than most.

The gray-furred creature chittered, and Grak decided this was the group's pet. It was strange that they'd bother keeping something around with so little meat on its bones, and such an irritating voice.

The large human noticed that Grak was still conscious and barked a laugh. In a blink, a knife was sailing through the air toward Grak. There was a wet and final-sounding *thunk*, and the world went black.

"My little lancet," Artem rumbled as he jiggled the knife out of the dead common orc's head. "Good for us close-ranged fighters to keep a trick or two up our sleeves."

"Good tip," I said, trying not to throw up. It'd probably cost me a few strength points if I did. I stared at the headless body. Despite its green-tinged skin, the creature looked far too human for comfort. I made to steady myself against a wall, found it slick with an unknown substance, and reconsidered. "These guys aren't sentient, right?"

"Nope," said Artem.

"I don't believe so," said Selene.

"And if they are, they're probably assholes," said El.

"Right then." I pinched my nose shut with my clean hand. "This corpse smells really bad. Can we talk shop somewhere else?" Selene wore a strange expression on her face. "Why are you looking at me like that?"

I turned just in time to see a shadow looming over me. The orc's headless body was still alive, driven by instinct or hatred or a desire for revenge. As I raised an arm to defend, it brought down a dirty-looking dagger and cut me, and I felt immediately sick. I threw a sloppy haymaker that pushed his body back to the floor, where it twitched and stopped moving.

You've been inflicted with Super-Tetanus! Your dexterity has decreased to Worm.

Suddenly, my muscles spasmed and I fell, arching my back. My plunger clattered to the floor. I could almost hear the rush of toxins through my veins as sweat drenched through my clothes.

Selene was at my side immediately. Her fingers danced, and violet light poured from her outstretched hands onto me. My fingers moved uncontrollably, and for a panicked moment, I worried I'd set everyone aflame by accident. My chest spasmed, and I couldn't breathe.

I couldn't breathe. Darkness crept in at the corner of my vision. I reached toward Selene with my hand and saw that it was black, too.

"Purge," I managed through gritted teeth. According to Kieran, who'd upgraded my plunger, it now had the ability to Purge me of afflictions. Could anyone use that or only me? *Should've tested earlier,* I thought with a pang of regret.

I kicked the plunger toward Artem, and he picked it up, looking confused. "Purge," I gasped. "Sign *Purge.* Then hit me with it."

Finally, he got it, spelling the word with his kada hand. Nothing happened for a moment, then I saw a mote of violet light drift over to the plunger's haft.

"Ready?" he asked.

I nodded and closed my eyes. *Plungerize me, cap'n.*

A klaxon blare drowned out my thoughts, and red lights began to strobe across the metal corridor. Some kind of PA system buzzed and cracked with what sounded like harsh static. I realized that it was a sort of language, all hissed sibilants and guttural throat sounds. I assumed they weren't reading the weather report.

Two orcs burst out of a smoky room, and Artem quickly stuck my chest with the plunger before turning around and swinging a *Power Striked* elbow that knocked one into the other. He gave the plunger haft two pumps, and I felt poison leach out of me. "Good," I croaked. "More."

He had to turn to fend off another band of orcs, and Selene took up plunging duty. She stood over me, and each pull of the plunger siphoned another stream of poison that looked like black tar as it dissipated. The color began to return to my extremities. "How much longer?" she said.

"Almost there, I think."

El was cackling as she ignited a circle of explosions around us, turning multiple orcs into a mess of flying limbs, but more closed in. Artem was almost surrounded, too.

You've been cured of Super-Tetanus! Your dexterity has returned to Una Poca de Gracia.

I got up shakily, my face flushed. "Thanks," I said to Selene. "I owe you one."

"Later," Artem shouted, indicating the oncoming mob. "Now, we run."

We didn't have time to loot any bodies; doors were slamming open all around, and shouts echoed through the maze-like passages.

El sent one last roll of thunder at the horde before we bounced. "This is fun," she cried. "Did you see that one's head explode?"

"Gray midget bear, if you have breath to talk, you aren't running as fast as you should."

"The fuck'd you call me?"

Artem seemed to know where he was going. He took us through side-alleys, up spiraling stairways, and past narrow passages. Many times, we had to press against a wall and wait for orcish patrolmen in cruel, spiked armor to pass. But slowly and surely, the tramping of boots and sirens fell behind us.

"One last turn," Artem said, and we rounded a corner into a wide open space. But there was no elevator to be seen. It was a wide open room, some kind of cafeteria or mess hall, the smell of roasted chicken filling the air.

"I don't think this is the right way, coach," I said, as a hundred muscled orcs turned from their lunches to stare at us.

CHAPTER THIRTY-FIVE

Food Fight

(*Strive 12:2*)

The orcs surged toward the four of us in a chaotic wave of green bodies. Their mouths opened wide, spittle-flecked, as they gnashed and snarled. Tables were upturned in the frenzy, food flying everywhere.

They cook their meals, I thought numbly. There was even a buffet line, formerly orderly, of orcs loading their trays with mashed potatoes and peas. Now they were scrambling over themselves to get at us, some of them still holding their forks and knives.

El was the first to break for the exit, but it slammed shut, and a heavy bar fell across it with an echoing boom, as an ear-piercing alarm began to blare. The only other way out lay at the far side of the room, past the horde.

Artem shouted something and his shield flared to life, but I was too close to activate mine—the heat would cook El and Selene if I tried. So I ran toward the massed lump of orcs, summoning Purgator into my hand as I went. I fired the cup at a nearby **Orcish Patrolman**, who was a few meters away, pulled hard, and the rope yanked the creature off his feet. Another whip of the handle caused him to slam into his companions, knocking them down as they cursed in fury.

Crackling explosions like fireworks strobed across the room. I turned back for a moment to see Selene and El behind Artem's shield. El was casting repeated Firecrackers, while Selene pulled a pile of health bars and refreshing drinks out and scattered them onto the floor between them. Then, she made three signs with her hand, and the whole room went white.

It was like the full moon had descended upon the orcish mess hall. Her immense Lux spell blinded the orcs, and they threw up their hands and shrieked. I cast Harden as I slammed into their front lines, and the sickly odor of burning flesh joined the food smells in the air. Even burning and blind, they grabbed and struck at me, and I felt the mass of bodies threaten to bury me alive. More weight was added every passing second, pushing the air from my lungs. My plunger was trapped against my side, and in a moment, I might not even be able to move my kada hand.

With a flash of my fingers, I detonated. A ringing sound in my ears replaced the din of battle as the pile of orcish bodies disintegrated around me. Those were the fortunate ones. The ones further back were left mangled, but still breathing, blood spurting from new orifices and stumps. I pushed myself off the ground, gasping for air, but not even two seconds later, more of the brutes were pressing forward to fill the gap, wading through a sea of their companions' body parts.

I aimed Purgator skyward and fired, felt a jolt through the rope, and flew up, one or two orcs still clinging to my legs stubbornly before I kicked them off. For a moment, I caught a glimpse of Artem chopping three orcs in half with an elbow strike, severed bodies falling to his feet. Through the mess of bloody explosions and strobing lights, I could see that our party was being overwhelmed.

As I sped upward, pulled by the retracting line, individual bodies below blended into a crowded mass, our small half circle by the door surrounded by a shifting swarm of green and black. My plunger slammed into the steel rafters, and I half-accidentally flipped up to land on top in a wobbly crouch.

The open door at the other side of the mess hall was now practically unguarded. All the orcs were clumped up near our party.

Downing a refreshing drink, I wished I had a ranged spell, like El's Firecracker. From up here, I'd be able to pick off the orcs at my leisure. Instead, all I had was a dumpster fire of an ability and my war plunger. Well, I'd use what I had. With a shift of my hand, my flaming cloak relit.

"I fucking hate heights," I said to myself, pushing off the rafters.

Wind screamed in my ears as I burned toward the ground like a flailing meteor. Then, after a second, or an eternity, impact.

The floor cratered, and a blast of wind and heat rippled outward to bowl over the nearby horde. I felt a searing pain in my kneecaps, but the unlucky orc underneath me splattered like a Fruit Gusher. I unwrapped a health bar with shaky hands and swallowed it whole.

The others were almost completely backed up to the locked door. Selene's light spell flickered, now and again obscured by a writhing mass of orcish bodies, and shakily I got to my feet and began limping over while my bones knitted themselves together. Almost immediately, I was set upon by a mass of orcs and forced to detonate again.

But more came, and while I tried to down a grape-flavored refreshing drink, they were on me. I didn't have Harden activated, and I panicked, flailing my plunger uselessly. A dozen claws and bites broke my skin, and dirty utensils stabbed at me. I screamed, and the orcs stopped for a moment and looked up.

For a moment, I thought they'd been shocked by my cry, but then I felt it—a low rumbling that grew more and more severe, as orcs dove under tables like frightened schoolchildren. I glanced at the others, and they all looked back at me with the same bewilderment that must've been on my face.

Now instead of the roar of combat, the only sound was the periodic wail of the siren. It was quiet enough for me to hear Artem's cry of "Towerquake!"

Gravity went sideways, and I slammed against the edge of a table, then careened off of it to knock into the buffet cart. I was coated in side dishes—mashed potatoes, gravy, a sprinkling of peas, topped off with cranberry sauce—before coming to a stop in an industrial-sized vat of vanilla pudding, which I knew was vanilla flavored because I landed in it face-first.

Then the second shock came, and I launched across the room again, but this time I stuck my plunger down onto a table and clung onto it until the shaking passed.

There was a moment of stillness as the sprinklers came on, then the floor where I had landed from the rafters collapsed. With a terrible squeal, it caved downward, and tables began to slide toward the bottom, orcs still huddled under them, now scrabbling to get free. That additional weight caused the floor to give way entirely, and it swung open like a trapdoor, revealing harsh tropical sun from the floor below. It was a long fall with nothing underneath but the sea, and choruses of orcs yelled and screamed as they went over, accompanied by tables still laden with food.

The floor began to tilt under me, and I shot my plunger toward the exit, pulling myself toward it. Selene and Artem were running in that direction as well, El riding on Selene's shoulder, as the three of them dodged runaway tables and orcs sliding toward the widening gap in the floor. We passed through the exit, slamming the door behind us. The alarm finally faded.

My vision blurred, and I staggered. In those last moments when I hadn't been Hardened, I'd taken more cuts and stab wounds than I'd thought. My own blood commingled with orcish fluid and gravy, and I prayed I didn't contract some weird blood disease.

"Selene," I said. "Can I get some healing over here?"

She was about to cast her spell on me when something burst through the doorway. From the gap emerged a monstrous green face, gnashing its teeth at us. It looked similar to the orcs we had fought, but was so large that only its head fit through the door.

"An ogre," Artem said after Examining it. "Floor boss. A bit late to the party, but unfortunately for us, it's here now."

The thing looked like it could eat me for breakfast and El for dessert. It strained against the doorway, pushing to get to us, cracking the hinges as they peeled away from the wall. I backed up slowly, peas falling from my coating of tapioca.

"I'm no expert," said El, "but maybe we should run?"

Artem yelled "Go!" and none of us needed further convincing. We half hobbled, half ran along the corridor as it became a catwalk, hanging miles over the tropical ocean. From our vantage point, we could see cafeteria furniture still tumbling down with live and dead orcs, until they shrank to dots and disappeared.

At the end of the catwalk, rickety stairs led upward, labeled with the number thirteen. We were so close. But there was a great roar as the ogre tore through the threshold behind us, sending the door flying off the ledge to flutter down to the sea below. We weren't going to make it.

Each step the ogre took shook the entire catwalk. The top of its head was bald, but long strands of filthy hair made a ring around its skull. The eyes were rheumy and filmed with white, and it leered at us with rotting teeth, swaying back and forth. It wore only rags, and its feet were soaked in orc blood and viscera. Uncut toenails protruded like lawn-mower blades.

Artem flung several knives at the monster's face, but they bounced off an arm the size of a tree trunk. As it covered its face, El launched a series of explosions at its kilt. The material lit aflame, but the ogre seemed unfazed.

I stepped toward the ogre, looking back at El, Selene, and Artem.

"Ain't no way you're pulling a Gandalf on us, compadre," said El.

"I don't intend to. Now back up. It's going to get hot."

I moved my hand, and the flaming mantle encircled me, forcing my friends to scramble away from the heat, toward the exit. The ogre screamed and leaped at me, and metal creaked and groaned beneath us. It was too heavy for the catwalk. Or maybe it would've been fine normally, but now, weakened by the heat of my shield . . . I caught Selene's horrified glance for a moment.

There was a crashing sound as the walkway collapsed, and the ogre and I fell.

CHAPTER THIRTY-SIX

Nemo

(Strive 11:5)

Fuck off!"

The islands of the eleventh floor were green-and-white pinpricks far below. Even as the ogre and I tumbled down toward the ocean, the hulking brute was still swimming through the air to get at me. It was ridiculous. Here I was, trying to enjoy my act of noble self-sacrifice, and this lunk was ruining it.

I kicked at the ogre with a burning leg, and it latched onto me. It howled at the pain as its hands burned but refused to release me.

"Let go, you stupid son of a bitch!"

My shield sizzled as we passed through a cloud, water droplets turning to steam. Sea and sky inverted as I twisted against the monster's grip. With my kada hand, I signed *I-N* for inventory and began swiping through for anything that might help. I didn't recall parachutes being on the packing list. Tent stakes, dry rations, water, bedding . . . I selected a large white bedsheet, and it bloomed in my hands, jerking me upward and righting me. That was enough, and the ogre, surprised, relinquished its grip on my leg as it fell past me.

Then the sheet burned to ashes in my hand, and I plummeted again, before summoning another one. *Thank God for overpacking.* I had a good dozen or so of the things in my inventory.

My vision threatened to fade as the heat shield continued to drain my energy, but I knew I couldn't deactivate it. The detonation would probably cause me to pass out entirely, and then even if I survived the impact, I'd drown.

In this stop-start manner, I descended through the tropical sky until slapping down in the ocean. The impact sent a jet of boiling water outward, and bubbles washed around me. Immediately, I felt cold, and my last thought was something about the specific heat of water before I passed out.

Bright white sunlight baking the asphalt. The laughter of children, the repetitive bounce of a slightly under-inflated basketball. It was an in-between time—right before summer break, when the world relaxed into a slower rhythm.

I didn't even panic much when my mother called out my name in that distinct, you're-in-trouble tone of voice. Sure, my heart leaped into my throat a bit, but that was normal. I rolled my eyes at my friends and went inside.

My mother was waiting at the dinner table. She threw a piece of mail down in front of me. "This is very not good," she said in Chinese. "After we took you to all those classes, spent all that money, and you still can't qualify for semifinals?"

So that was what this was about. I fought the urge to grin.

My father was there, too, shaking his head in anger. "Whole this year," he said in English. "Not concentrate on schoolwork. Brain always in game world." He jabbed a finger at another sheet of paper. "How can you save world if you can't even save GPA?"

"USA*MO*, USA*BO*, USA*CO*." My mother listed out the competitions as if they were charges brought against me. "Not a single one passed."

"*USAHO*," I said mildly. "I didn't qualify for that one, either." I didn't expect the backhand swing from my father that struck me on the side of my face.

"You must get some punishment for this," he said.

My jaw stung, but I acted as if I hadn't felt anything at all. "You know, they say corporal punishment doesn't work—"

Another slap cut me off. "Always talk smart, like you know more than us," my mother cried. "If so smart, then why not qualify for competition?"

"You're saying we shouldn't hit you," my father added. "To be honest, we don't want to hit, either."

"Seems like there's an easy solution here," I said.

"But still, you must have some punishment." My father went over to the fish tank where Finneas swam about in his toy castle, none the wiser, and scooped him up.

"No," I said. Finny wasn't much for conversation, but I cared about him. I was the one that fed him every day, cleaned his tank. He would nibble at my fingers for food whenever I trailed them in the water.

But now he was struggling, flopping in my father's grip.

"Put him back," I pleaded, rebelliousness forgotten. "I'll do better, I'm sorry."

But my father just stood there as if deciding what to do. With each passing second, Finneas's flopping grew weaker. I rushed at him, and he put an arm out to hold me off, but my pinwheeling arms smacked him and he dropped Finneas on the hardwood floor. He lost his balance, and as he stumbled, his foot came down on my pet with a sickening squish. Even my father looked stricken for a minute, and then his face turned to disgust as he tried to scrape the fishy mass from his sock.

"Better this way," he said, as if it had all been part of a grand plan. "Less distraction from school."

I cried. Not then, of course, not in front of them, but later in my room. It sounds fucking stupid, but at the time, part of me resolved to harden my heart, to build a kind of barrier around myself. So I wouldn't feel the pain that I had on that early summer's day, when I watched my father scrape the guts of my beloved Finny off his foot and onto the laminated hardwood.

(Strive 10:10)

I coughed and sputtered, vomiting out water from my lungs, and it streamed into the sky. Something was wrong. I looked up, expecting to see the sun, and saw instead, with a sudden sense of vertigo, the glowing light-spell of Shinar, the city hanging upside down above me. A steady stream of utensils, bowls, and half-eaten pieces of food floated gently to the surface, then fell up toward the city.

Something pushed against my feet, and I jerked back to see that it was the ogre's massive corpse, its eyes glazed over. I watched in horror as it breached the surface, hurtling upward toward Shinar. A transparent disc flickered into existence, and the ogre evaporated as it struck the safety zone protecting the city.

While fighting the ice whale, I had seen Shinar below the sea, but I'd thought then that the ocean floor was just made of some kind of solid, transparent material like glass. Now, I realized that it was in fact a strange inversion of gravity, so that the sea had two surfaces, and my momentum from the fall had carried me to the underside, which was the ceiling of the tenth floor. My head, floating above the water, seemed to be trying to lift off my shoulders and fly up to Shinar, which was a discomfiting feeling.

Treading water, I pulled a refreshing drink from my inventory and slammed it, feeling its energy course through my body. Then I dove into the water, dodging dining tables and dead orcs as I followed the brighter tropical sun.

But it was too deep, too far away, and I soon flailed to get back to the Shinar side of the two-faced ocean. I came up, gasping for air. Checking my inventory, I saw that I still had some red Swedish Fish—**Fish of Fortitude**, my udjat called them. Maybe if I finished enough of these, I'd be able to unlock a skill that would help. The trick would be to do so quickly without vomiting.

One by one, at a measured pace, I began eating. Each one was like a punch in the gut, but I forced myself to chew and swallow as more orcish corpses rose out of the water around me to break against Shinar's shield. For a brief moment, I thought I saw a glowing figure in the distance with its arms crossed, but it vanished.

You feel strong! You feel strong! You feel strong! Your strength has increased to Unthreatening! You feel strong! You feel strong! You feel strong! You feel strong! You feel strong—

I choked, and a thin sour-sweet liquid rose up out of me, red like blood.

You feel weak!

I cursed myself for wasting resources, then continued shoving the candies down, at a slower rate. I lost count of the notifications as Shinar's enchanted sun swapped out for a less-bright moon. By the measure of the epoch command, it'd already been hours since I'd fallen here. I wondered if El and the others were looking for me. We were stuck in here, true, but it was still a big world.

I was absentmindedly chewing on one of my last red candies when my strength swelled. **Your strength has increased to Milquetoast!**

Your strength and Corpus aspect have unlocked a new technique!

You've learned the basic technique _Power Strike_, a spell of selective self-enhancement.

Energy consumption: Moderate.

Six characters, ending with a clenched fist, like a suggestion of how to use it. But that wasn't what I wanted it for.

Carefully, I made the signs, and my bracelet, now orange, flared. I wondered if for a brief moment, I looked like the birth of a red star in the evening sky of Shinar. Then I turned away from the city and dove.

(Strive 11:6)

As I kicked out with augmented strength, my newly unlocked technique rocketed me up toward the eleventh floor surface of the ocean. Orcish body parts streamed past me, and I cast the spell again and again, feeling the hollow gnaw of energy drain. Finally, after several casts, I broke the surface, gasping.

Something grabbed me.

I was going to scream before I realized it was Artem, his ruddy glow illuminating the water. For his part, he seemed as surprised as I was.

"You're alive. Power Strike?" he said in his low voice, not quite a question. "When Selene's reading turned up your location underwater . . . we thought . . ."

"You guys came back," I said, rubbing water out of my eyes.

"Don't get blubbery on me." Artem turned and began paddling.

"I'm not," I protested, but he didn't listen. I sighed and started to follow.

El and Selene weren't hard to spot; her Lux spell was like a floodlight in the evening sky. As I got closer, she snapped it off, and I saw both of them standing up, El on her hind legs. We waded out of the water, and I felt my legs wobble.

"Don't ever fucking do that again," said El. "That hero shit is so whack."

"I'm sorry. I didn't mean to, I swear—"

Selene punched me in the stomach half-heartedly. "That was for El." Then, looking into my eyes, she slugged me again.

"And that was for me."

She readied another fist. "And this one's for Artem—"

"Okay," I gasped. "I get it, I get it."

She pulled me in tight. El jumped on my shoulder, and it felt good to have her fuzzy warmth there. Artem stood aside, and I looked at him for a moment until he rolled his eyes and joined, patting me on the back.

For a brief moment, things were good.

CHAPTER THIRTY-SEVEN

Small Magic

(Strive 11:7)

El unlocked a new spell that evening as we rested in the Atlantis Resort lodging. We didn't have any tokens left and, possibly for that reason, the entrances to the restaurant and Midway had actually disappeared, leaving only a solid wall where they'd been. No restaurant meant no breakfast bar, which meant no piña coladas and mai tais. It was a sorry state of affairs.

"Hat Trick," El read, as she lay on her back on the corner of my bed. "Fires illusory rabbits from a hat, number fired dependent on magic level, blah blah blah. Rabbits do not interact with physical matter."

"So that makes four now. Along with Firecracker, Airbrush, and Pickpocket." I was noodling on my Aetherphone as I leaned back on an abundance of pillows. "Try it out, I guess."

El brought her hands together and signed, and the room flashed with blue light. Suddenly, I was staring into the brim of a large magician's hat, pointed at me like a cannon.

There was a sound halfway between a squeak and a boom as something fuzzy and white shot straight at me. I instinctively covered my face to defend myself, and a stream of illusory rabbits passed through me, evaporating through the wall. I heard a muffled yelp from the adjacent room as they appeared on the other side.

El cackled with glee and prepared to send another wave of rabbits in the other direction, toward Artem's room, when our door burst open.

Selene stood in our doorway, toothbrush in hand, wearing an oversized T-shirt. Her gaze flicked between the two of us, then settled on the raccoon rolling around in chaotic mirth.

"Really?" she said. "Some of us are getting ready for bed."

"My bad," El managed through tears of laughter. "It was an accident."

Selene's mouth twitched. "You are not very convincing."

El dropped down to the floor to nuzzle at Selene's ankle in contrition. "Honest, I swear. Minimal amounts of rabbits, from now on."

Now that we had a moment to rest, my mind returned to the combat in the mess hall. Something about it still did not sit right with me and made it hard to relax.

"Hey," I said, sitting forward. "About those orcs."

Selene nudged El aside to sit down on a chair, folding her hands in her lap. "What about them?"

"I know they were trying to kill us, but they seemed . . . intelligent, if not outright self-aware. They had a buffet line, for Chrissake."

Selene leaned her chin on her hand. "You hadn't seen anything like that before? In your climb."

"No," I said. "Is there more like that? Humanoid monsters."

"There were some on my fourth floor." She paused, as if trying to put something delicately, then grimaced. "But if we can't communicate with them, and they always attack us on sight, what's the difference?"

"It feels like there's a difference," I said. "Maybe I'm just soft."

She smiled. "Maybe."

"Right. No sense turning the other cheek if they're gonna stick a fork in it." I sighed and rubbed my forehead. My words felt hollow to me.

Selene nodded, then reached down to scratch behind El's ears, and for a while, the only sound was the raccoon's sniffing. "We didn't have raccoons, where I came from."

"Consider yourself lucky," I said. "They're a menace. Like big rats with kleptomania."

El rolled over for Selene to rub her belly. "What do you mean?" purred the raccoon. "I'm all sweetness and light."

"Sweet'N Low, more like," I muttered.

Selene lifted El to her face. "Don't pay any attention to him. How about you spend time with me instead? What do you say?" She wiggled

El's paw affirmatively, and I felt sure the raccoon would've slapped the shit out of me for trying that.

"I can't believe my raccoon is being abducted by a wicked sorceress," I commented. "At least pretend to put up some resistance."

"I don't belong to anybody," El said, looking back and forth between me and Selene. "What's in it for me?"

"Couple candies and some leftover roast chicken," said Selene.

"Deal."

"It's settled then." Selene looked at me and smiled in triumph. "Sleep well." I stuttered a goodnight in response as she carried El from my room and gently closed the door.

It was only a few minutes before the barrage of phantom rabbits started from the other side of the wall.

(Strive 12:3)

"One hundred and forty-six," I said in a low voice to El.

"What?"

"A hundred and forty-six rabbits you sent over last night while I was trying to sleep. I counted. Not quite as restful as counting sheep."

El snickered. "You're the one who's always talking about practicing new spells." She signed *Airbrush*, and her hand left a glowing trail in mid-air. She used it to draw a rabbit.

"Great. Hello, rabbit number one hundred forty-seven." I waved my hand through the picture, and it dissolved. "Goodbye, rabbit number one hundred forty-seven."

We sat in a quiet room on the orcs' level. There was a well-worn poker table in it, and El and I were playing Go Fish. Well, I was attempting to play Go Fish, and El was pocketing the playing cards when I wasn't looking.

"Almost?" said Artem.

"Don't rush me." Selene's fingers danced as shining symbols formed a sleeve around her right arm. She sat cross-legged in front of a giant crab shell she'd pulled from her inventory. Apparently, she and El had gone hunting on the beach while Artem was searching for me in the water. The shells were perfect materials for oracle bone reading, and

Artem was insistent that too long had passed since we last checked on Mia's whereabouts.

Just as the two of clubs was disappearing into El's mouth, Selene drove her hand down onto the shell, and the script flowed into it with a lick of blue flame and a *whip-crack* sound. Artem and I leaned over to see. Even though the network of cracks must've been equally meaningless to both of us, we pretended to look for something in the randomness.

Selene traced the lines with a slender finger, her lips moving silently, eyes closed in concentration. We were painfully quiet as she interpreted for what felt like a whole minute, before she opened her eyes, clear and sharp.

"She doesn't seem to be aiming toward the other Willstones in Strive. It seems she's headed for the bridge back to Eramai."

Artem breathed out slowly and sat.

"That's a good thing, right?" I asked. "The tower won't be weakened further."

"Maybe," said Artem. "But it will be harder to get to her, as well."

"She'll have the home field advantage," commented El.

"Yes," said Artem. "Eramai is mysterious and ancient, much older than our Tower Strive. And we still know very little about it. To travel there would be very dangerous."

"We have our powers, too," I pointed out.

"They won't necessarily translate. This . . ." Selene held up her amethyst bracelet ". . . petty magic of hand and eye is tethered to Strive. The further we stray, the weaker we get." She seemed a bit shaky from the heavy toll of the oracle spell.

"So what do we do?"

"Well," Selene said, "she's not there yet. As far as I can tell, she's somewhere on the thirteenth floor. The bridge is on fifteen, so it's still possible we could catch up in time."

"Are you sure she's going for the bridge?" El asked.

"Yes," said Selene. "That's why I just cast the spell."

I wasn't completely sold on the idea of being able to predict someone's future actions, but obviously things were different in a world where magic existed.

"Although," I said, "it seems it would be difficult to catch up to someone who can move so quickly."

"The ability Interchange requires direct line-of-sight," said Selene. "That should be to our advantage now, since the thirteenth floor is almost always pitch-black."

We passed through the orcish hallways and the lunchroom, now emptied of bodies and newly pristine. It felt odd, like a high school on a Saturday, and it suddenly occurred to me that none of the orcs had dropped any shiny game tokens or stat candy as they died.

CHAPTER THIRTY-EIGHT

e

(Strive 13:1)

We mounted the stairs to the utter darkness of the thirteenth floor. Each of us chewed leftover candies from floor eleven in silence—Artem red, myself green, and Selene and El blue. As we came to the same level as our quarry, our party's mood seemed to darken as well.

"I should've known that the tower would take this chance to throw some spooky bullshit at us," I said, and my voice felt too loud somehow. "Lucky number thirteen."

Selene's Lux spell illuminated a muddy swamp, before the darkness seemed to push back at it, compressing it to a small orb. I tried casting mine, and it was a mere candle, wisping in and out of existence.

"Stay close," Selene said. "I'll lead the way." She stepped forward, and her foot squelched as it sank ankle-deep into the mud.

"El, you'd better ride with her." I couldn't use my flaming Harden spell if the raccoon was too close to me. As a matter of fact, if I were within the reach of Selene's light, any usage of that spell would be a danger to everyone. But if I were too far away, I'd be prone to ambush in the gaping darkness.

Then again, I was more durable than Selene and El. "How about this: I patrol around the outside. Artem can be the up-close defense for our spellcasters."

"Don't presume to make plans for me," grunted Artem, looking even more menacing than usual in the half-light. Despite his words, he moved in closer to the two mages.

I stepped away into the darkness, activating both Harden and my pitifully weak Lux. Mud burbled around my ankles as it boiled, throwing up a stench of decay. My shield of flames combined with my magic lantern to create a flickering light that enabled me to see a few feet. Nothing but mud and scraggly weeds. I swept the perimeter around our party in a wobbly orbit until I bumped into a looming wall.

"Tree trunks," Selene said when I asked. "They go up all the way to the next floor."

The trunk was vast and hard as iron, and my burning aura did nothing to it. I squinted upward and didn't see anything above us other than pitch blackness, then got a bit dizzy and refocused. The surface of the swamp rippled near us, and a bubble popped. I shivered and tried to keep moving. A few seconds later, I shivered again. My hair seemed to be standing on end.

"Feels like we're being watched," El's voice said.

"What?" Artem stopped walking, and there was urgency in his tone.

"I said, someone's watching us."

We stopped moving. There was a splashing sound in the distance, and I tried to cast Examine on it, blindly indicating the rough direction.

???

Error*: *Unable to scan entity. Please ensure that lighting is adequate, and/or approach the entity for better results.

"El," I said, my heart thumping. "Firecracker on three. One, two . . ."

"No!" Artem shouted, a second too late.

BANG! El let loose a Firecracker somewhere in the distance, illuminating the entity briefly. Just as she did, I pointed a curled finger to Examine it.

? Witness

This ?????? ??? ?? ??? floating eye ?? ?? ???? deadly.

???? ?????? ?????? paralytic gaze ?? ??? ??? mental attack ???????

The brief glimpse I caught was of a floating orb with far too many eyeballs. There was a screech, and then a strange whirring sound that grew louder and louder, along with muddy splashes. Artem's voice came rapidly, and he sounded as nervous as I'd ever heard him. "Lights off. Now." The light in Selene's hand went out, and the group of three vanished, replaced by darkness. I deactivated Lux, but a dim red glow still suffused me.

Shit. "I can't—"

The eye was on me. I looked at the floating eye and the eye looked back at me. I looked at the floating eye and the eye looked back at me. My mind turned inward on itself like a snake eating its own tail, like a painting by that surrealist artist. What was his name? Escher. That's right, M. C. Escher, he of the impossible staircases that went around and around and around and around into eternity, and the other one, too—the pencil rendering of the hands drawing hands drawing hands drawing hands drawing hands drawing hands drawing hands drawing hands—*oh God, let me out*—hands drawing hands drawing hands drawing hands drawing hands drawing hands drawing hands—*somebody, please help*—drawing hands drawing hands, and then the world seemed to *jump.* Everyone was gone, and I stood alone in the darkness.

I felt a sudden stab of hunger. Looking down, the mud had completely boiled away, exposing hard-cracked dirt around my burning ankles. A significant amount of time had passed. I'd been frozen, locked in a loop in my own head, for how long? Hours, possibly.

"Artem? Selene? El?" I called each name in turn. "Is anyone there?"

My voice was swallowed up by the infinite dark. It sounded muffled and childlike, and it suddenly seemed to me an attractive idea, if only for an instant, to retreat to the warmth and artificial sun of Shinar, or even the beach with its murderous crabs. Master Shaw was a reasonable man; he would understand.

There was a sound like the riffling of a deck of cards, not far off, and I froze. Inching toward the source, I twitched my fingers, ready to set off an explosion at a moment's notice. The ground rose up out of the muck at a shallow angle, and on that cracked earth, I saw a body lying prone, illuminated by a weak Lux light. *Selene.* I backed up a good distance away to detonate my shield, then ran up next to her.

Her eyes went in and out of focus, and her white robes were stained red and gray. She lay on top of some scrawled characters on the ground that I couldn't read. Sharp burrs stood up out of her skin, and I saw that they were needles. Her braceleted hand looked like a porcupine, pierced through by hundreds of spines. The other hand was unharmed, and I felt a sudden chill. It was almost as if whatever had gotten her had aimed to disable the biggest threat, her spellcasting. There was an uncanny intelligence behind that reasoning. Selene looked at me like she would say something, then her eyes rolled back up in her head as she passed out, her mage light winking out at the same time.

I desperately fumbled a health bar from my pocket, broke some bits off from the corner, and rolled them in my fingers. They crumbled easily, like granola, but as I placed them in her mouth, she hacked violently and turned from me, still unconscious. *Too dry.*

After some thought, I scrounged in my inventory to find a bowl. Using the tail end of Purgator, I ground up the remainder of the health bar in the bowl. The contents of a can of refreshing drink joined the powder, forming a kind of rough slurry. I gently poured a little of the mixture down her throat and waited to see if she would choke. It seemed okay, so I added a little more.

Her eyes fluttered open, and I was surprised at how glad I felt, as she began to cough. As the mixed restorative took effect, two or three needles squeezed out from her skin and fell away.

"Tastes . . . bad . . ." Selene strained.

I squinted at the labels on the bar and soda. "Tofurkey and cherry cola. Sorry."

She said nothing, just closed her eyes, leaving her mouth open, and I fed her another sip of the evil-looking mixture. More needles popped out of her flesh to lay in the muck.

"What happened?" I asked. "The eyeball froze me, and next thing I knew, I was alone."

"We were . . . attacked. Separated."

"By what? Where are El and Artem?"

"Don't know," she murmured. "Tired."

"We can't rest here," I said.

She looked at me, and I saw a deep sadness, more than fear or anger. The resignation that I perceived in her eyes scared me more than the dark.

"Is there an anti-depression candy or something?" I asked.

Selene started laughing weakly, and then she punched me in the stomach as hard as she could, which, somewhat concerningly, didn't hurt at all.

I was alternating feeding Selene painfully small sips of my improvised potion and chewing on candies myself, when text bloomed on my udjat. Another spell unlock.

Your dexterity has increased to Mediocre!

Your dexterity and Corpus aspect have unlocked a new technique!

You've learned the basic technique _Quicken_, a spell of ephemeral speed.

Energy consumption: Minimal.

"Good," said Selene when I told her about it. "Any power we can get will be helpful."

It was the same green aura that Mia had used during our encounter. When I used it, my movements were so quick that they were uncontrollable, and I almost knocked over the bowl of healing gruel. There was a slight drain of energy, but less so than the fiery variant of Harden. When I had time, I'd need to practice with it more. But for now, the priority was finding the rest of our party, so I deactivated it.

"Would an oracle reading help us figure out where El and Artem went?" I asked.

"I'm all out of crab shells," said Selene. She'd recovered enough to talk more, and propped herself up on one elbow. Even in the dim light, I could tell that her eyes had recovered some of their usual clarity. "We need to find something hard and organic, like a bone."

I felt the intensely inappropriate urge to make a that's-what-she-said joke.

CHAPTER THIRTY-NINE

Sound Judgment

(Strive 13:2)

Selene's orb of floating light drifted over the two of us as we waded through the muck. "The only thing the floating eyes can do is paralyze," she said. "They won't hurt you themselves, but there are a myriad of other monsters in the dark." She spoke calmly, as if she were a nature guide on a wilderness safari.

"Fuck." I shivered as I imagined being devoured by some unknown beast, unable to move a muscle. "Do you remember what happened?"

"El shot a Firecracker at the eye as it chased us. She must've panicked, and I caught a glimpse of it in the resulting flash. That was just enough for its paralytic gaze to take effect. Next thing I remember is waking up to the taste of ground-up imitation turkey and soda." She made a *tsk* sound and changed direction slightly, almost bumping into me. "Judging by the spines, I must've been attacked by a hedgeboar in the interim."

"Maybe if we find one of those, we can get you the raw material for your oracle reading?"

"That's right," she said, and clicked her tongue again.

I figured it would be good to activate Quicken again while we searched for enemies. As I formed the seven signs, the world was lit *Matrix*-green. "Sounds like so far on this floor, we've got a big, paralyzing eyeball creature and an unknown spiky thing. Oh, and mud. A metric shit-ton of mud. Anything else?"

Selene stared at me. "What?" she said, and her voice was a slow-motion drawl. "Why are you speaking so quickly?"

With a start, I realized that Quicken had altered my perception, making the whole world crawl like molasses. As Selene blinked at me, I could see her eyelashes move down, then up, in two separate motions. I recalled how fast Mia had grabbed my hand when I had tried to Examine her. She had interrupted me between two signs, which was, in retrospect, an almost inhuman reaction. Her right eye had been green then.

I wondered what my speech had sounded like to Selene just now. Probably a lot like Alvin the chipmunk. Disabling Quicken, I repeated the question.

"Oh," she said. "This is a floor of unknown unknowns. I've passed through before, but never stayed long enough to catalogue the monsters that live here. The floors change, but it's always dark here, and always unpleasant. The only good thing is that Mia's Interchange is effectively neutered without vision. We may recover some lost time."

"That's good," I said. "By the way, what's up with the tongue clicking you were doing earlier?"

"Sound's better than sight here." Selene made the short, sharp noise again. "Echoes can tell you a lot about the environment around you."

"Wow," I said, impressed. "You're like a bat."

Selene looked at me, her eyes impassive in the low light of the Lux spell. She clicked loudly, seemingly more to make a statement than anything, then turned and kept walking. "Multiple trees at thirty meters ahead, fifty meters ahead—right, twenty meters behind . . . and half a meter to the left." She reached out and knocked on the wood next to us. "No sign of a staircase or elevator."

"How did you learn to do this?" I asked. It wasn't a skill as far as I could tell, her kada remaining dark when she demonstrated the ability. This was raw talent and training.

"I was bored a lot as a child." She shrugged. "This was one of the ways I amused myself. I made a game of it, walking around with a blindfold on while I tried not to bump into things."

"I should've played fewer video games," I muttered to myself. "Maybe I could've learned how to echolocate, too."

"I can show you the basics," said Selene, "if you don't mind being a bat."

"Maybe later," I said, thinking of El and Artem lost in the darkness. "I'm batty enough as it is."

There was silence for a moment. "I can only assume that was a pun. You know those generally don't translate, right?"

"Ah." I scratched my head. "Duly noted."

A soft whir in the distance announced the return of the floating eye. I Quickened myself and pulled Purgator from my inventory.

"No lights," Selene commanded, voice lethargic to my ears, "and close your eyes. I'll direct you."

"Are you sure?" I said slowly.

"Do you trust me?" she asked.

"Uh . . ." I trusted her judgment on some things, but I wasn't sure if that extended to life-or-death fights with magic eyeball monsters. "Alright." I shut my eyes as she turned off the Lux spell. "Let's give your way a try."

A series of sharp clicks pinged through the darkness. "It's not just one enemy. There are more incoming," said Selene's voice. "Multiple entities, small and four-legged. Not hedgeboars or eyes. Nearest one at two o'clock, distance ten meters, five meters, three . . ."

I fired to the right and felt my plunger strike true, a jolt running up my arm. There was a desperate yelp as I blindly yanked my catch toward me. "Get over here!" I growled, more for myself than anything.

Something impaled itself on my fist, showering me with steaming innards that metamorphosed into red licorice. Its companions yowled in fear, giving away their positions.

"Four o'clock, nine o'clock," came Selene's voice, calm as always, and I was already firing my plunger to the left. This time, though, I hit only air.

"Which one's closer?" I yelled.

"Four—" Something cut her off, and I opened my eyes by instinct. All I could see was a furred snarling thing, lit by dim white characters scrolling around her wrist. I leaped for it, but there was a sharp crack, and the monster went limp. In the near-pitch black, I perceived a shape like a wolf, half-sunken in the mud, with endless teeth and only bumps where its eyes should've been.

I clamped my eyes shut. Silly of me to even open them at all, but it was hard to break lifelong habits.

"That eye's back," Selene said, "at six o'clock. We're good on bones, so let's run. Just don't look."

But I wanted satisfaction. I shot Purgator behind me and felt it stick, the whirring louder than ever as the eye let out a mouthless screech. Feeling the resistance of the eye's weight, I grappled myself toward it. Hardening at the last second, I pierced a jelly-like layer and found myself in a warm world of vitreous fluid. All around me was the organic smell, the feeling of blood pumping. An ear-shattering vibration came through the body, conducted by solid tissue directly into my ears. I could feel the tissue around me writhing and twisting in a disgusting manner.

Though my eyes were shut and I held my breath, I couldn't shut my nostrils. The smell was revolting, but more than that was the texture of gristly flesh all around me. I pinwheeled my arms inelegantly, trying to do maximum damage before I'd have to surface to breathe. *Carving out a niche for myself?* I'd have to use that one later, when I wasn't inside an eyeball monster.

All of a sudden the tissues around me went slack, and everything collapsed to the ground. I fell heavily and dug my way out of the smoking eye. Selene had turned her lantern back on, and was staring at me in shock. I knew I must look like hell, covered in burnt white jelly and dark ichor.

"Good teamwork," I said.

"More or less."

Selene butchered one of the wolves, peeling back the skin with a knife and cutting through flesh to pull out a skull and immense breastbone. She inspected the breastbone, rapping at it with her knuckles in satisfaction.

"It should suffice for a small reading," she said, seeming pleased, as she filed it away in her inventory.

"You really took that thing down." I wiped myself off with a towel. "I thought you were a healer."

"I'm a lot of things," said Selene, wiping the knife off. "Fragile is not one of them."

"I didn't mean—" I thought for a moment. I didn't mean that women should be protected. Was it considerate or patronizing to feel that way? If someone told you they didn't need help, did it take away their agency to act as if they did? "Never mind," I said. "We held our own pretty well there."

When Selene looked at me, I could almost feel her gaze penetrate the veil of my thoughts, and I had to wonder if a minor form of telepathy wasn't part of her arsenal.

As we finished cleaning ourselves up in the muddy darkness, a torrent of rabbits poured straight down from the abyss above us.

Either El's learned to fly, or she's already on the next floor.

CHAPTER FORTY

Quickening

(Strive 13:3)

As we ran toward the stream of rabbits, the ground began sloping upward out of the mud, turning into blissfully solid earth. My pant legs were crusted over, and I had to call for a break to change out of them for a fresh set. Once again, I mentally thanked the commissary for having the forethought to pack spares.

"Penny for your thoughts?" I asked Selene, who'd been quiet for a while. I didn't feel winded at all from the run, another boon of the increased stats.

"Mia was here," she responded without changing her gait. "When I did the reading on the last floor, it indicated she was on the thirteenth floor. But we haven't seen her at all. No trace." More phantom rabbits drifted down like a flurry of snow, closer to us now. "Now that we know where El is, I'm tempted to use this breastbone immediately to pinpoint her location. What do you think?" I could see the shine of her one purple eye in the dark, fixed on me intently.

"Oh," I said. "Well, I agree knowing her whereabouts would be good. But I don't know if I alone can defend you if we're attacked while you're casting. And given that El's already on the next floor, we'd probably need to catch up first regardless of what the bones say. Artem might be there, too."

"That reasoning seems sound." Just like that it was decided, and we continued running up the slope. Every once in a while, spectral rabbits cascaded down, like furry smoke signals, assuring us that we were heading in the right direction.

The hard ground became cracked with scraggly weeds, then a carpet of grass, and the outlines of trees began to appear further up the knoll. A dim gray light overcame the darkness, until finally, at the peak of the hill, we came to a massive trunk that stood as solid as a castle tower in the pale half-light.

"Is the elevator inside this tree?" I asked Selene.

"It's possible," she said doubtfully, "but not every floor transition is the same. Sometimes it's stairs, sometimes it's another kind of conveyance."

"So what should we do now?"

"Now, we climb." She began rolling up her long shirtsleeves, a look of determination on her face.

"Wait," I said. "Let me try something first." I took several steps away from her and Hardened, the flames leaping up. She flinched slightly at the heat, and I moved even further away. I augmented my aura with Quicken and felt my energy drain frighteningly fast from the combined spells. Finally, I cast Power Strike and threw my fist at the tree trunk. Empowered by the dual enchantments of speed and strength, the strike sounded a sharp whip-crack as it broke the sound barrier.

That wasn't the only cracking sound, as the bones in my hand shattered on the tree trunk. Blinding pain shot through me, and I gritted my teeth to keep from screaming, letting out a small groan instead. "What are these things made of?" I gasped. There was no indication of any damage left on the tree.

"You can't just punch everything," Selene said, starting to sign as characters scrolled around her amethyst bracelet. It flashed with light, and she took my wrist in her hand. A warm violet glow enveloped my limply dangling hand, and I felt the bones grind back into place. "No more hitting trees," she said before releasing my wrist. "Doctor's orders."

"Alright," I sighed. "We climb."

Selene immediately began to lag behind as we ascended. She was a more technically skilled climber than me by far, but my investments in strength and dexterity allowed me to power through even with terrible form. In addition, Purgator allowed me to swing from branch to branch with ease.

I levered myself up to a bough wide enough for a two-lane highway and looked over the edge. Selene was still climbing a few meters below. The Quicken spell made her seem like she was moving through molasses. I reached a hand down to assist her, and she extended a hand to grab mine—

There was a slight humming sound, and a second later, the whole world lurched sideways with a hollow boom.

I had plenty of time to appreciate the sight in slow motion as a thousand leaves startled at the shock of the towerquake and spun crazily into the air, making the gray dappled light swim on the ground far below. A single phantom rabbit was trailing down in the distance. But worst of all was the look of slow horror filling Selene's eyes as her hand slipped, and she began to fall backward. Her kada hand twitched, and a single character bloomed on her bracelet. She wouldn't make it in time, whatever spell she was trying to cast.

I whipped Purgator out and fired it at her, my other hand gripping the branch beside me. The rope uncoiled like a darting snake, and the cup struck her in the chest. I had time to register a twitch in her left eye, an opening of her mouth like she was going to speak, before I yanked upward and retracted. Her body arched backward as she was flung toward me, and I put out an arm to catch her. The second jolt of the towerquake almost threw off my aim, but I adjusted and caught her around the waist.

It was the fault of Quicken that I had ample time to feel her softness against me, even though I let go as soon as possible. To my surprise, she looked as abashed as me. Though she recovered quickly, every emotion lingered on her face twice as long due to my slowed-down perception of time.

"Are you alright?" I asked.

Selene stared at me and began laughing, every gasp a second apart, and I realized I was still in chipmunk-voice mode. The stuck plunger cup rose and fell with each breathless exhalation. After the spell had passed, she said, in a slow deliberate voice, "I'm alright. Remove the plunger, please."

"This is embarrassing," Selene said.

"Sorry."

We were standing on the same wide bough, her behind me, and she hesitantly put her hands over my shoulders. I grasped her wrists, holding them like backpack straps, then squatted slightly and lifted her up. A few experimental steps showed me that this was feasible for walking, at least. We'd have to see if climbing was possible. "Shouldn't take too long. We've got this."

"Inspiring," said Selene dryly. She turned her head away and cleared her throat. "Let's get it over with, then."

We'd come to the conclusion together that this was the best way to avoid being thrown to our deaths by another towerquake. Quicken made it so that I could react to any quakes in time, theoretically, and stick the plunger to lock myself in place. But I couldn't both do that and use it to save Selene, and besides, I had the advantage of increased strength and dexterity for better climbing. As convincing as the arguments were, and despite the fact that we'd both agreed on them, I couldn't help but feel like I was somehow taking advantage of the situation.

Leaves brushed my face as I climbed the well-worn grooves of the great tree trunk. It was dark and cool in the thick of the canopy layer, and the gray light warmed to a verdant green. From all around came the rustling of foliage in the wind. It was pleasant, although lacking in the small sounds of life that I'd normally associate with a forest—the chatter of squirrels, the squawking of nesting birds. Buoyed by the scenery and my enhanced strength, I honestly could've forgotten I was carrying Selene if it weren't for her long hair on my neck. That was distracting.

Purgator and my aura of Quickening made the ascent easier than I'd expected, and after some time, the regularity of the climb became a comfortable rhythm. The leaf cover was now thinning out, green giving way to flecks of sky blue as neighboring branches parted ways to their own destinations. Finally, the last few hangers-on fell away, and I could see the fourteenth floor's cloudless sky. We came up to the last wide branch, and I staggered forward onto it as Selene let go of me.

Was it just me, I thought, *or did she wait a little too long to release her grip?* But it could've just as easily been due to my accelerated perception.

CHAPTER FORTY-ONE

Above the Treetops

(Strive 14:1)

The fourteenth floor was a world of treetops, connected by high-flying rope bridges that tossed in the wind. Diffuse, rainbow-colored light emanated from bunches of glowing fruit that dangled from the trees like Christmas ornaments. Up here, evidence of the recent towerquake was clear as day. Half the trees were barren of leaves, and trunks leaned as if about to topple over.

But some trees still had fruit clinging to them. **Peaches of Power (Unripe)** hung next to **All-Up Apricots (Unripe)**, and I plucked one of the latter, taking a bite. The acidity nearly burned a hole in my tongue, and I didn't even receive a stat increase for my trouble.

"Don't bother," I said, as Selene reached for one. I tossed the bitten fruit, and it disappeared soundlessly into the bottomless void.

"I could've told you that was gonna happen," chittered a voice above me. "Shame I didn't feel like it."

A familiar weight of something fuzzy landed on my head, and I put one hand on it. The bulk, the slightly coarse fur, the rounded ears—I'd know them anywhere. Selene gave a rare smile.

"My favorite dumpster diver," I said, ruffling El's fur.

"That's all you gotta say to me? No 'thanks for distracting the giant floating eyeball, El'? 'We owe you our lives, El'?"

I sniffed. "You smell like mud."

"Yeah," she said. "You would too if you'd been wading in it up to your ears. I just barely got it all cleaned up." The raccoon leaped over to Selene, who hugged her tight to her chest.

"Where's Artem?" Selene asked. "I thought you two were together."

"We finally caught a glimpse of her, and the madman insisted on charging ahead by himself," said El. "This floor's so broken, I couldn't follow him."

"She's here?" Selene's smile vanished, and she held El at arm's length, staring at her. "Where?"

"That way." El pointed a paw, then wriggled in the uncomfortable grip. "Across the broken bridge."

"Show me." Selene's tone was tight and controlled as she placed the raccoon down. There was no hint of anger in it or on her face, but her eyes seemed to glow brighter than before with something feverish. It worried me.

El led us to a spot where a tree stood at a precarious slant, a crater on one side of its trunk, next to the remains of a bridge that hung limp over the abyss. "We saw her across here. Thought we did, anyway. I think it was an ambush to try to take us down on the climb up, but I sent a few sparks flying her way and she ran."

I thought of how vulnerable we'd been on our ascent, and had to admit that it would've been a good strategy. "Then what?"

El indicated the damaged tree and bridge. "Artem boosted off of the trunk," she said. "Told me to wait for y'all here. Next thing I knew, he was gone in a flash of red. I couldn't go after them if I wanted to."

"He's using Power Strike for movement to catch up with her. Like when I used it to swim." *But*, I thought, *it takes a heavy toll to use it repeatedly that way.*

"Anyway," El continued, "after that, I just sat tight here and sent rabbits down till you two showed up."

"And now we're here." Selene's demeanor was robotic. "So let's go."

"Wait." El screwed up her snout and covered her eyes. "Hold on a second."

"What?" Selene said. "For God's sake, what?"

"I'm afraid!" El burst out. "You didn't see when we fought her, what she tried to do to us. You didn't see—"

"I saw the jar," said Selene in a voice like steel. "I saw enough."

"—us raccoons are supposed to be scavengers." El was speaking over her. "We run away and live to fight again. But nowadays, you'd think my name's *El Goddamn Hero*. I didn't have to come on this grand quest—"

"So why did you come?" I asked. "Just to get away from the city crowds?"

"At first," El Bandito said unhappily, looking up at us, "but at this point, you're my people."

And Selene's eyes softened.

I aimed Purgator at the far side of the broken bridge and pulled the trigger. With a hollow *thwip*, the rope fired in a lazy arc before sticking to the tree on the far side. I stepped backward until the line went taut. Selene wanted to use the same tactic as with the beachside cliff, walking across like a tightrope.

"What if there's another quake?" I asked, digging my heels into the ground. "I feel like they're happening more and more often."

"And they're getting worse and worse," said El. "Last one nearly ended me."

"I could power-jump across, reel you two in with Purgator," I offered.

"No," said Selene, at the same time El said, "Fuck that."

"Just a suggestion. Look, I don't see what the problem is."

"Plunger's a plunger," El said, scrambling backward, and Selene nodded in agreement.

"Suit yourselves," I muttered. "But if you're going to walk across the rope, you'd better do it quick."

We were fortunate enough that no towerquake struck as the two crossed the plunger line like a pair of acrobats. I retracted the line and fired it at a branch high up, then willed myself to leap. My feet pedaled in midair as I swung across, landing on the other side.

A crater on the far side of the trunk showed where Artem had gone. Looking in that direction, I saw the trail of destruction he'd left, a neat path for us to follow among the treetops. They were dense enough here that no rope bridges were needed, as the boughs of neighboring trees interlocked with each other to form wide footpaths.

Selene looked ahead, then back at El and me. "Shall we move faster, then?"

Instead of answering, I Quickened.

"*Vámonos*," said El.

Selene sped up the pace to a jog. Both El and I kept up easily, the raccoon dashing across smaller branches alongside us. Seeing this, she took us to a run, then a sprint, following the wake of Artem's destruction. No normal athlete ever made that pace on as twisting a terrain as we did, leaping from one treetop to the next, as a rainbow of colors blurred past. We saw a group of screeching enemies like crazed chimpanzees, but passed them before they could do more than holler at us.

Once, there was a gap too wide for me, and I pulled out Purgator, plunging headlong across the chasm like Tarzan, and after that I realized I could just keep swinging, without ever touching the ground, whooping as I went, until I passed through a waterfall with a spray of white foam, launched, flipped, and skidded to a stop on the branch of another tree.

"Showoff," said El as she and Selene caught up to me.

"I didn't know I could do that," I panted, resting my hands on my knees. "Damn. I might be kind of awesome."

"That's one word for plunger-based parkour," El said. "Not the one I'd have picked, though."

"Focus, both of you," Selene said. "I see him."

There was an immense clock face set into the side of a tree trunk. The two hands of the clock spun crazily, and the numbers along the edge of the dial weren't any that were familiar to me. The surface of the clock appeared somewhat like liquid, and looking at it made my gut churn. I scanned it with Examine, and, as I'd expected, my udjat read **Floor 15 Entrance.**

"That was easy," I said.

"I guess sometimes Sender throws in a freebie," El responded.

Artem sat under the portal cross-legged with half his inventory laid out in front of him. He finished polishing a wicked-looking knife, held it up to the light, then stored it with a flick of his kada hand.

"About time," he rumbled, and his low voice was reassuringly familiar. "Thought I lost you, midget bear."

"What happened?" Selene demanded, her voice cracking slightly. "Where is she?"

"Be calm." Artem held up a hand. "I had hoped to catch her before she left the floor, but given that we're now approaching the bridge, we should reassess. I don't want to press forward blindly without some idea of what's coming. Could you perform a reading, Selene, and see what she's up to on the other side?"

Selene twisted her fingers brusquely and brought out the wolf's breastbone from the previous floor. Using a nail, she punctured the bottom of a can of refreshing soda and pressed it against her lips, cracking the top and downing it in a messy gulp. She sat, holding the breastbone on her lap.

"I almost had her," Artem said as Selene began to sign, the sleeve of characters rolling around her wrist. "But the girl said something that gave me pause."

"What?" Selene demanded.

"Before she disappeared into the portal, she said that she hoped to see all four of us on the other side. That she had something to show us."

CHAPTER FORTY-TWO

Sendoff

(Strive 14:2)

Selene stumbled in her signing, and the glowing white characters blew away like ashes in the wind. I gave her a look of concern as her gaze became steely, and Artem glanced at me.

"I don't know how much more obvious it could be that this is a trap," I said, "with a capital T."

"That much seems clear," said Artem, sharpening another knife.

"Is there another way to get to the next floor?" I asked.

"Not that we know of," he replied.

There was an ear-splitting crash and the whole forest shook, sending us sprawling to the ground. A second jolt of the tower dislodged a flurry of flower petals, adding to the carpet already surrounding us. Selene's cast was interrupted once again, and she snatched a leaf out of her hair, crushing it in frustration.

"Ignore the quakes," Artem advised. "We are in no danger of falling here—"

"The trees," said El. "Something's happening to them."

All around us, leaves curled and dried up, turning from green to brown in an instant. Fruits dropped out of the canopy like severed heads, splatting to the ground and releasing a rotten scent. There was a low groaning sound that seemed to come from all directions at once, and each of our udjats flashed twice, almost blinding, with a warning message.

High instability detected in this area. Environments may not function as intended.

The world went twilight-orange as if a cloud of dust had passed over the sun, and I shivered.

"That's the color of nothingness," said Selene in a controlled voice. "The outside world's leaking in. We were too late."

There was nothing to do but stand and gape, as the sky began to shear open with an unearthly screech, like the voice of the tower itself was screaming in pain. A band of dusk sliced through the gaps in the leaves above us, widening into an open wound. *So close*, I thought with a pang of remorse. *We almost had her.*

Everything shook, more violently than any of the previous quakes, and we all ducked down. Selene uttered a short, sharp word that I didn't need my translator to understand. But when the shaking cleared, there was another figure standing with us by the portal, a being made of light that exuded waves of pressure.

He looked exactly as he had so many floors ago when he'd saved us from Death. The golden outline of a male in peak physical condition, but with all the features washed out by light. This time, as close as he was, I noticed hovering bands of rings around each of his arms, each lit up with power. I Examined him again, to be sure. As before, ornate serifed characters bloomed into view:

First Sender of the Tower Strive. Creator of the kada-udjat system, and the high authority of this tower.

Selene and Artem immediately knelt in respect. It wasn't hard, since we were all on the ground already, and after a moment, I moved to copy them. El remained standing, although on all fours, the difference wasn't obvious.

Sender looked upward. "Fuck," he said, and his voice was again less intimidating than I'd expected, neither especially loud nor authoritative. He seemed to be speaking to himself, not having noticed our presence. "What is it this time? No, not Death this time. Something else?"

He lowered his gaze at me, staring not so much at me as through my body, to the place in my chest where a fragment of Will resided, and I knew he was rapidly coming to the same mistaken conclusion that Artem had on our first meeting.

"I can explain—" I started.

"You again," he said with shocked anger in his voice. "This is how you compensate me for saving you from Death? By trying to ruin everything that I've built?" He raised his hand and a light began to gather on his wrist. A gale of dark wind blew from the gash in the tower, and it smelled like an ending. The deep rumbling note had reentered his voice in an instant. "I should have cast you out earlier, let you be devoured by the shadows that live in the lands between the towers. No matter. I'll take back that fragment of Will and do it now."

The light on his arm began to glow hotly white, and the force it exuded buckled my limbs, pressing me face-first into the ground. Around me, I saw that the same thing was happening to everyone.

"Tell him what really happened," growled Artem, "before he crushes us all to paste."

The pressure felt like a vice gripping my chest, making it nearly impossible to speak. "*Wait!*" I tried to cry out, but it came out as a hoarse whisper. "Sender, please. If you can see inside me, look at how little power there is there. I don't even know how to use it, really. Someone else has the rest."

Somehow he heard me, and the overwhelming pressure relented slightly. Gasping, I chanced a look upward. Sender had his arms folded, still staring at the space below my sternum with frightening intensity. "Explain."

My eyes are up here. "I was tricked," I panted, "by someone from another tower into helping her steal the stone. Didn't know what I was doing. I ended up with this fragment, but the lion's share is with her."

"An interloper?" said Sender skeptically. "From where?"

"A girl from Eramai named Mia," Selene said, propping herself up onto her knees. "She's close by, waiting for us."

"She took most of it and ran." Seeing that Sender's anger was cooling, I was eager to show that we were on the same side. "She could steal even more in the future. That's why we're here, to try and capture her. If you like, you can recover my portion. I've got no complaints about that. And if you could assist us in any way—"

"Okay, I understand." Sender paused for a moment. "Well, that is certainly a problem. Stand up, all of you."

He turned to the widening hole in the sky, where shadowy figures now hovered outside, watching and waiting. With his hands, he made a zipping motion, and a network of light raced along the trees, up into the sky, surrounding the void. There were uncanny screeches of disappointment from far away as the hole shrank, before it popped out of existence. Then, with a motion of his arms, he sent up vast bars of light that reinforced the sky like girders. Finally, he turned back to us.

"There are rules that I must respect where other Towers are concerned," Sender said heavily. "I am not supposed to involve myself directly in conflicts between my climbers and their agents."

"With all due respect," said Artem, "this is an existential threat to all of us. Surely exceptions can be made."

Sender shrugged, the gesture oddly casual. "There are rules," he repeated. "The lord of one tower attacking a child of another—I can't do that."

"So you're going to sit here," El said, "while everything goes down in flames?"

"I can support this world for some time." Sender eyed me. "And while I can't directly help, I can give you all some advice."

"Please instruct this clumsy one on the proper path forward," Selene said. I blinked, wondering if there was a hint of sarcasm in her voice.

If there was, Sender didn't notice. "You said that the girl is from Eramai. The good news is that their magic tends to not be as powerful from a combat perspective. It's more emotional and internal. She probably won't be firing any magic missiles at you, if you catch my drift."

We all nodded. *The guildmaster mentioned something similar,* I thought.

"But if she's crossing the bridge, that's bad news. The closer you get to her home, the stronger her magic will be, and the weaker yours will be. You see, in general, power is inversely proportional to the distance of your own Tower. Get far enough from here, and your kadas won't function at all."

"Well, at least we won't have to worry as much about her bracelets," said El.

"The bridge on the fifteenth floor," said Selene. "She may be there already. That must be the trap. Get us where we're weaker than she is. If our magic doesn't work as well and hers does . . ."

"Try to catch up before then," Sender said. "Go now, and best of luck. I'll hold down the fort here. Heh. Maybe you can take out that bridge while you're at it, stop these supposed interlopers from coming in."

While he spoke, I slowly removed the translator from my ear, out of curiosity. "Could you give us anything to help?" I asked. "Might make it easier for us to take that bridge out."

"Your reward is that you get to keep the Will you stole from me. For now. Maybe it'll help you where your kadas cannot. Besides, I really don't believe in rewarding theft with handouts."

I could still understand him, even without the device. *Huh*, I thought. *The lord of the tower speaks Standard American English.*

Selene said something I didn't understand, and Sender turned to her as I refitted my earpiece.

"Yes, it's only appropriate that you're the one to do it, Mingyue. Am I right?"

He had knelt down to stare at the top of Selene's head until she looked up at him. Whatever she saw, she averted her eyes quickly, like she'd been burned. I felt more confused than ever as the being made of light stood upright. "Once my Will is restored and the bridge is closed, the climb can continue," he said, almost to himself, before a kaleidoscopic flash announced his departure.

"What was that about?" Artem sounded as bewildered as I was.

Selene was trembling slightly as she slumped into a sitting position. "It was me," she said. "It was my fault the girl from Eramai was here in the first place." She drew a deep breath, then said dully, "This is not the first time I've been here. The one who built this bridge to Eramai was me."

CHAPTER FORTY-THREE

A Remembrance of Home

In a time long ago for some, not long at all for others, there was a young priestess who lived in the city of Feng. She was considered wise beyond her years, if a little cold, and known for the infallibility of her readings. Her fame grew to the point that the king himself consulted her on all matters of importance, and he even provided her a small house in the royal gardens, so that he might have ready access to her prophecies at all times.

It was spring, and lotus pads floated on the surface of the tranquil pond, while swallows chirped and spun in the sky above. The priestess sat in a pavilion on the water studying with her husband, who was a man of letters. A brilliantly colored koi breached the water nearby and made bubbling noises, opening and closing its mouth.

"And here is the character for 'fish,'" said the scholar, drawing a flowing line of ink on a piece of parchment, "since you seem more interested in that one than in our lessons."

The priestess darted her eyes back from where she had been gazing at the margin of the pond. "Nature is the best teacher," she said smoothly. "I've learned much by observing the movement of the goldfish through water."

"And what have you gleaned from your study?" He arched an eyebrow.

"See how greedily it gulps at the water's surface?" said the priestess, pointing, "and yet, if it were to attain the realm that it so craves, it would surely perish."

"Just as we often seek our own destruction," mused the man. "This was to be a class on writing, but I fear we are verging on philosophy."

Suddenly, there was a loud sound that scared the fish away, and the two looked toward the massive gong that indicated the king's arrival.

"I apologize," said the priestess. "It seems I'm needed."

"Remember your letters," said the husband. "Written in the cracks, they are often ambiguous, but they are always there."

The priestess passed over floating wooden walkways toward the garden entrance, before kowtowing in front of the king and his advisors. "This humble one asks how she may be of service," she intoned.

The king was beside himself with excitement. "I have heard that in the mountains to the west there is a heavenly garden tended by none other than the Queen Mother herself. The fruits there are said to bestow immortality upon those who consume them. Tell me how to reach this place."

"Your Majesty does this one great honor by this question," said the priestess, holding her gaze downward to avoid being blinded by his radiance. "I will consult the oracle bones at once."

The priestess led the king and his entourage to the ceremonial cauldron and lit the ritual fire. Then, in another room, she changed into her robes and brought out the ceremonial turtle, Slowpoke, the twenty-seventh of that name.

In those days, turtle shells were considered the best material for accurate fortune-telling. For reasons unbeknownst to the priestess, the king required that all readings be done with turtles that were slain in front of him.

Therefore, the priestess did so, prying the plastron off with forceps and washing it thoroughly with fresh water. One didn't argue with the Son of Heaven. The king tapped his foot impatiently, but he too recognized the importance of a clean reading.

By this time, the fire had heated the bronze cauldron so that the bottom glowed red-hot, and the priestess held the flat white shard over it until cracks began to form. She waited a moment longer, then drew the oracle bone out before it became too brittle.

She peered at the characters, copied some onto a scrap of parchment, and nodded to herself.

"Well?" demanded the king.

"Yes," said the priestess. "These unworthy eyes see that in the mountains west of here, there is indeed a garden where peaches of uncommon sweetness are grown, purported by some to grant the power of immortality. However, this is a great exaggeration, spread by the savvy owners of the orchard to attract high prices for their crop. In fact, the high sugar content means they should only be consumed in moderation, Your Majesty."

The priestess couldn't help but notice the king turn to stare daggers at one of his eunuch advisors, who cringed. "We will be having some words," said the king to him. "The rest of you are dismissed." The band of men and half-men scattered, leaving the priestess to tidy up the ashes of the reading.

The king's next visit was that summer. The heat was oppressive, although the water of the pond dispelled it slightly. The priestess was swimming when the gong sounded, signaling the king's arrival. She darted into her living quarters to change and dry her hair as much as she could, before approaching the entrance of the shrine.

The king's entourage was one member smaller than it had been before, and the priestess couldn't help but notice a few of the advisors glaring at her. It wasn't often that she noticed the emotions of others, so she decided their hatred of her must be quite strong indeed.

"If this lowly one may inquire," began the priestess, "what happened to the other advisor?"

There was a scoff from somewhere in the king's presence, and one of the robed men behind him said, "You dare to ask? After your actions—"

"Quiet." The king's voice was low, and the priestess felt a thrill of fear at someone who could dispose of a person so easily. Had the advisor been exiled, sent out into the wilderness? Or subjected to the thousand cuts? Or crushed under the Thumb of Heaven, which was said to be the king's new favorite toy?

"This one patiently awaits the Son of Heaven's query," said the priestess, her head bowed low.

"My beloved has passed away," said the king, and his voice cracked. "I don't know what to do."

The priestess was stunned. It was like hearing that a god had been stabbed and blood had come out. "W-well," she said. "This one is very sorry to hear that. This one is unsure what the king would request of her—"

"Perform a reading asking what I should do next," said the king.

"Yes, Your Majesty."

The twenty-eighth Slowpoke was shortly dispatched, bled, and cleaned. The flames were built up, and the reading was done. The priestess's hands shook as she looked at the cracks. They seemed ambiguous and unclear to her, and tears threatened to cloud her vision even further.

"Your Majesty, the reading is unclear . . ." Always before the answers had come right to her, but the knowledge that her words had such dire consequences for others made her feel deeply unbalanced. Under such circumstances, the void-like state needed for the reading seemed to elude her. But she knew that the king brooked no excuse for failure. She had to come up with something that would satisfy the king and not cause harm to any others.

Hoping she sounded convincing, the priestess intoned, "It was unclear, but it is resolving before me now. Your Majesty must concern himself foremost with the repair of his heart, for a nation's spirit reflects the spirit of its ruler. Time and distraction are the cure—one month of hunting and fishing may help to take one's mind off of troubles. Trust in your advisors to keep the ship steady, for they are good and wise."

Winter saw the little pond freeze over, and the shrine maiden and the husband had tea as they watched snow drift by the window. When the gong sounded, they thought they had misheard at first, but then the sound became insistent, and the priestess sighed and composed herself to meet the king. The ceremonial robes were not made for winter, so she wrapped her robes tight as she crossed the floating wooden walkways.

The king was alone, and the priestess knelt before him, shivering. The robe soon began to soak through with snowmelt. It was odd that he was alone. *Where were the advisors?*

"I took your advice," said the king. "Good advice, and I felt better for it. But I still felt a hollowness inside. So I asked my advisors what the best cure was for missing a woman."

The priestess saw a strange expression on his face and quickly looked away with a premonition of fear.

"Another woman," the king said, as if he'd unlocked the mysteries of the universe. "So I come bearing not a question today, but a gift. The gift of myself."

The shivers could not be held back any longer.

"Look at me," demanded the king, and she did so. "You are lovely, you know, and still youthful. I would be kind to you, and you would have everything you ever wanted at your fingertips. The finest jewelry, servants to cater to your every whim, and only the tenderest cuts of meat."

"There is someone," the priestess said, "who is very dear to me. And I'm vegetarian."

"It's a figure of speech," snapped the king, ignoring her first objection. "Refusing a royal order is punishable by death, you know."

The priestess was at a loss for words. The best she could manage was a whispered "Please . . ."

The king made a disgusted noise and walked away.

The priestess was not entirely surprised when, a day later, palace guards kicked in the door of her little house in the gardens of the shrine and dragged her and her husband to a pagoda in the center of the royal palace. It was the tallest building in the city, with balconies stretching up into darkness. The center of the floor was marked by an enormous circular dent. Looking up, she saw a log of enormous girth dangling from a thick rope, with myriad upon myriad of dark rings recording its great age.

It was said to have been shipped in from a distant forest where the lumber was as hard as steel. According to legend, it had taken multiple generations of woodcutters a hundred years to fell the tree. Now it hung overhead as a symbol of the king's potent authority, but it was also used for executions.

The priestess and her husband were bound back to back, kneeling in the center of the floor, so that they could not see each other. She reached for his hand to hold, but he jerked it away. Raising her head, she saw the full moon framed by the doorway of the pagoda. Then there was an echoing snap from high above, and the Thumb of Heaven came down with the force of a falling semi-truck.

CHAPTER FORTY-FOUR

Moonrise

The priestess and her husband awoke in an otherworldly chamber finer than any monarch's palace, crafted from stone as smooth as glass and illuminated by candles that never flickered. They were greeted and offered face towels by a manservant with a strange name who dressed in strange tight-fitting garments.

After their initial bewilderment had subsided, the servant gave them each three gifts. This, more than anything, helped put them at ease, for they knew that messengers of the gods would often present three objects to favored mortals.

The first gift was a bracelet, and the second was a glassy lens worn over the eye. The third wasn't exactly a gift, per se, but rather the return of something lost—a pair of matching flutes from their previous world, one of ebony and one of ivory.

The two were both proficient musicians, as most members of the court were. The priestess had written some pieces of modest renown, and her husband was a strong player in his own right. Her most famous work was a melancholy duet, whose melody was said to have spread to towns hundreds of *li* distant from Fenghao, although usually under other names and with minor variations.

So, they were thankful to have their instruments restored to them, and with that, they began to climb the tower. The casting of spells was a slight complication, since the language of the magic was unknown to them, but they learned the foreign words and the foreign signs well enough to carry on. In fact, they found that the foreign language was quite intuitive, with its compact set of twenty-six characters, and so they picked it up relatively quickly.

Nonetheless, the first nine floors were harsh. Burned and bleeding but alive, the pair stumbled onto a strange city with high walls and were gladly accepted into the gates. There they found a semblance of peace, and their lives began to take on a new routine. The priestess found productive work in a scholarly institution that quested for information beyond the walls of the world, but her husband began spending his time frequenting the many drinking establishments in the city.

One night, they were playing their instruments together on the walls of the city.

"You sound a bit flat," said the priestess. And she thought, *Do you blame me for what happened?*

"I think yours is sharp," said the husband. And his eyes said, *I don't mean to, but I do.*

The priestess rolled her flute outward from her lip, blew a few notes, then stopped. "I fear you drink to excess these days."

"Maybe you should have thought of that when you got us killed. Maybe you should've given the king what he wanted."

The priestess said nothing.

"I'm sorry," said her husband. "I shouldn't have said that."

The priestess left to take a walk alone. It was dark, but here, it wasn't frowned upon for women to walk unaccompanied in public. That was a refreshing change of pace, and the priestess was thankful for it.

She had meant to wander, but her feet habitually led her to the place where she spent most days, the center of learning in the city's guild quarter. Here, in the laboratory, they had bored a small hole in the wall of the tower, and a strange miasma of orange and black lingered in a tightly sealed chamber. They studied chaos here, and the power of outside, and the priestess felt somehow drawn to both those things. As she stared into the brumous vapors, her mind clouded over with a vision that spoke to her. The priestess had ample experience in receiving divine instruction.

There is a ritual that aids with the opening of hearts, the mists whispered. *Only three ingredients are required. A man and a woman. A place where the walls are thin. And the marriage of two appropriate spells. Performed correctly, it will serve to bring new closeness to a pair in conflict.*

The priestess shook her head, and the vision evaporated, but the memory remained as clear as day.

"I had a waking vision," said the priestess to her husband later, "of a way to bring us closer."

"Is that so?" He seemed not much interested.

"I think we should try," she pressed. "Lately, I feel a growing distance between us. I feel . . . alone even when we are together."

"Worth a shot, I suppose," he replied, taking another swig of cheap beer. He had started to grow a gut, the priestess noticed. But she was thrilled that he would try, for her.

"Not here," said the priestess, thinking about the requirements for the ritual but also with a desire for privacy. It felt like it would work better if it were only the two of them. "Let's move upward a distance."

So they began their ascent from the city on the tenth floor of the tower. The eleventh floor was too bright, the twelfth too dangerous, the thirteenth too dark. The fourteenth had walls that were far too thick. Finally, the pair stumbled onto the fifteenth floor of the tower.

"This should serve." The priestess raised her bracelet, and it shone violet. Her heart was suddenly beating very fast. "A man and a woman. A place with thin walls. A spell of opening and a spell of moving. All the elements are in place."

"I never knew these spells could be used this way," her husband wondered aloud, with a hint of his old curiosity. "I wonder if it was an intentional design or something else."

The priestess looked around for monsters that might interrupt the ritual and found none. She felt a sense of dread and suddenly wanted to finish the rite as soon as possible. "Take my hand in yours. We need to do this quickly."

The priestess and the scholar joined hands, then they each signed with their other hand, placing it against the walls of the world. At first, it seemed like nothing would happen, but then a tremor began, like a distant drumbeat, growing louder and louder. *Da-dum, da-dum.*

Then the world shattered, like a turtle shell over a brazier, like a dropped porcelain bowl, like human bones under a great falling weight.

Cracks spiderwebbed from her fingers as the air broke like glass, and the web formed a bridge that linked their world of endless stairs to the world that beat like an undying heart.

Then, with a blinding flash of indigo from the scholar's bracelet, they moved through space, crossing the chasm from Strive to the other tower.

It was a strange place, beautiful with columns of pure white inset with red gemstones. A glittering jet of water sprayed up from the center of the great hall, reflecting light. But these were mundane compared to the emotional effects.

As the priestess looked at her husband, she felt she could see everything in his heart. A roiling pain, sadness, homesickness, anger, and love for her, though the last was nearly buried under resentment and anguish. The mists had not lied about the opening of hearts; there was a closeness in knowing the exact way he felt.

Therefore, she was painfully conscious of the rising bewilderment in him as he looked at her, deeper than he had in years. "It's different," he murmured, almost to himself. "The way you feel . . . feels muted, less . . ." His bewilderment turned to panic. "You don't love . . ."

"But I do," she said. The priestess knew what he meant, without the need for words, because she could feel what he was feeling, and she knew that he could do the same to her, spiraling into entangled infinity. And she had known for a long time that the way she felt things—pain, fear, happiness, love—had always been different, maybe even less than others. But that had been perceptible only to herself before. It was painful to have that fact confirmed. "I do," she pleaded, but words could only do so much.

Suddenly, he turned and fled, down, down, back to the other tower, back to the city of walls, leaving the shocked priestess to slowly trek back across the new bridge alone, wondering what exactly he'd seen in her heart that had been so damning.

The next time she saw him was in a jar of glass.

(Strive 14:3)

We all sat in silence for a moment after Selene finished her story, then she got up, dusting off the hem of her dress. "One thing we didn't expect is that once the ritual is performed, the bridge stays open. I couldn't fig-ure out a way to close it. At some point, Mia must have stumbled upon it and came into our tower from Eramai. And you know the rest."

My chest was tight. "It wasn't your fault, Selene. None of that was your fault."

She turned her palms upward, as if to say, *Oh well, what can you do?* "I hope this at least helps prepare you for the emotional effects of Eramai. It was quite a shock experiencing that connection without knowing, even with someone I knew well."

"Can't believe they made you kill like a hundred turtles," said El. "That's messed up."

"Thanks for saying that, but it was only forty-six," said Selene. "Anything else?"

Artem clapped her on the back. "Ever the pragmatist, eh? I'll ask a pragmatic question then. Will we have to worry about suddenly all becoming telepaths once we get to the other side? If being there with one other person was so bad, four sounds like it'll be a shitshow."

"I don't care if everyone sees what is within me," Selene said impa-tiently. "I have nothing to hide."

"Me neither," said El. "Why bottle it up when you can just do what you want?"

"Mm," I said.

"What was that?" Artem said.

"It was a noise of assent." I paused. "Mia's powers will be of that nature, too."

El piped in. "Doesn't matter; we'll get her. She fucked around and now she's going to find out."

"There will be no fucking of anyone," Artem said firmly, and El chit-tered in nervous laughter. "Given the inherent unknowns, I suggest we approach the situation like this . . ."

Once the plan was settled, we turned to the face of the clock that led to the fifteenth floor. A towerquake rumbled our tree, but Sender's sup-pression was still in effect; it was only a minor tremor. I wondered if that meant he was listening to every word of our conversation.

"Now what?" I asked.

Instead of answering, Selene reached out and pushed herself into the face of the clock. It admitted her with a strange rippling effect, and she was gone.

I put my hand against the clock and it warped, clinging to my fingers in a way that made me queasy. I pulled away, and it snapped back into place. El was looking at me, so I was forced to put on a brave face.

"Okie-doke," I muttered under my breath, stepping into the face of the clock.

CHAPTER FORTY-FIVE

Time After Time

(Strive 15:1)

The fifteenth floor was a mess of gaudy clockwork gadgets that clanked and rotated in every direction. A stuck gear made a juddering racket somewhere in the distance, and I could clearly see that this floor had suffered from the tower's instability most of all.

"The bridge is on this level," said Artem. "Do you all feel that?"

There was a sharp ozone bite to the air, and El's nose wrinkled in response. Then there was another scent, more like the memory of a smell than anything tangible itself. "What is that?" I asked.

"It's the wind from another world," Selene replied, "passing over from Eramai."

It was barely perceptible, the ghostly breeze with a light scent of roses, but it seemed to come from a specific direction, so we started walking that way.

Coils, springs, and sprockets lay strewn on the floor, along with shattered bits of metal that had fallen from the mechanisms. There was a high tinkling sound as a screw popped loose from somewhere high above, bounced once on the metal floor in front of us, then dropped through a gap to disappear below.

Selene led the way to a massive rotating gear the size of a building, and we rode up inside one of its teeth before hopping off onto a platform that spun horizontally like a giant turntable. At the other end of the platform was a mess of gears and rubble that my udjat identified as **Clockwork Golem, a living construct of gears.**

The gears shuddered weakly as we approached, but remained on the floor, crushed under fallen rubble. Another message appeared in my vision: **Defeat the Clockwork Golem before the timer elapses—**

Before I could blink, the text was replaced in quick succession. **Clockwork Golem defeated. Please collect your reward.**

A treasure chest fell from the sky and crashed down on top of the golem. Without a word, El looted it and we moved on.

Reach the end of the obstacle course before the timer elapses.

Not long after the Clockwork Golem, the message appeared before a timer began to count down from one hundred seconds in the upper right corner of my vision. Unfortunately, the obstacle course in front of us was so damaged by towerquakes that it was practically unrecognizable as a path, and fully impassable.

"What happens if we don't make it?" I asked.

"Don't worry about it," said Artem. "We just need to make it to the bridge in time."

"And if we don't?"

"Then we won't be around anymore to worry about it."

The tower rumbled again, and I looked up. "Really making it easy on us, huh?"

"We'll make it," said Selene. "It's in that direction."

I used Purgator to swing up to a higher walkway. At first, I saw nothing, but then it seemed like there was a familiar orange and black fog in the distance, a mirage like a heat haze on summer asphalt. Our destination.

"I'll scout ahead," I called down at the others, and flared my aura shield. It would save precious seconds if I could go forward and clear the path, and besides, my combat abilities were most effective with ample distance between me and the rest of the party. I leaped down and began clearing debris off the path with Power Strikes.

The timer had reached sixty-five when I was accosted by another Clockwork Golem, this one intact and uncrushed by rubble. No quest pop-up appeared this time, but it sensed my approach with whatever senses it had and rose up, forming the rough shape of a man twice my size before shambling toward me.

A fist made of spinning gears smashed the ground where I'd been standing. I rolled and sent a rope at it, but a gear shot out of the golem's chest and knocked my shot astray.

I yanked the plunger head back and ran at the golem. Gears flew at me in a hail of metal, and soon I was surrounded by a pinging mass of steel and chrome. But by enclosing me, the golem had made a grave mistake.

I detonated.

Gears flew outward like an exploding suit of armor. Without looking backward or taking the time to inspect what rewards it had dropped, I advanced further toward the portal, chugging a refreshing soda with a picture of a jelly bean on it.

No, that was a pinto bean. It was a pinto bean-flavored soda.

It was kind of annoying, since I'd been saving some of the ones that I thought would taste less unpleasant as a treat. All the ones I'd drunk so far had had unfortunate flavors like blood sausage, or they were undecipherable. One had a picture of an ear, which was very confusing to me. I still had a loose juice from the fifth floor that I had almost forgotten about. I'd saved it because it looked just a bit too radioactive and dangerous for me at the time.

The timer was at thirty seconds when I reached the tunnel's entrance. Tunnel seemed like the right word to describe it, but I wasn't sure what it was. It was different from anything else in the Tower Strive, and looking at it hurt my eyes.

Everything about it seemed to change whenever I blinked or looked away for even a second. It might've been small or large, red or green or blue, night or day. If I unfocused my eyes, I could just barely see cracks like hidden writing spiraling out of the corners. It made me deeply uneasy, and I felt my heart synchronizing to a strange pulse that came from somewhere deep within it, the same frequency of the tower's rumblings.

The only constant was the miasma that leaked from the tunnel like off-gassing from a mine shaft. It had a feeling of twilight about it and made me recollect vividly the sensation of looking outside Death's classroom at that in-between world where chaos reigned.

I looked back and saw Selene and El scrambling onto the platform, with Artem climbing up close behind.

"What are you waiting for?" Artem demanded. "Go!"

The timer was at fifteen seconds when we left Strive and entered the bridge to another world.

(*Interstices 3*)

She stood at the far end of the bridge, waiting for us. Two bracelets—one blue, one green—shone on her wrists, and the same two colors sparkled in her eyes. The rest of her attire was light and sheer, carefree as a summer holiday. She didn't seem any the worse for wear after my explosion on the tenth floor. Her posture was relaxed, almost insolent, as she gazed outward over the lands between the towers like a tourist at an observation deck. Well, that was fair enough. She was no local.

"*Finally,*" she said, drawing out the word petulantly as she turned to us. "I was starting to wonder if you all would show."

"Could've been sooner if you hadn't run like a coward," El said.

"I missed you, too, El!" Mia smiled. "But I'm afraid being taken prisoner doesn't really agree with me. I'm more of a free spirit."

"How does she know your name?" I asked El, and she shrugged.

"Oh, I can see into all your minds, at least a little bit." Mia winked at me. "Enough to get the gist. Now that we're halfway between your home and mine, more of my own powers are returning to me."

"Drop your bracelets to the ground now," Artem said to Mia. "You won't escape me a second time."

"Oh, Artem," she said. "Always so serious. Learn to let loose a bit, and maybe people would like you more. You, too, Selene."

I tried to blank my own mind, but it was a futile exercise. Selene and Artem had faces like stone, and El was crouched, ready for violence.

"I should be thanking you, actually, Selene," said Mia. "If it hadn't been for you opening this bridge, I wouldn't have known how vast and wonderful this world is. Eramai's great and all, but you know what's better than one tower? An infinity of different towers!" She beamed. "So many people to meet. I love meeting new people. The best thing in the world is winning people over."

Selene remained silent.

"Your man was pretty torn up about you," Mia continued. "You must've known that he blamed you in part for his death. Even then, he still loved you. The straw that broke the camel's back was really the little couples' therapy trip you guys made out here. Before he saw what was in your heart, I think he expected to find more love there than he did." She turned her hand over to examine her nails. "But then, I've always thought that we each love in our own ways, in our own amounts. It was unfair for him to look for his own love's mirror in you. But he did, and he was badly hurt when he didn't find it." Mia smiled sympathetically. "The least I can do to help is to bring you closure. Do you want to know what his last words were?"

Selene said nothing, but her silence became deafening, like the moment before a storm. El began to hiss loudly, and looking down, I saw the reason why.

Selene's shadow looked grotesque, twice as large as mine and growing. It writhed and coiled like a living thing, then boiled outward in all directions until it rose up around us, enclosing the five of us in a sphere of utter darkness.

Flames leaped up, illuminating a scene from hell. I saw an image of a water pavilion engulfed in flames, a baleful red moon glaring down at me with its bloodshot eye. Everything burned, and as I cried out, I felt my throat being scalded. I tried to Harden myself, but the shield wobbled unsteadily and sputtered.

The source of the flames was Selene. She sat stoically in a meditative position at the heart of the pavilion, even as fire consumed her.

"Guess she doesn't want to know," said Mia's voice next to me. I swung at her, but she was on the other side of me, bracelet flashing blue. "Whew! I'm glad that one still kind of works here. Definitely not as effective as before."

"What's happening?" Artem roared.

"I'm glad you asked," Mia said. "This is Selene's guilt and anger. Her internal world projected onto the external. In this place, outside the walls of the towers, even the abstract can be made solid . . ."

El triggered multiple explosions that went wide, and they seemed weaker than usual. "Does she ever stop yapping?"

"You might be wondering why I waited for you all here," said Mia, tapping my shoulder mischievously before vanishing again. "If you listen, that and other mysteries will be revealed to you. Even you all must be aware that outside the walls of the towers is a realm of chaos." Mia patted El on the head affectionately, and the raccoon twisted around to snap at her, but she was no longer there. "And there's nothing us humans love more than turning chaos into order." Mia whispered this in Artem's ear, and he lashed out with a powered fist, striking empty air. "Whenever we strongly feel or suffer or desire, we bend the primordial energies of the world to our whim, and they gladly follow."

The water beneath the pavilion was boiling, fish drifting to the surface on their sides. Lotus pads and flowers shriveled and blackened.

"This is what Will is," Mia continued, seemingly unworried, "and there are so many uses for it. Crystallize it and you have a Willstone, or you could even be the proud parent of a new baby tower. Selene here is learning that firsthand."

"She's making a tower?" I said. If this was how towers were formed, that meant Strive and Eramai and all of them could've been created by people like us. Even the god-like Sender could've been mortal at some point. It explained so much . . .

"Even if I let her go through with it, it would be a pretty unimpressive one," said Mia. "A person only has so much raw Will-power. But here would be the best place to start."

"You can't," thundered Artem, leaping with a burst of red at his feet, but he stumbled short as the spell only worked with half its usual power. "It's forbidden to use that power directly."

Mia tsked. "Did your tower's creator set down that law? He sounds like a bit of a buzzkill, if you ask me. It's true that the Will inside of us is normally suppressed by a Tower's Will. But we're not in Strive anymore, and you're not beholden to Strive's rules." A translucent sphere surrounded Mia, grew to surround all of us, including Selene, and the burning night split open, dumping us back onto the bridge between the two towers. "You see? It's as easy as that."

"Each tower is aligned to its creator's Will," I said, wiping sweat off my brow. "And now that we're out here, you have the freedom to do what you like with it." Thinking back, I remembered using my Will to pass through the rubble of the smithy, but that was all I'd been able to muster. "It must be far more flexible and powerful in this in-between place."

"Yes," Mia said simply. "Out here, everything changes. Not only can we express our innate Will, as Selene was doing before I interrupted her, we can convert opinionated Will from other sources for our own purposes."

"You brought us here so you could use Sender's Will on us," El said.

"No," I responded, with a sudden realization that came too late. "She brought us here to take ours."

"That's exactly right," Mia said, and flashed a charming smile.

CHAPTER FORTY-SIX

Will They, Won't They?

(*Interstices 4*)

Selene lay on the floor, her skin charred and peeling. Artem's red aura flickered like a dying neon lamp, while Mia easily sidestepped his blows. El's explosions were more like those novelty bang snaps they sell at dollar stores.

All the while, glittering particles of Strive's stolen Willstone drifted out from Mia's sternum, transforming into a golden flower bud that floated in front of her waist. "I promised to show you all something," she said, dancing around another punch from Artem. "And now, ladies and gentlemen, it's finally time for the big reveal. Right . . . about . . . now!"

With a brilliant white flare, the flower bloomed, unfurling giant sail-like petals of light. One feathery petal wrapped itself around me, and despite my struggle, I found myself being taken in by Mia's Will.

The whole world shifted and darkened, like with Selene's domain before. But while that burning vision had been murky and dreamlike, this one felt pretty real.

Smooth golden walls around us sloped up to the rim of an enormous bowl—no, a chalice. That seemed like the right word for the metallic crater in which we found ourselves, with intricate designs sweeping around the circumference in three great circles. A sloshing sea of sweet-smelling nectar came up to our knees. El surfaced from it, coughing and sputtering, and I put her on my shoulders. Selene floated in the sticky sap, seemingly unconscious, and Artem and I now stood across from Mia, who stood at the center of the cup.

Three rings of elaborate carvings decorated the walls of the chalice, far above us. The outermost and highest depicted finely dressed men, very obese, at a great banquet. They feasted on animals and plants that were entirely alien to me, and poured decanters of drink directly into their mouths. Some seemed to be emptying their bowels at the tables as they continued to eat.

The middle ring was a knot of limbs, men and women entangled so that it was hard to tell where one body ended and the next began, like a human ouroboros. All the faces bore blissful expressions, and looking closer, I realized that they were in the midst of some kind of orgiastic festival.

The inner ring was the most disturbing to me. It showed every kind of torment I had ever heard of, and some that I hadn't. Stabbings, flayings, boilings, crushings were among the tamer ones. The bronze bull, the iron maiden, the rack and wheel, and a thousand other instruments that we use to inflict pain on one another. I looked at the images and knew them all somehow, even though some had never been practiced in the history of Earth, as far as I was aware.

"Welcome in." Mia smiled demurely. "I hope you like it. I worked really hard on the aesthetics."

Selene. I fumbled in my inventory for a health bar to help her.

"How . . ." Artem started.

Mia laughed, a pleasant sound. "Eramai magic is pretty close to this. To be honest, I was much more confused by Strive's system. All the strange techno-magical gobbledygook. Contact lenses. Sign language." She held up an azure kada bracelet—Selene's husband's—and grimaced. "It's more of a shackle than anything. Your First Sender must be an interesting guy, to design a system like that."

I tried to feed Selene a piece of the restorative, but it crumbled apart in my hand.

"Oh, those things are a part of Sender's system, too," Mia said. "I guess they don't work very well out here, either. Too bad for you."

If only we could break out of this thing somehow and drag her back to Strive, I thought. *At least we'd have more of a fighting chance.*

"Anyway," Mia continued, "can you guess what the theme of my little pocket world is?"

"Fuck if I know," said El. "I'm starting to think it has something to do with trapping us here so you can keep talking at us."

Mia covered her mouth and giggled. "I do enjoy the pleasure of your company, but no." A stray popping explosion from El landed on her skin, and she brushed at the spot absentmindedly. "And the most that's going to do is tickle. I hate to be cliché, but your powers are useless here."

"Desire," said Artem in a voice like grinding rocks. "Your domain is that of desire and seduction. You've employed it on your former victims."

"*Ding*!" she clapped her hands. "Double *ding*! You guys love that, right? That's exactly correct. Although, it was very weak when I was hanging out by that city of yours. My powers were quite suppressed there, so I had to rely mostly on my natural charms." She batted her eyelashes coquettishly. "I don't mean to brag, but I've never been lacking in that department."

"So now what?" said Artem. "You've got us where you want us. Kill us then."

"Speak for yourself." I raised my head from where I was still trying to get the health bars to work their magic on Selene. "I'm trying to stay living."

"Ah, don't worry," Mia said. "I'm not going to kill any of you here. Better if I extract the Will while you're still alive."

There was a feeling of immense pressure, and then a new light bloomed from Mia's chest before suddenly she was all I could think of.

She had always been attractive. Cat-like eyes in an innocent face, at once both predator and prey. A long single braid that she now undid to let her hair fall naturally. The sheerness of her garments that hinted more than they revealed. A slim, athletic form, and a way of moving that suggested dance or something more.

But now she was desire made flesh. She rose up from the crimson sea, Venus-in-the-Red, beckoning with an outstretched finger. Even that gesture was shapely, suggestive. My heart felt like it was in my throat. **"Come,"** she said.

I will shower you with affection, her eyes told me. *I will smother you with softness, anoint your head with kisses.*

I took a step forward, and a searing pain in my leg made me tear my eyes away. El had bitten me, hard. Looking up, I saw that Artem was still fully fascinated by her spell, wading toward her unsteadily. I cried his name, but he made no response, not even turning to glance at me. She beamed in delight, hung her arms around his neck, and whispered something in his ear before turning to me.

"**Come**," she repeated.

The rational part of myself was screaming, but it was oddly muted, displaced by an animal desire that felt a hundred times more real. Lust, desire, and even jealousy. *What secret had she whispered to Artem?* I wanted to know.

"Xavier," came Selene's voice, "if you take another step forward, I swear I'll castrate you myself."

I looked down to see that she was pushing herself up, one hand gripping my ankle tightly. I hadn't even noticed before, enchanted as I was. Some crumbs of the health bar were on her chin, and her skin was still peeling from the burns of her domain.

I felt a dull relief from the conscious part of my mind before pulling Purgator and enabling the Purge ability. Purple motes of light entered the plunger cup, and I fired it at Artem in a last-ditch effort. It landed on his chest and stuck.

Emotionlessly, Artem removed the plunger from himself as Mia gave me a beautiful, teasing smile. "What did I say about Strive magic? Those things are toys compared to the power of a Willstone— keep them indoors where they belong. I'll give you one last chance. **Come**."

I felt an almost physical pulling force from how much I ached for her, so I tried to think of anything else. *The parabolic shape of the chalice around us. A simple parabola is defined by the equation $f(x) = x^2$, meaning its second derivative $f''(x)$ equals 2 everywhere. Positive concavity. Which means all points on the curve slope toward Mia at the center, and once again I was thinking of her curves—*

No, no, no.

I dove inside myself, trying to find refuge in a memory or a feeling, and at every turn, I was met with her seductive smile, until at last I stumbled on a decrepit door hidden deep in my subconscious. In my desperation, I opened it, and that was where I found my Will.

It was a living room, set up for a house party, but there was no one there. *For most people,* I thought, *this would be where their cherished relationships would live in their minds. But for me, nothing.*

No family that I talked to. No friends. No acquaintances—even my neighbors avoided me when they saw me on the street. Was I lonely? No. This was what I wanted. Closeness always led to pain.

The fragments of Will swirled about the room, still aligned to Sender's principle. They bumped up against the ceiling, trying to climb up higher, to ascend. But now I understood how I could make use of them. The pieces hesitated, frozen in midair, then began to turn.

You couldn't reject me if I rejected you first. And I rejected it all.

When I opened my eyes, Mia was still looking at me with the open invitation in her eyes, the exhortation to come to her, live all my desires with her, die in pleasure with her.

I opened my mouth and found enough power in me to utter a single word in response.

"No."

CHAPTER FORTY-SEVEN

Cup Runneth Over

(Interstices 5)

S ilver rain began to fall from above, pitter-pattering into the red liquid around me. I bent to inspect a droplet and saw that it was solid,
a glittering metallic teardrop-shape that felt heavy in my hand.

Holding the droplet, I was suddenly overwhelmed by a vision of
myself in the seventh grade. The first day of school, I remembered, at
lunchtime. It was hard to balance the tray of food on my knees in the
narrow bathroom stall. Someone had shouted that it smelled like fried
chicken and banged on the stall door, peeking through the gap, asking
if they could borrow a nugget, before laughing and leaving with their
friends.

I hated them, but more than that, I hated my own weakness. I wanted
to rage at them, but all I could do was sit silently and wall the feelings
out. *Wall everything out.*

As the memory faded from my mind's eye, its physical form rose from
my hand and pressed itself to my chest, fading through my shirt. I gasped
at the sudden coldness of metal on my skin. One by one, its brethren
rose from the water and clinked into place, linking with the first. The
scales interlocked like a suit of armor until they fully enclosed me, each
one a reified memory reminding me of the cold, hard truth: Human contact only led to pain. It was better to block the world off altogether.

To be honest, I couldn't help feeling a twinge of disappointment. If
this suit was composed of all the Will I could muster, it was an

underwhelming amount. But that made sense, I supposed. It wasn't an inner world that could be shared like Mia or Selene's.

It was a domain meant for one.

I looked up at Mia and felt the snare of her enchantment wash away, along with a whole sea of human emotions. Fear, desire, melancholy, hope. *Why was I doing this again? For my friends?* I looked at them and tried to feel the affection that I knew was normal, but could not. This new armor seemed to make me numb to everything. *How could stoic Artem have fallen so easily?* I sneered. *All that talk of duty and honor, and he'd folded like a cheap suit.*

Currently he stood zombie-like at Mia's side, while her ever-present smile grew into carefree laughter. The metallic faces inlaid in the sloping walls of the chalice turned to laugh, as well, a hollow ringing sound.

"Oh my," Mia said, looking me up and down. "What have we here? I didn't know they were doing a casting call for the local ren faire. Forsooth, thou appear'st to be some sort of strange armored fish." She giggled at her own joke. "Wilt thou swim to me, fish-knight?"

I didn't dignify that with a response. Instead, my armor flexed outward on its own, sending red waves away from Selene, El, and myself. The waves rose, higher and higher, as they surged toward Mia, but as they reached her they split apart, rolling gently to both sides. Her arm was outstretched in a knife hand. The waters hadn't touched her at all.

She grinned, and there was something of the fae in her expression. "You're being a very bad houseguest, you know. But I have to admit I'm enjoying this. Your heroism against my villainy." She rotated her wrist so her palm faced upward, a challenge or an invitation, and the pulling force intensified. El and Selene froze, not drawn to her exactly, but paralyzed by the psychic strength.

Still I felt nothing. *Our party is weak*, I thought mechanically. *With El and Selene useless right now, it'll fall to me alone to do what has to be done.*

But was some part of me deep down enjoying this, too? The chase, the danger, the banter? I suppressed those thoughts, the scales of my armor fluttering uneasily. "I'm no hero," I said. "I'm just doing what has to be done. If that includes ending your life, then so be it."

She stuck a perfectly pink tongue out. "Can't kill me if you can't touch me."

I signed Quicken out of force of habit and rushed forward. To my surprise, the green aura held long enough to give me a burst of speed, and I lashed out with a scaly fist, grazing her cheek. She seemed as surprised as I was, clapping a hand to her face as a thin line of blood appeared. It dripped into the sweet liquor of the bowl, and for a moment, that *drip-drop* was the only sound in the world, echoing off the gilded walls.

"You hit me," said Mia in wonder, looking at her hand.

The liquid below me frothed, then became a geyser that threw me back and away from Mia. While I was in midair, another wave struck me, slamming me into the hard wall in a continuous torrent that rattled my armor. My fish scales were flexible and did little to cushion the impact. All the air went out of me. I couldn't get a new breath. I was drowning in warm sweetness.

With a feral instinct, I lashed out, not physically, but with an all-encompassing rejection of what was happening, of the world around me, and the scales of my armor oscillated. A sphere of emptiness pushed outward, and the pounding of the liquid reduced into a fine mist, then died away entirely.

It felt colder than ever now. Each scale of painful memory that pressed against my skin was like ice, but at least I could breathe. Next to me, contained in the sphere of emptiness, Selene shivered, and El muttered "What the fuck" under her breath.

Mia's expression was unamused now. As she focused, she looked more fae than ever, and I could believe she was a creature of another world. Something golden grew from within her, reflecting brilliantly off the golden walls. From her waist, petals of light unfurled, waving in an invisible wind, and one reached out to ensnare me. I didn't know how, but a ghostly hand pushed its way out of my chest and met that first petal in midair. God, even that contact sent an uncanny thrill of pleasure through me, quickly suppressed, a shock of softness and warmth as her emanation wrestled against mine for control. I gritted my teeth and sent forth another phantasmic limb which was met by another lush petal of light.

Invitation and rejection. Push and pull. Warmth and coldness. We went back and forth until five bands of light entwined in the air between us like dueling snakes. Space began to fracture as we strained, orange light from the outside world leaking into the pocket dimension, and I felt something begin to give way. It wasn't her overpowering me, or me her.

It was the two of us breaking space itself.

There was an annihilation of opposites, and we each flew backward, crashing into the walls of the chalice. The world rumbled, and sediment began to fall from above into the liquid, then chunks of rock. Orange light peeked into the world through gaps, and I saw that Mia's domain was beginning to unravel at the seams. Seizing my chance, I began to rip and tear my way out, like a chick from an egg.

El and Selene saw what I was doing and joined in. As we emerged, we beheld a scene of destruction.

Sender would be pleased. Selene and Yao's bridge, once spanning between the towers, was well and truly broken, cloven into two halves with a giant fissure between myself and Mia. Orange mists streamed in from outside, inflicting me with a strong premonition of approaching death.

Selene, El, and I stood on one side of the bridge, while Mia and Artem stood on the other, the latter still ensorcelled. Mia waved as their half of the bridge seemed to recede physically from us, growing smaller and more and more obscured by autumnal vapors. This tenuous bridge, it seemed, had been the only thing holding Strive and Eramai together. Now they were mere specks, and I could see nearly the whole form of Strive behind them—a narrow, noble tower whose peak was obscured by clouds above. *Wait a second . . .*

I wheeled around. Behind me was a series of layered red curtains in an archway, with a single shining ruby set at the apex. It was all very yonic in a way that I found a bit heavy-handed, and was certainly not the entrance we'd come through. The door pulsed with a familiar *ba-dump, ba-dump* sound.

"Xavier . . ." El put a paw on my scaled foot.

"Don't touch me," I said dully, and she pulled her paw back as if the armor had burned her.

We had ended up on the wrong side, and even my armor couldn't block out a subtle stab of fear. With every passing moment, the tower called Strive shrank further into the distance, until it was a thin dusky line on the horizon, and finally, not visible at all.

About the Author

Walsh Bear can be found rummaging through a dumpster near you. He enjoys chicken nuggets and dislikes opposable thumbs.